Big Cats Don't Purr

by

J. R. Moir

Grosvenor House
Publishing Limited

This book is published by
Grosvenor House Publishing Ltd
Link House
140 The Broadway, Tolworth, Surrey, KT6 7HT.
www.grosvenorhousepublishing.co.uk

This book is a work of fiction. Any resemblance to
people or events, past or present, is purely coincidental.

A CIP record for this book
is available from the British Library

Paperback ISBN 978-1-83615-274-3
eBook ISBN 978-1-83615-275-0

For all my friends... Human and animal.

Lankin Moors Wildlife Park

Walled Garden

Musth is a condition in a Bull elephant, where it becomes extremely violent. Its testosterone levels rise up to 60% more than its normal state.

It is believed that during musth, an elephant remembers its days in the wilderness, and longs for freedom.

Elephant Protocols, Manuals, and Proceedings
Practical Elephant Management:
A Handbook for Mahouts

Prologue

He sensed their approach. He heard the clink of a chain – brittle and sharp like the pain that stabbed relentlessly inside his head.

He forced his forehead further into the metal, leaning in with all his immense weight until the bars strained against his bulk, but the cold steel no longer soothed his temples. Taking a step back he unfurled his trunk, raising it high in the air and drawing in the scent of danger.

His gaze settled on two shapes. He studied them, inhaling their aroma without recognition, only resentment, the burning sensation in his temples intensified, enflamed by a rush of hate, anger, confusion.

Turning, he took a step towards the intruders, then another, the heaving metronomic rolls of his head increasing with each advance.

Another step. He was towering over them, tasting their odour. His ears billowed, he raised his trunk again… then he halted, staring down at them as a familiarity slowly seeped into his consciousness. He continued to stare, struggling with an innate shred of reason that contradicted the urge to attack. Laboriously, he began to turn away.

A sudden flair of orange light ruptured the darkness, the brief ferocity of the flash seared through his brain. He roared, his head swept back, his trunk flaying wildly towards the intruders.

'Christ…What the…'

Then darkness.

PART ONE
CHAPTER 1

One year later

Saturday 28th August 1976

In the arid evening heat even the crickets were lethargic, waiting until the very last moment before reluctantly throwing themselves clear of Matt's footfall.

Further up the lane a crow was greedily plucking the eyes from a slab of carrion. It paused; its senses pricked by the distant roar of a leopard. Its brazen eyes tracked the sound as it floated past, then settled on Matt, regarding his approach with savage irritation.

Matt looked away; the raw insolence of the bird's glare was the last thing his fragile confidence needed. He rummaged deep into the pocket of his jeans for his last roll-up. He found it, dry and disfigured after its confinement, but salvageable. Massaging it until it once again resembled a cigarette, he put it between his lips and lit it.

'Here we go,' he sighed as he rounded the corner of the lane and The Hunters Moon Inn came into view.

The air inside was so dense that Matt felt its resistance as he pushed open the door and waded through the stench of stale shag tobacco, wood rot and musty carpet.

A clique of old heads with flat caps and consumptive complexions briefly looked him up and down as he weaved his way passed the stained beer kegs fashioned into tables, and headed towards the bar.

Waiting to be served, Matt sensed the scrutinising stare of the man standing next to him. He glanced over and smiled apprehensively as the stranger's wary expression brightened with recognition.

'Hey, you're Matt…Matt err Flynn, right?' said the man, 'we met at your interview, I'm Andy…remember? Small mammals keeper.' He passed a tray over the bar. 'Fill it up will you, Annie, and five packets of cheese and onion. You getting this round in…cheers.'

'What? Oh, sure…I guess,' said Matt, noticing with slight irritation Andy's gaze fix on the crisp pound note that he'd pulled from his wallet.

Casting his mind back, Matt searched for some recollection of his new acquaintance. To the curly black hair and quick, ferrety face, not unlike the animals in his charge. He recalled being struck by how many of the keepers that he had seen that day had, in some way, resembled the animals on their section: the skinny bird keeper with spiky hair, the doe eyes of the deer keeper, and he wondered whether some subconscious force had guided them to animals with similar features or whether, as it is said of old married couples, they simply merged over time.

Of all the faces that he had been introduced to, Andy's had obviously made no impression, but like the small prey mammals he looked after, survival meant an ability to make themselves forgettable, and it was their skill in avoiding attention that helped keep them alive.

Matt scanned the room. 'Am I early? It's just I was told most of the zoo staff would be here on a Saturday and I don't recognise anyone.'

'Including me,' replied Andy, his narrow shoulders slumping.

'Sorry, was it that obvious?' said Matt.

'Not your fault I s'pose, guess you saw a lot of new faces that day. No, everyone's here, we just don't like to mix with the riff-raff.'

'Riff-raff indeed!' cried the barmaid rolling her eyes with mock despair. 'Because they work with animals they acts like animals, so we makes 'em go out in the annex, calls it their den. Kind of a home from home you might say.' She placed the tray, sloshing with spilt beer, onto the bar with the dexterity of a bricky with his hod. 'That'll be one seventy-five, my lover.'

Matt rummaged in his wallet for a second pound note and passed them both over.

'Hey, speaking of new faces,' Andy almost squealed as though he had committed some unforgivable faux pas, 'let me introduce you to Lucky!'

A second later Matt was looking into the startled eyes of a white fancy rat.

'Matt, say hi to the best friend a man can have.'

The rodent's red, bulbous eyes blinked.

'I know what you're thinking, surely a dog is man's best friend...Don't get me wrong, I like dogs, all animals in fact, but with a rat you can get a really strong bond, it's almost symbiotic, there's something about feeling her little heart beating against mine, it's like we're the same being, and what they say about rats being dirty, that's crap, you can toilet train them to –'

'Andy! What have I told you about bringing that vermin in here?' Annie's voice was precise and controlled as she grappled to maintain her honey-soaked drawl. Andy shrank back. Sulkily, he replaced Lucky back down inside his T shirt and beckoned to Matt who, picking up the tray, smiled faintly to Annie and followed Andy out through a door that opened onto a large cobbled courtyard.

On the left was a parking area that at first glance could have been mistaken for a junkyard, with its collection of rusty, dented vans, mini's, and mopeds, the poor condition of which was highlighted by the centrepiece, an enormous Harley Davidson, blazing high above the rest like a chrome phoenix blushing gold with the shame of the association. Behind them was an old stone barn that looked like it had recently had some work done on it, none of which was cosmetic. The entrance was a stable door so old that the wood had shrunk and warped leaving large gaps between each panel through which Matt could hear clinks and clanks, laughing, swearing and the dull, repetitive thud of music. He looked over to Andy with a fondness forged from the relief of not having to enter on his own.

'So, is the Harley yours?' It was a flippant comment, Matt doubted that Andy's feet could even have touched the floor, but he had hoped the assumption might lighten Andy's mood after the rat incident.

'Mine! You kidding...Why would I need that? All that "my cock's bigger than yours" bullshit, that's all a Harley's for. That's my bike, there.' He nodded in the direction of a push bike, set slightly apart from the rest. 'It's got twelve gears,' he added proudly, 'come on, let's get inside.'

Matt dutifully followed as Andy yanked opened the door.

'Whayhay, about bloody time,' bayed a small crowd above the sound of Hawkwind's 'Silver Machine' that was blaring distortedly from the jukebox. Unlike the bar, which was exactly as Matt had expected, this den was a complete surprise. It shouldn't have been, it lived entirely up to its name. A wolf's den, foxes den, den of iniquity, it was bursting with animalistic order. Three groups were strewn around the room in various degrees of hierarchy. The youngsters were tussling and grappling with each other over the pool table, reminding Matt of juvenile chimps, anarchic and simply content to live in the moment. At the far end of the den there was a different dynamic. A more mature troop, (some of whom Matt vaguely recognised from his interview tour), was lounging around an abused looking table, their careless attitude conflicting with the shifty looks that they occasionally threw into the corner of the room.

And in the corner sat the Alpha male – a Silverback in a leather jacket and cowboy boots. Scattered adoringly around him, captivated, was a small group of adoring women, and at his feet, sphinx-like, sat a German Shepard.

'The Harley?' suggested Matt, nodding towards the corner.

'Yeah…that's King.'

Andy's indifference was betrayed by his obvious attempt to avoid King's gaze, Matt, however, couldn't resist looking back. King's glare now rested on Matt and he quickly hurried over to where Andy was distributing the drinks, just as Silver Machine was finishing its turn on the jukebox. Andy paused, and with obvious pride, he took the opportunity to introduce Matt, clearing his throat in an exaggerated manner to evoke the gravitas of the occasion.

'Hey you lot, this is Ma–' but he was too slow, the jukebox clunked and whirred back into action and Silver Machine started again, accompanied by groans from all around the room.

One of the men closest to Matt slammed his fist on the table. 'For Chrissake Al, this is the fourth sodding time in a row!'

A man, presumably Al, was sitting at the table, hunched possessively over a pile of belongings that included rizla papers, tweezers, roaches, matches and the largest lump of Lebanese Resin that Matt had ever seen. Al smiled with apparent satisfaction, shamelessly exposing stubby, mossy teeth that jutted from his gums like a row of neglected tombstones, and turned his attention back to rolling a joint.

Andy cleared his throat for a second attempt at an introduction but once again was cut short. This time by a man in his twenties who was half buried beneath a blonde girl sprawled across his lap.

'Yeah, give us a break Al, why don't you stick on some Bay City Rollers.'

Whether he meant it as a wind-up Matt couldn't tell, but that was the effect.

The smile dropped from Al's face and he stood up, tipping over a chair as he rose. Matt had never seen anyone so tall.

'Bay City Rollers!' Al's deep Scottish brogue regurgitated the name like a dog trying to sick-up a trapped bone. 'That fucking bunch of big girls' blouses give tartan a bad name, 'she sang-shang-a-lang,' I mean, for fucksake, I'll slit my own throat before I listen to that shite.' He drew a long, thick finger across his neck for emphasis, then looking down he noticed Matt for the first time. 'Hawkwind, best band in the world, yes or no?'

Matt took an involuntary step back and looked over to Andy who was nodding his head enthusiastically. Taking the hint, Matt did the same.

'Good man. You see, even the wee skinhead likes it.' He leaned over until Matt's nostrils were filled with his rank breath. 'And by the way, who the fuck are you?'

Andy opened his mouth, but another voice got there first.

'You remember, it's the new bloke, Matt isn't it? We met briefly at your interview.'

Matt leaned across Andy and shook the man's hand.

The man spoke with a slow drawl as he flicked a curtain of lank fringe away from his eyes. 'I'm Roger, Paddocks. The ogre with lousy taste in music is Big Al, carnivores.'

Al grinned and sat back down, scooping up the heavy oak chair like it was made from papier-mache.

'And buried down there somewhere,' continued Roger, 'is our wayward sea lion trainer. Jez.'

A deeply tanned arm appeared from under the blonde girl's T-shirt and gave him the thumbs up.

'You forget Tommy!' Andy squeaked in triumph at Rogers's omission.

'Calm down, I didn't forget, just saving the best 'till last.' Roger winked fondly at a small, hunched figure who, until that moment, had been hidden in the shadow cast by Al's massive frame, 'This is Tommy – Bird section.'

The boy smiled shyly back as Matt shook the limp, boneless hand and tried to hide his shock at the boy's appearance. He was young, but in some ways ancient. His translucent skin was stretched tightly over his bones like cling film and clumps of sparse ginger hair sprouted from his scalp, drawing attention to a fin-like bony ridge that jutted out from his skull.

A forceful nudge from Big Al shifted Matt's attention to a large joint being waggled in his direction. He took the spliff and dragged on it greedily, exhaling a thick cloud of smoke that obscured the boy's features and, with it, his thoughts on what could have caused this.

CHAPTER 2

Hours had passed. Matt neither knew nor cared how many but he guessed it was well past closing time. Not that it mattered, he knew that most rural pubs felt it their duty to flout such laws. *Silver Machine*, along with Al's monopoly of the jukebox, had ended peacefully in favour of *'anything I can bang my fucking head to,'* (Al's one concession). Alcohol had flowed, joints had been shared, and all Matt's earlier insecurities had floated away on the warm, amiable air. He was too stoned to join in with the conversations, content to sit back and watch his new companions. Occasionally he glanced over to King, only to quickly look away from the stare that had been seemingly focussed on him, or at least his table, for most of the evening.

Al, slumped in his chair, gave in to a loud, exaggerated yawn, interrupting Andy's attempts to tell the group about something he'd seen on TV. 'Shut up Al, it's true,' Andy continued. 'I swear, it was on Nationwide last night. This reporter, you know, the one with the moustache.'

'Wears glasses?' said Jez, with a knowing wink to the others.

'No!' Andy's voice leapt up an octave, causing his rat to bury herself amongst her master's mass of curls, 'It was the other one, anyway, he cracked an egg on the pavement, I think it was Oxford Street, and it bloody well cooked. He even ate it!'

'What's wrong with a café?' asked Roger.

'Nothing…that's not the point, the point is that the pavement was so hot that –'

'Sounds pretty disgusting to me,' said Roger, 'you know, dirty, eating off the pavement, you don't know what people have walked in, dog shit, puke, ugh.'

Al grinned. 'Dunno, reckon I've eaten worse.'

'Course you have, dog shit's like caviar up in Scotland. Haut de cuisine when it's battered.'

'Fuck you, Roger. Anyway, what the fuck do you know about Scotland, you've never even set foot out of this county.'

'True. Guess I must've seen a programme about it – Fanny Cradock cooks shit in Scotland. Something like that.'

'You're all missing the bloody point,' Andy persisted, 'what he was saying was how hot it is, hottest since records began, in three hundred and fifty years. Apparently if it doesn't rain soon then-'

'Aw, Andy give it a fucking rest. It doesn't take some overpaid hack frying up on the street to tell us it's hot. I can just stick my head outside for that.' Al ran his hand over his thick mane thoughtfully. 'Reckon Matt here's got the right idea, might get myself a crew cut next week, what do you think?'

'I think you'd look like Boris Karloff's love child,' said Roger.

Al grimaced. 'Yeah, guess you're right.' He slammed his empty glass down on the table. 'So, whose round is it?'

All eyes turned to Andy who shifted nervously in his seat. 'Don't look at me, its Jez's turn.'

'Like hell it is, I got the last one in.'

'Then it must be Matt's.' insisted Andy.

'No problem, what do you all want?' Matt began to stand up.

'No, you don't!' Al lent his hand on Matt's shoulder, and with a gentle push sent him crashing back down into his chair, then he turned to Andy. 'That little fucker's been avoiding buying all night.'

'No, I haven't, you know I haven't. I've got at least two rounds in.' Andy looked imploringly over to Tommy. 'Tell him, Tommy. 'You've seen me, at least twice…remember?'

Roger suddenly whipped his arm across the table and grabbed Andy's rat. She squirmed and tried to wriggle free, her pop eyes staring desperately back towards her owner.

'Hey, get off her, she doesn't like it!'

'You know it's not fair to ask Tommy,' said Roger ignoring Andy's plea. Forming a pistol shape with his fingers he aimed them at Lucky, whilst forcing his large round eyes into a narrow Clint Eastwood squint. 'You've got till the count of ten before I shoot. One, two, three…'

'Better do what he says, Andy, he ain't kidding,' cried Jez with exaggerated urgency.

'Stop messing around you lot, it's not funny, you're scaring her.' Andy retrieved the traumatised rodent and smoothed down her spiked fur. 'Bunch of nerds.'

Al reached over and ruffled Andy's curls. 'Calm down, we're only joshing with you.'

'Well, it's not funny!' he snapped back, cradling Lucky and standing up to leave. 'I'm going to have to get her some pork scratching's now, try and calm her down.'

'And don't forget our drinks while you're there,' Roger called after him.

Matt, muttering an excuse about needing the toilet, followed Andy out. As irritating as he was, as his 'first contact' Matt felt a nagging loyalty which had been amplified by the others' taunts. And besides, the dope was starting to really get to him and he felt some fresh air might do him good.

'I knew we'd be friends the moment I saw you,' Andy declared after Matt asked if he was okay. 'You're not like those other bastards...all they care about is themselves, where their next joint or beer's coming from. Well, they can bloody well wait for all I care; we'll teach them not to mess with us.'

Us! thought Matt, instantly regretting the bond that his pity had created.

With Matt in tow, Andy set about taking his time: he talked to Annie (with Lucky hidden well inside his T shirt), chatted for a while to some vague acquaintance in the corridor and told anyone who'd listen how 'the bastards' had upset Lucky, and how he and his new friend Matt were going to make the bastards wait for their drinks.

Andy was strutting like a kitten returning with his first kill by the time they finally arrived back at the den, kicking open the door and seeming to care little as the drinks sloshed over rims and into the tray. Al would drink it out of the tray anyway, he told Matt; he'd seen him do it before – 'dirty bastard.'

The moment they entered Matt was immediately aware of the change of atmosphere. A lethargic kind of unease seemed to hang in the air, mingling with the layer of yellow smoke.

After scanning the room, trying to pierce through the smog, he finally settled on the source. He rubbed the sting out of his eyes, causing the image to blur and slowly to refocus onto the unblinking gaze of King.

The man's expression was blank, pure poker, but there was something about him, perhaps the curl of his lips or the tightness of his jaw that Matt felt was dangerous.

Feeling a growing sense of menace in the air, Matt watched as the American nodded to the two boys who'd been playing pool, a signal that brought them immediately to his side. Like predators casually closing in on their quarry, the three of them sauntered over to where he and Andy stood.

'Hey, Andy, I wanna word with you.' King's voice was lazy and toneless and carried a weary American twang. 'You've been snooping again, ain't you.'

Andy gave a little yelp as the colour flowed out of him. Matt thought even his hair seemed a tone lighter as he whimpered a denial that King cut short.

'Don't lie to me boy, I hate liars as much as I hate cowards...seems to me you're both. Know what we used to do to liars and cowards in Vietnam?'

Andy's pleas were almost inaudible above the noise of glasses that clattered in his shaking hands. 'I swear it, honestly, I wouldn't...not after last time.'

'Don't bullshit me,' barked King. 'Gary here spotted you last night with that camera of yours.'

Andy attempted another denial, the trembling in his hands spreading over his entire body and the weight of the tray clearly becoming unbearable, unbalanced by the tide of beer that sloshed over the edges.

'Hey, careful.' Al's arm reached over the gathering, lifting the tray to safety.

King flashed a look like a cougar being disturbed from his kill by a bear. 'This is personal business, Al.'

'Too fucking right it's personal, that's my beer he's spilling.' Andy's pale deflated form became eclipsed as the giant moved in, planting his feet defiantly between Andy and King like a Scots pine bracing itself against a coming storm.

King stood motionless, broad and solid. His expression was impenetrable, the look of a professional soldier unwilling to give any advantage of insight to his foe, whilst Al loomed over him, his eyes brimming with wild, lustful glee.

A wolfish grin crept over King's face. Looking over to his two companions he gave them a 'stand down' nod. 'Sure...you're right. I forget how important this warm beer shit is to you English.'

'I ain't English, I'm Scottish!' said Al with feeling, 'Come on, Andy.'

But Andy had disappeared, leaving nothing but a Warm draft as the door of the den closed in his wake.

Handing out what was left of the beer Al sat down and began slurping noisily at the tray's contents.

'Christ, Al,' said Roger quietly, so only Al and Matt could hear, 'I thought King was going to go for you for a minute. I can't believe he backed down.'

Al shrugged at Roger's concern and wiped away the sticky droplets that ran down his chin. 'Shite, Roger, he didn't back down.' He paused and looked over to where King was easing himself back into his throne. 'He just wasn't in the mood.'

Matt was also watching King, his curiosity unrestrained by the alcohol and cannabis in his system. He turned back to his table. 'What the hell was all that about?'

His question was met with bland indifference, a shrug from Al, a roll of Roger's large eyes.

'Come on, tell me. What was it about?'

Roger sighed as if placating an insistent child. 'Just some ancient history that rears up from time to time. Andy doesn't help himself, winds up King, but like I said…ancient history.'

Matt ignored Roger's reticence. With the drugs in his system reacting to the excitement of the last few minutes, the den was no longer a slovenly, inanimate museum; it erupted with a life of its own. Light bulbs burst with swirling colour, snooker balls collided, sounding like a crack of a whip, and tact was the last thing on his mind. 'But what ancient history…what happened?'

If you ask me,' said Jez, 'he's been in a lousy mood ever since the boss decided to get that mahout to sort Uddanda.'

Matt attempted to focus on Jez, trying to work out where the sea lion trainer began and his girlfriend ended, 'Uddanda?' he said. 'What's that?'

'Not a what, a *who*,' said Jez patiently. 'He's our bull elephant, largest in captivity as a matter of fact. Anyway, last year he…ow, fuck! What was that for?' Clutching his shin Jez looked accusingly from Al to Roger and then followed their eyes to Tommy. The boy's expression was still gently vacant but a slight rocking motion suggested a growing agitation.

'Like I said,' Roger repeated with force, 'ancient history.'

CHAPTER 3

The rat slowly awoke from her deep sleep, dimly aware of being lifted from her shredded paper nest. Her mouth opened wide, exposing long yellow incisors that should have bitten down on the hand. Instead, she just yawned. Wildness had been bred out of her many generations before.

She knew she was safe. She knew the room, the scents and sounds, and she knew the hand; it was her world and she understood her world, when she was agitated, scared or content. She had that much instinct left.

Anger was not something she was able to comprehend, but she understood agitation, and with a sudden start she sensed it. His pounding heart, the chemicals in his sweat, even the salt from his tears. The event was not unfamiliar to her but that didn't make it any the less fearful. It confused her, adding to her fear. She was fully awake now, her senses on high alert trying to find a cause, a predator.

She was on his lap and the hand was smoothing down her fur, but even this felt wrong. The hand was too forceful, held no rhythm or tenderness. It pushed her down and dragged her skin until it hurt. She attempted to get away; her world wasn't safe and she had to get back to her nest. She twisted and contorted against the hand but it kept dragging her back, then finally it gave up. She was free.

Andy watched vacantly as Lucky tumbled from his lap and scurried across the floor towards her cage. Briefly she turned and stared at him with pop-eyed alarm before darting into her den.

He didn't mind that she'd left him. He wasn't even bothered by the rhythmic bangs of Jez's bed in the flat below. He was used to Jez's conquests and it no longer taunted him. All he cared about was justice, justice and revenge. The incident in the den had shaken him badly, but that was now hours ago, long enough to re-write the event in his head, to imagine an alternative ending where he had stood his ground and fought back. Where a perfectly placed blow had felled King, dropping him to his knees and causing him to cry out to Andy for forgiveness.

He smiled at the idea, rubbing away the last of his tears with his knuckle.

On his desk was a collection of Polaroid photos. Dark, shadowy scenes of figures with elephants, images so blurred and distant that it hurt your eyes trying to bring them into focus. He considered them for a moment longer before collecting them up into a tidy pile. Taking them had been a risk, almost got him caught and they proved nothing. But he didn't need to take any more. He had a new plan.

CHAPTER 4

'*Ouch! Fuck!*' Matt flopped back down onto his pillow, his forehead stinging from its impact against the beam two feet over his bed.

It took a few confused seconds for his mind to adjust to his surroundings, to make sense of the unfamiliar sounds that chattered and whooped outside. The pain quickly subsided leaving the dull recognisable throb of a hangover.

He lay still, allowing his mind to assemble all the information available.

The noises... familiar, yet not fitting his concept of the English countryside.

Human made?

No.

Animal? Cow, sheep, dog, duck. Johnny Wiesmullar... shit, where did he come from?

Tarzan, jungle, jungle noises. Whoop, whoop. Monkeys? Whoop, whooooop. Gibbons... That's a gibbon!

In England?

He peered blearily at his watch, eight-thirty, and rolled out of bed – the only safe way to exit he had discovered – his torso leaving a damp, sweaty imprint on the mattress as he stood up.

Another beam two feet up from the other collided with his crown.

'*Fuck! Shit! Fuck!*'

What was it a friend from university had once told him? If your first word after waking up is *fuck*, you're best-off staying in bed.

Clutching his head in both hands, he backed cautiously out of the alcove. In the centre of the room, he tentatively stood erect, contemplating whether the flat had been built by an agoraphobic, a contortionist or some Alice in Wonderland nut.

He surveyed all the cardboard boxes piled around him, some empty or almost empty, most full, with *cooking, records, clothes* or *misc.* scrawled on the side. He ran his hand around his throat and let it trail down his chest.

'A coffee, then a shower, then you lot,' he said.

Ducking through the doorway he walked along the narrow, tapering corridor that ran the length of the flat. At the far end was the primitive kitchen area consisting of a sink and a primus stove. He stepped up to the sink and ran some water into a saucepan, placed it on the stove and lit it. Automatically he made a roll-up, put it between his lips and bent down to the blue flame until the tip flared into life. Noticing the envelope that he'd left on the draining board the previous afternoon, he shook out the letter, flicked it open and re-read it.

18th July 1976

Dear Mr Flynn,

Following your interview, it is with great pleasure that I can formally confirm your appointment as Education Officer, commencing on Monday 30th August.

As I previously explained this is a new position and as such it will take time for you to become established, and until then we will expect you to carry out other keeper duties whenever possible.

I am also delighted to inform you that we can provide accommodation within the park in the form of a rather charming self-contained flat, (the rent for which will be deducted from your monthly wage), which will be available from the morning of Saturday 28th August.

May I take this opportunity to say how absolutely super it is to have you on board and how we are all very much looking forward to working with you.

Yours sincerely,

Dr Julian Meads
Curator

'Raaather charming, self-contained flat' said Matt, feeling the bump that had risen on his head. 'Absolutely suuuper to have you on board.' Immediately he felt guilty.

The truth was he had liked Julian. He reminded him of a chubbier, version of…What's his name from that kids show Animal Magic – Johnny Morris.

Hearing bubbling, he chucked a spoonful of coffee into a mug, poured in the steaming water and took the drink into the bedroom, squatting down on the floor so that he could peer through the small gash in the wall that passed itself off as a window. Despite the hour the sun was blazing down from a cloudless sky, burning into the morning dew and creating pockets of mist that hovered in the valley below.

From this vantage point Matt could just about make out the shapes of deer plucking at any nutritional foliage they could find growing in the sun-baked earth.

They only had a of couple grazing hours before the midday heat would drive them to shelter beneath the dappled sanctuary of the beech trees.

He sat watching for a further ten minutes whilst the white mist evaporated, revealing a small flock of flamingos who, one by one, unfurled their long necks and looked around them as though searching for their African savanna.

Pokey little dive, but what a view, he thought, throwing back the remains of his coffee and flicking his fag butt into the empty mug. He felt revitalised, not completely, but enough to consider phase two of his recovery programme.

Walking stooped-fashion out of the bedroom, Matt peered down the other end of the corridor and into the tiny shower cubicle as he wriggled out of his jeans that, after two days of continuous wear, clung obstinately to his sweat damp skin.

Punctuated by his yelps as the water fluctuated from scalding to freezing with the tiniest adjustment to the tap, he managed to take a shower. Using the jeans he'd dumped on the floor, he mopped up the water that had escaped during his struggle, then he rummaged through a box until he found some new clothes, creased but at least fresh.

He considered unpacking, but the invigorating effect of his shower combined with the sunlight that was now bursting through the little east-facing crack proved too enticing. He grabbed his tobacco, removed the key from the lock and stepped outside. *'Christ, it's going to be the hottest day so far!'*

CHAPTER 5

Apart from the occasional animal sounds and the distant hum of a tractor, the park seemed deserted. It was still too early for the public and although the keepers must have been well into their morning rounds Matt saw no one, the freshly-stuffed hayracks and troughs brimming with food pellets the only clues that anyone had been there. He followed the paths without any sense of exploratory purpose, simply enjoying the fresh air and solitude.

The camels mooched aimlessly amongst the clumps of wool that lay scattered around their paddock like tumbleweed. Antelope sprawled lazily in dusty bowls. Two tapir squeezed themselves into the shade of a small tree, forcing out a capybara who ambled amiably off to seek sanctuary elsewhere. The wolves were absent, presumably dozing in the relative cool of their den.

Matt wandered on, pausing on a footbridge that crossed the stream which divided the valley. Judging by the steep shelves on either side it must, he decided, at certain times of the year be six or more feet deep and fast flowing. Now it was reduced to a small trickle that fed shallow pools thick with flickering silver flashes of what looked like minnow and stickleback.

Continuing up the path, Matt entered the walled garden. Here, access to sprinklers had halted the encroaching brittleness. The baked, cracked earth crept up as far as the perimeter wall but dared go no further.

The garden was an oasis of lush green shrubs; laurel, magnolia and rhododendron sprouting plump shoots that burst unhindered through the wire mesh enclosures, taunting the occupants who, unlike the foliage, remained captive. Common marmoset, emperor and cottontop tamarin, goeldi's monkey, rows of callitrichid all followed Matt's movements with dark, insolent eyes. Blankets of ivy as thick as thatch tumbled over the roof and down the sides of the long reptile house. He could picture the snakes, lizards and spiders lurking inside in timeless suspension.

Matt wandered contentedly on, following along the path that led deeper into the menagerie. The otters, on hearing the snap of a twig under his footfall, screamed with opportunistic anticipation of a treat. Finding their stares and hysteria unsettling Matt hurried past, glancing at the sign directing him to 'small cats and aviaries'. As he neared the enclosures he tried softening his tread, but his weight on the gravel, however tempered, only seemed to prolong the grind of stone against stone, alerting the cats who vanished into a thicket and hissed mistrust at Matt's presence. By contrast, he could have been playing a bugle for all the notice the lynx took of him, pacing their perimeter with a vacuous detachment that left him with a sense of pity rather than thrill.

After passing a ramshackle building with the word 'curator' painted on the door in an ancient-looking font, the path straightened out into a long run of aviaries whose inhabitants warned each neighbour of his approach with shrill alarms. Still Matt met no one.

Eventually, the path led to a set of double doors, large enough to drive a tractor through. It had the kind of solid foreboding that Matt associated with the gothic castles of Hammer horror movies, mysteriously swinging open to Bela Lugosi's greeting of 'velcome to my home.' Nailed onto the right-hand door was a deer skull that helped to accentuate the warning sign beneath, 'NO ADMITTANCE STAFF ONLY.' He glanced at his watch – nine-thirty – and quickly dismissed the idea of returning to his cramped, stuffy flat.

'Well, I'm almost staff.' Grabbing the handle, he heaved open the door and stepped inside.

CHAPTER 6

The short lane was littered with signs of recent activity, indicating that he was entering the heart of the zoo. Abandoned trolleys, half-empty food crates, large humming fridges and freezers, which lined a row of squat buildings and deep alcoves, all ending at an enormous barn.

But Matt was only semi-aware of his surroundings as he stood motionless, distracted by the scene ahead of him. There was a girl, about his age, battling to untangle a hosepipe that resembled a child's slinky toy. An apparently frustrating task made all the worse by a mass of shaggy red curls that kept tumbling over her face. With growing impatience, she repeatedly tossed her hair back over her shoulder, whilst muttering what she would do to it, as though it were an unruly and persistent puppy. Matt sensed that if she had access to a pair of scissors she would have hacked it off there and then.

The girl looked up and Matt involuntarily jumped back, concealing himself behind the door.

'If you're going to stand there gawping all morning,' she said, 'I'm going to have to charge you.'

Sheepishly, he emerged into the full stare of the girl. 'Hi, I'm Ma—'

'Matt Flynn, the education officer.' Her confident voice hinted at being local. 'Don't panic, not much goes on around here that isn't common knowledge within a few hours. You'll get used to that, people knowing your business, your likes, dislikes, your voyeuristic perversions.'

Matt blushed and tried to stammer out an explanation.

Her green eyes sparkled impishly. 'Relax, give me a hand with this goddamn hose and we'll forget about it. Start afresh, how's that sound?'

He was momentarily taken aback by the word 'goddamn,' it seemed so out of place with her local dialect, but her suggestion seemed genuine, and he approached her with enthusiastic relief.

Next to her, suspended by a hook, hung the carcass of a new-born calf. The hook pierced its jaw, forcing out the tongue to create a baffled expression which would almost have been comical, were it not for its sliced-open innards, severed limbs and the pool of semi-congealed blood, faeces and urine that dripped onto the floor beneath it.

As he passed, a cloud of flies leapt into the air with an agitated buzz, a hundred, maybe a thousand individuals reacting together to become one lustful, carrion-devouring demon guarding its rotten feast. Matt backed away. 'Yuck,'

'Tell me about it,' said the girl. 'I keep telling Al he can't leave stuff like that lying around, especially not in this heat. He'll be sorry as hell if Beth gets sick, and it'll be me who'll have to sort it.'

She stood up and stretched her back, causing her T-shirt to rise above her naval and expose her toned, olive skin. With effort, Matt tore his gaze away, aware that he was on probation.

'See that handle, when I say, you start pumping, okay?' she said.

Matt looked around, unsure what she meant.

She rolled her eyes, let out a sigh and pointed to a long, metal bar. 'No chance of mains water way out here, we pump direct from a reservoir which, by the way, is almost empty, another few days like this and... I don't know. Get pumping will you.'

Matt started raising and lowering the handle trying to find a rhythm. 'So, are you a keeper?'

'Quiet,' she barked, 'I think I can hear something.' She placed her thumb over the end, causing a jet of yellowy water to splutter out, spraying and saturating the black mass of flies that fell sodden into the puddle.

'That's better,' she said with satisfaction. 'You can stop now...sorry, what were you saying?'

'I was just wondering what your section was?'

The girl, winding the hose back up, hesitated before answering. 'Section? Oh, I'm not a keeper. I'm the vet,' she announced with unconcealed pride. 'I work in a practice in Bridgeworthy, mostly livestock and a few pets. I come out here when I can for the experience.' Adjusting the last coil she briefly studied her handiwork then turned to face Matt. 'Ideally, I want to work with elephants, try and find a job in a sanctuary in India, just for a year or two and then, who knows.'

'An elephant doctor. Sounds cool.'

A hesitant smile crept over her face and she looked him over with inquisitive eyes. 'I'm surprised Julian employed a skinhead, not his kind of thing at all.'

Automatically Matt ran his hand through the bristles on his head. It had been two weeks since the barber had got Matt's usual (a Bowie style feather cut), mixed up with another client's usual, and although initially devastated, he had now almost forgotten about the resulting crew cut. 'It was an accident, a case of mistaken identity. It's normally longer.'

The girl laughed. 'Boys and their hair! I don't care what anyone says, you're the vainest sex. Don't worry, it suits you.' She turned to leave. 'And it's practical, I like practical.'

He couldn't be sure, was that a 'come on'? Her back was now to him, she was walking away. 'Anything else need pumping?' *'Christ!'*

She turned back to him, furrows forming in her forehead as she looked him over with keen, questioning eyes. 'Have you met the eles yet?'

Matt shook his head.

'I'm going there now, come on. I'll introduce you.'

Susie led him down the short lane, passing a row of shabby doors with 'zoo kitchens,' 'wash room' and 'Incubators, keep door shut' hand-painted across them. At the end of the lane she stopped at a rusty gate, beyond which was a narrow lean-to corridor that ran a short way along the side of the huge barn. Parked next to the gate was the Harley Davidson, dazzling in the morning sun, and at its side lay the German shepherd.

'You're the education officer,' she said. 'Perhaps you can start by educating Al about the importance of food hygiene.' She bent down to greet the dog, who licked her face, then she tugged at the gate, but it just clanked against the lock.

'I'm not sure he'll take much notice but I'll give it a go if you want,' said Matt, imagining the giant's response to a lecture. He attempted to pat the dog but quickly snatched his hand back as it silently bared its teeth. Worried that she might be the sort of person who believed dogs sensed character flaws he urgently looked over to her, relieved to see she was too absorbed by the padlock to notice. 'I just realised, I don't even know your name?' His question was abruptly answered by the sudden appearance of a broad, tall figure on the other side of the gate.

'Hey Susie, you get my message?' King flicked his fingers over the padlock, yanked open the gate, and with one swift movement, he lifted the girl onto him. Wrapping her legs around his thick waist and her arms around his broad shoulders they kissed, a deep, wet kiss that left a string of spittle that snapped as they separated. King wiped it away with his huge forearm, like a lumberjack downing a beer and wiping away the head. 'Thanks, baby. I needed that.' He let her slide slowly to the ground, 'Come with me, I've got a surprise to show you.'

Turning to go inside Susie paused, as though remembering some mildly unimportant item that she'd left behind. 'Sorry, Matt, I almost forgot. Hey King, I bought someone along. He wants to meet the eles, if that's okay.'

King glanced back at Matt and pushed his mirror sunglasses up onto his forehead. His expression was hard to read; it could have been smug or superior or predatory like a shark. Or it could just have been a look of indifference.

'The college boy, I'm surprised to see you up and about this early after all the shit you put in your system last night. You sure got in with the wrong crowd there, should have come sat with me, could've shown you some true southern hospitality, and gotten yourself a lift back on a real machine and not that goddamn popsicle Al rides.'

'Goddamn.' That word again. Matt felt a simultaneous sting of shock and despair as he realised that, not only were they an item, but they had been together long enough for her to adopt his phrases.

'I'm not sure Shadow would have been too pleased to share her seat,' chipped in Susie, looking thoughtfully at the dog. 'She rides pillion.'

'Shadow does what I say, don't ya girl.'

The dog gave one thud of her tail, then looked at Matt with the same unsettling, enigmatic expression that King had greeted him with.

'Anyways, you're here now so let's see if we can't get you back on track, teach you how things are really done around here – the right way.' He looked down at Susie and winked. 'The King way.'

Matt looked at Susie, expecting her to recoil at the comment, but she merely rolled her eyes with mock despair, then grinned as she tugged King towards the entrance of the elephant house. 'Come on, I want to see what this surprise is.'

Like a kid on Christmas morning, she rushed ahead of them both, down the short corridor and disappeared through another gate. King swaggered after her, leaving Matt on his own, staring at the easy, relaxed roll of the big man's broad shoulders.

Despite the obvious age difference, he reluctantly understood the attraction. There was something compelling, almost mesmerizing about King. Tall and solidly built, he looked like a sandy-haired version of Robert Mitchum. But most striking of all were the eyes. Pale and chalky blue they should have been weak but instead conveyed immense power. Matt felt a growing dislike for the man.

He shook himself from his thoughts and, in his haste to catch up went sprawling over a hard, metallic object.

'Mantraps,' said a mocking drawl.

Matt, sitting on the concrete floor of the corridor and rubbing his shin, looked back at the obstacle, an obscene-looking collection of springs and serrated iron, and then over to King who had mysteriously re-appeared by his side.

'Kind of a hobby of mine, got some that go back to your Queen Victoria. I keep intending to clean them up, mount them somehow, you know, like a display, but a part of me likes them all weathered up like that, makes them look... more in use, know what I mean.'

Matt glared back at him, picked himself up and brushed the dust from his jeans.

'Come on boy, let's get inside, see the girls. It's hotter than a bitch in heat out here.'

As they walked to the end of the corridor the sweet aroma of hay and molasses reached Matt, enhancing his awareness of the strange environment he was entering. Low rumblings, emanating from the building echoed all around, penetrating his skin and agitating the hairs on the back of his arms.

Above the rumble, the shuffle of huge feet punctuated by the sharp clanking of chains added to Matt's mix of apprehension and exhilaration. He felt as though he were walking into a lost world, where prehistoric monsters would lumber and make the earth quake – a place where mythology replaced reality. He hesitated at the door, half-expecting to see a sign above it saying *'Here be monsters.'*

'Don't you fret, boy,' said King. 'As my Pa used to say, what don't kill you makes you stronger,'

Slipping down his sunglasses he then tapped his side, drawing Matt's attention to an object that hung from his belt – a long, smooth handle with a steel hook at one end that was sharpened to a vicious point.

'Anyways, nothing's going to get you, not when I've got this baby. It's all about respect – respect, and understanding your place.'

Matt felt this last point was personal.

'The natives call it an *ankus* – that's elephant hook to you. I won it in an arm-wrestling bout in Vietnam. I'll tell you boy, there's nothing I prize more.'

He un-holstered the goad as though it were a Winchester rifle, gliding his hand along the cream-coloured handle. 'See that, pure ivory.'

Matt shuddered.

'Yeah, kinda ironic, huh?' said King. 'But turning an opponent's weaponry against them – that's the first rule of battle.'

'Battle? You handle elephants – what's that got to do with battles?' He probably should have kept his mouth shut. He could imagine King's eyes darkening behind the shades.

'I'd say taking on four tons of muscle, fat, skin and bone was a battle, but hell, maybe you know better, huh, college boy?' He paused, letting his point sink in and caressing the hook as though Matt had hurt its feelings. 'And as for *this*...If you made me an offer for my Harley I'd say 'sure, a thousand bucks and it's yours', but *this*, no way. Take this from me, I'd snap you in two. Like I was saying...respect – that's what's important.'

They stared at each other. Matt knew that some half-arsed macho line had been drawn and King was daring him to cross it – and for a second he was tempted, incensed that King had spoilt this moment, insinuated that he was afraid, challenging his manhood. Behind the sunglasses Matt felt he could sense King's glare, the force of those impenetrable pale blue eyes draining him of his resolve. Finally, Matt looked away, King smiled.

'Wow, King! It's fantastic; she looks beautiful,' called Susie from inside the barn.

'Coming baby.' replied King, and he strode off in her direction, 'Oh, and college boy,' he said, pausing, 'I'm a trainer. You don't handle an elephant you train 'em, remember that.'

Matt followed, his bitterness quickly evaporating as he stepped from the corridor through a gate. Entering the barn, he was greeted by a thick, fleshy, outstretched trunk reaching eagerly out for contact.

'Kali back, piche!' King barked, whacking the inquisitive trunk with his beloved goad.

The immense creature recoiled in pain.

'Watch ya self there, boy,' said King. 'That's Kali – name means dark one, and that's not just 'cause of her colour, she can be mean as a sack of snakes when the mood takes her. Come over here.'

Matt instinctively did as he was told, following King cautiously past Kali to another corner of the barn, separated by a row of thick steel columns.

Susie was already there, standing next to two young men who Matt recognised as the pool players from the pub. His attention shifted towards the images that stood swaying in the shadows behind them. Two elephants, paler and chunkier but not as tall as Kali, looked down at the visitors, their trunks separately caressing the girl who giggled as she dropped Polo mints onto their eager tongues.

'King, they look great, really fantastic,' she said.

'Hang on, baby, it's too dark to see them properly.'

He pressed a green button on the wall, causing the large steel door to squeal for lubrication as it grudgingly opened.

There was a gasp of delight from Susie as sunlight flooded inside, illuminating the elephants and allowing Matt to see the surprise in full.

Both the elephants were painted in hues of the brightest blues, greens, yellows and reds. Impressionistic flowers adorned their trunks and ears, and on their foreheads burst the sun, its rays reaching over their crown and cascaded down their backs. On each cheek was painted a large blue eye that stared unblinkingly back at them, in stark contrast to their real eyes – two small, dark sunken holes that blinked rapidly against the shaft of sun that bored into them through the open door.

The cracks around King's eyes increased as a grin crept over his face. 'So, what d'ya think?'

'It's bizarre, magnificent. I've never seen anything like it' said Matt, still scrutinising the artwork around their ears.

'Not you college boy,' snapped King.

'It's great. I had no idea you were going to do it,' cried Susie, gazing open-mouthed at the elephants. 'When did you do it? It must have taken ages.'

'Started last night after we left the pub.' King turned to his minions, Colin and Gary, who were covered in almost as much paint as the elephants. 'Been at it since then, haven't we boys.'

Matt let out a short, involuntary laugh. The two scrawny teenagers had modelled themselves on their mentor, right down to the mirror shades that obscured half their faces. They nodded in unison.

'We're knackered,' said one of the boys with feeling.

'And starving,' added the other.

King ignored the hint. 'It'll need a bit of touching up for tomorrow, but most of the hard graft is done, speaking of which, you boys better get mucking out.'

The teenagers started to open their mouths but, thinking better of it, slumped off towards a grubby wheelbarrow and some forks in the corner of the barn.

'So, what are you going to do, rides?' asked Susie.

'Thought about it, but Joti's been playing up a bit lately and you know what Devi gets like when there're separated. No, just take them walk-about, show and tell, a bit of touchy feely for the kids, know what I mean, baby?'

King stepped up behind Susie, wrapping his arms around her waist and resting his chin on her head. They both gazed at the elephants. Matt decided to take the opportunity to explore the barn, which appeared to be a cross between a small aircraft hangar and a reinforced cow shed. Absently, he wandered to the far end, a place still stifled by shadow and, judging by its position, rarely touched by the sun. Still preoccupied by thoughts of King and Susie, he felt resentful that she could be involved with a man that said stuff like, *Do things the King way,* someone who carried an ivory stick with pride, someone who collected mantraps. A man who, for no reason, had challenged him.

But slowly these feelings began to subside, replaced by a slight sense that he wasn't alone. He peered deep into the darkness, and then he saw it – a tiny flap of movement, eleven maybe twelve feet in the air, perhaps a bird nesting in the rafters.

Gradually, as his eyes became accustomed to the darkness, a large, dim shape began to loom out of the half-light, a shape that was instantly familiar and at the same time almost unbelievable. Matt could only stare in the presence of such power and magnificence. It was as though he had strayed into the domain of a deity and his mind was bewildered, unsure of how to react to such a vast being. He felt both fearful and thrilled, feeble in comparison and overcome with wonder. And yet, despite its enormity, he felt no threat.

He took three paces forward and reached up, thrilling with the anticipation of touching and making physical contact. Then he remembered what Jez had said about the Bull elephant; he struggled to recall its name and then it came to him, and in reverence he said it out loud. 'Uddanda.'

'Shit, boy, have you got some kinda death wish?' King's voice cut through the spell, severing Matt's thoughts. 'That's Uddanda, and he's a bad elephant, a killer. Why d'ya think we got him shackled like this? It's to stop kamikazes like you getting splattered from here to kingdom come.'

Colin and Gary appeared, shifty smirks on their faces. They caught each other's eye; one of them let out a peculiar rasping kind of laugh.

King swung around. 'You two get back to work, this ain't no fucking circus.' As the two scampered away he turned back to Matt. 'And it's no fucking petting zoo either; he's got over one hundred thousand muscles in that trunk, could squeeze you into pulp, or he might decide to step on you, all six tons of him, squish you like a piece of rotten fruit, just waiting for the opportunity, for some sucker to waltz up to him and say 'howdy.' His face glowed with anger.

'I didn't sense that from him,' Matt said. 'If anything, I think…' He noticed Susie's downcast eyes. Grudgingly he turned back to King. 'Sorry, I guess I got a bit carried away. I've just never seen anything like him before.'

'Yeah, well, like I said, if it don't kill you… look, I'm not saying you can't see him, it's just you gotta know what he's capable of. Remember, it's about respect.'

Matt knew he should listen to this advice and experience, and was almost ashamed of his arrogance in believing that King was wrong, but looking now at Uddanda and, distanced from his initial surprise, he still felt no fear, only wonder. He looked again and noticed for the first time the thick chains around a front and hind ankle, red raw from where the hessian sacking had slipped from its protective position, and he shuddered, imagining such a life chained in perpetual shadow.

'It's pitiful isn't it,' said Susie, guessing his thoughts. 'If you could have seen him before… before all the trouble, he was superb, spectacular.'

'Does he ever get out? I mean out of doors, into the sunlight.'

'Can't be done,' King answered. 'About a year ago he was in *musth*, that's when a bull's at his most dangerous – testosterone floods through them veins and there's not a damn thing you can do about it 'cept let them sweat it out and stay the hell out of their way.'

'The duration depends on the elephant,' said Susie, 'in some cases up to a few months.'

King smiled at her like a proud teacher. 'And for that whole time all the sons of bitches wanna do is kill you. But this boy, I ain't seen nothing like it, gone into a kinda trance ever since he got Jack and Tommy, over a year now, won't react to nothing, not even the girls.'

'Kali used to spend hours just touching Uddanda with her trunk,' said Susie. 'Devi and Joti too, but mostly Kali – they were closest. It's like she was trying to comfort him. She hasn't done it for a while now, I guess she's given up.'

'Just being nosey is all.' King's smile faded. 'You'll have to forgive Susie, she gets a bit involved; you'd think a vet would know better. Anyways, to answer your question, no, he doesn't go out, not the way he is now. You gotta be able to read an elephant, understand their behaviour, predict their moods and stay one step ahead, but this boy...nothing. Just a blank page, liable to do anything.'

Matt's mind was racing, trying to catch up with the information.

'Jack and Tommy... is that the same Tommy I met last night, the one with the...the weird skull thing?'

Susie flinched. 'That's right, that weird skull thing is my brother.'

King, glaring at Matt, rubbed Susie's shoulder.

'I'm so sorry, I didn't realise that he...I didn't mean...'

'You weren't to know,' said Susie with a sigh. 'I guess I'm just a bit sensitive, you know, baby brother and all that. It could have been worse, he could have been killed, like

Jack… and he's a lot better now. Since King got Julian to give him the bird section he's improving every day.'

Matt noticed her squeeze King's arm.

'Anyway,' she continued, 'the boss has arranged for someone to help with Dan, some elephant expert, a proper mahout apparently and—'

'The mahout is coming as a fucking PR stunt,' said King, 'and if the boss or Julian think I'm going to take advice from some gook then they can stick it. Bullet through the brain, that's the only thing left for Dan. Shit, it's the kindest thing, but the boss is too scared of the bad publicity, so he sends for Jungle Jim to make it look like he's making the effort.'

King paused, breathless and red in the face. He glanced across to Colin and Gary. 'And what are you two gawping at, it's bank holiday tomorrow, busiest one of the year and I want this place fucking spotless.'

Susie glanced at Matt and nodded her head towards the exit.

'I'm sorry,' said Matt. 'I've taken up loads of your time and I should be getting back as well, still haven't even unpacked.'

King ignored him, his eyes were angry and lost in thought.

'Maybe see you tomorrow?' he said to Susie.

She smiled back faintly. 'Maybe.'

Stepping out from the barn, the force of the late morning sun hit Matt like a blast from a furnace, sapping the last of his reserves. He felt vulnerable, out of his depth, an up-turned bug under a magnifying glass. He didn't want to think anymore…he just wanted to sleep.

CHAPTER 7

King resented chasing. Hunting, that was his style, his passion. Deer, mountain lion, bear, even people... especially people. Hunting was a skill that had to be honed and perfected, needed stealth and patience. It set you above others. Proof of supremacy.

But chasing, that was different. It was a response that stank of desperation and weakness.

He caught sight of Matt a hundred yards ahead of him and slowed down. If he was going to turn this situation to his advantage then he didn't want to be red in the face and out of breath, and he wanted a time to think, work on his strategy. He was questioning Susie's motive for wanting him to befriend the college boy. Her plea's to *'go and be nice to him...he seemed sweet ...he's only young...'* heightening his paranoia over this new buck's presence. Sure, he's young, he thought, young like Susie, an academic like Susie, sweet, according to Susie.

Once the gap had closed to ten yards King was ready. 'Hey Matt, wait up.'

With his dog at his side, King sauntered toward him, his smile widening with each approaching step.

Shadow let out a long growl that caused the boy to take a step back. The dog was suspicious – proof, thought King, that his own gut feeling was right. He silenced her with a snap of his fingers.

'Hey, Matt, just wanted to apologise – guess you caught me at a bad time back there. What'ya say we start over?'

He reached out and shook Matt's hand, soft in contrast to his own thick and calloused palm. Yet he knew the roughness was an example of his superiority; it told of a life lived, hard and raw and tough. And yet he couldn't shake an image of Matt's hand gliding smoothly over Susie's curves. 'Tell you what, Matt. I've gotta go and check the store room, how about you come with me? Give us a chance to get to know each other.'

King watched Matt's response keenly. Earlier in the elephant barn he thought he'd noticed a look of defiance in the boy. Only fleeting, but he was almost sure of it. He didn't like that. He was used to respect, compliance, and fear when he demanded it. Standing in front of him now, Matt was sweating. But for all he knew it could be due to the heat, or the narcotics Al had shoved down him the previous night.

'Thanks, King,' said the boy,' but to be honest I'm pretty knackered.' He gave a wide, exaggerated yawn. 'And I've still got loads to sort out. 'Sorry, maybe another—'

'Hell, you can sleep enough when you're dead.' The boy didn't know him. If he had he would have realised it wasn't an invitation, Matt was going with him. He gave him a firm slap on his back, propelling him in the direction of the park entrance, 'Come on, let's go.'

Julian was at the kiosk dealing with a small queue of visitors. King saw the curator raise his hand to him, trying to get his attention like he was flagging down a cab, but King had his own agenda. Blanking the curator he and Matt passed through the entrance and out into the car park which was starting to fill up. In the distance King could see a steady stream of new arrivals, kicking up trails of dust as the vehicles bumped and lurched their way down the rutted track.

'Amazed anyone ever finds this place,' King said. 'Guess the boss got lucky, making a zoo work in an isolated bit of swamp in the back of beyond like this.' He watched Matt who was briefly surveying the surrounding moorland with tired, dark-ringed eyes.

'I guess it is a fairly out-of-the-way spot,' agreed Matt.

'I'll say.' King laughed and patted Matt on the shoulder. 'Pretty as a postcard to look at. But hey, reckon there's more corpses out there than a graveyard.' King looked pointedly at Matt. 'Quicksand. Place is riddled. Put a foot wrong and you'd be sucked in like a goddam spider down a plughole. Hell of a way to go.' He nodded towards the track, 'That's the only way in or out, bit of snow or flooding and we're fucked.' He flicked a drop of sweat from his brow. 'Still, ain't much chance of that happening anytime soon.'

Matt smiled and King turned away, sensing Matt trailing behind as he and Shadow headed off towards a large timber shed that served as the zoo's store room.

King heaved open the door, its creaking accompanied by the sound of hundreds of scampering feet.

'Goddamn rats, disgrace ain't it…gonna have to chuck half this stuff.' King looked at the pile of feed sacks which were leaning against a row of large metal hoppers. The corners of the sacks were chewed through and little piles of corn and pellets were spilling out and on to the floor, mixing with a sprinkling of rat faeces.

'Told Julian to speak to them delivery drivers,' said King, 'make sure they come and tell someone when they make a drop instead of dumping it on the floor and scooting off. But he's too shit scared of confrontation to make the call...rather hide in his office or skulk behind the kiosk.' King looked directly at Matt. 'I mean, what the hell is a curator doing selling tickets, ain't a manager's job.' King paused, but the boy simply yawned and muttered what sounded like 'I s'pose.' Either he wasn't taking the bait or he wasn't interested. King decided to change tack. Be less subtle. Casually he began hoisting up the sacks, putting the intact ones into one of the hoppers. Automatically Matt did the same. King noticed with satisfaction how the boy was using two arms to lift what he was managing with just one.

'So, you got a girl?'

'Huh, what do you mean?'

'A girlfriend. Good-looking kid like you must have a girl or two knocking around.'

'No, not really. Well, not at all. There was someone at uni but nothing serious.'

'Shame, it's good to have female company, makes a man complete...ain't that right, girl.' King looked over to Shadow who was, as usual, hanging on his every word. 'Go on then.' He clicked his fingers and she darted off into the recesses of the shed. 'Won't catch 'em...wrong breed, she just enjoys the hunt.' He watched her proudly for a moment. 'Take me and Susie, for instance. Bet you never put us together?'

Matt said nothing. Just stifled another yawn.

King was starting to feel irritated. His mission, as he saw it, had been to find out how much of a problem

43

Matt was going to be. Not just with Susie, but with all the other hassles that were going on in his life: this mahout that the boss was bringing in, Andy's snooping.

'Come on Matt. I saw the shock on your face when you saw she was my woman. Gotta pinch myself sometimes, great-looking girl like that...brains too, but the truth is she ain't done too badly herself.' He watched Matt closely as he spoke, hoping it would stir some reaction, and he was right. A tell-tale twitch. Most people wouldn't even notice it. But King wasn't most people. He smiled inwardly. Hooked him, he thought, just got to land him.

'I know what you're thinking,' he continued, 'typical arrogant yank, but it ain't arrogance. Fact is, I prefer female company and they sense it. Guess it comes down to respect, never met a *man* yet who earned it.'

He put the last of the sacks in the hopper and closed the lid. 'Reckon a lot of it's gotta do with my pa, beat ma to a pulp one night, would've me as well, except I got to the bread knife first. Aunt took me in after that... fine woman, cancer got her. Wouldn't take a genius to figure out why I'm more prone to the company of women.

He looked over at Matt and read the interest in his expression. Almost there, he thought.

'Reminds me a bit of that story Jimmy Stewart tells in that film. What the hell was it called? Anyways a kid's taken before the judge and the judge says to him, 'Sonny, you've been found guilty of murdering your ma and pa. Before I pass sentence is there anything you'd like to say in your defence?' And the little boy looks up at the judge, all big eyed and innocent, and he says, 'only this your honour, won't you take pity on a poor orphan boy?'

King chuckled… 'Shane! That's the film.'

'Destry Rides Again,' said Matt.

'What'ya talking about…it was Shane. Don't presume to teach me about Westerns. I was raised on them.'

'Shane's Alan Ladd. Destry is James Stewart. I promise you.'

He held the boy's glare, wanting to see if he would look away, cave in like he had earlier. But this time the kid stood his ground, staring back with a look of self-righteous defiance. King relaxed into a smile. 'Guess I could be mistaken.' He looked down at the mess on the floor. 'Think I'll send Colin and Gary over to clean this stuff up. S'pose you'll be wanting to get along now. Sort out your own stuff…hope I didn't keep you none?'

'Like you said,' replied Matt, 'I can sleep enough when I'm dead.'

Summoning Shadow to his side with a whistle, King watched Matt trudge back towards the park entrance. 'Well, girl. Looks like we were right. The kid's gonna be a problem.'

The dog looked up at her master then back at Matt, her lip curled up in a silent snarl.

CHAPTER 8

Monday 30th bank holiday

'Wake up sleeping beauty.' The voice was nasal and familiar. 'Wake up or I'll huff and I'll puff and I'll blow this house down.'

Matt awoke in a sudden fluster and knew straight away what had happened, he squinted at his watch… eight-thirty. 'Oh Christ!' He ran to the door, swung it open and was greeted by Andy, grinning smugly, with his rat perched on his shoulder.

'Not big on mornings then?' he said sarcastically.

'Christ, has anyone noticed that I'm not there?'

'Hmm, let's think – last bank holiday of the season, traditionally the busiest day of the year, everyone, even Julian's in the kitchen preparing feeds to get everything ready in time. You may have been mentioned once or twice.'

'Oh Christ!' Matt said again, heading for the bathroom. He ran the cold tap and submerged his face, scooping handfuls of the discoloured water over his head.

'I should've warned you about Al's dope; it has a long-lasting effect.' called Andy.

'So, I see,' replied Matt, gargling and spitting out the last remnants of toothpaste. 'Last I remember I was having a lie down yesterday afternoon.'

His stomach lurched. 'You know, I haven't eaten since God knows when. I'm starving.'

'Lucky's got a few seeds and nuts left, I'm sure she wouldn't mind if you wanted some,' suggested Andy as Matt reappeared from the bedroom.

'Lucky? Oh yeah, your rat, err, no thanks.' He contemplated the rodent for a second, whilst drying himself. 'That's a pretty risky name to give something isn't it? I mean, no sooner do you call something Lucky than irony rears its ugly head.'

'You've seen too many movies; I think it suits her, and we're lucky to have each other, aren't we girl.'

He said this in a nuzzly, cosy way that you would expect to hear from a parent addressing their baby, not, thought Matt, as he scrabbled through his suitcase for a fresh T-shirt, from a man to his rat.

'Anyway, you can always grab an apple or banana from the zoo kitchen, if we ever get there that is.'

'Okay, I'm ready.' Matt tugged out a creased, slightly fraying green top and they left the flat, or rather Andy left and he stumbled out in his attempt to lock the door whilst pulling the T-shirt over his head. 'So, what happened to you at the pub, I didn't see you after you spoke to King?'

'Huh? Oh yeah, Saturday, I just had something to do is all.' Andy was momentarily quiet. 'I heard you met King yesterday, what did you think?'

'Of King? I don't know, he's quite a character.'

'Yeah, I know – he had Colin and Gary working till past six last night without a break, you must have had quite an effect. Hey slow down, my legs aren't as long as yours.'

Matt was half walking, half jogging up the steep path trying to make up for lost time. He grudgingly stopped at the top of the hill to give Andy a chance to catch up.

'Slow down will you,' said Andy breathlessly, 'it's going to be a full-on day, and another hot one, you need to pace yourself. If you're worried about Julian, don't be, just leave him to me…So come on, tell me what happened yesterday with King?'

Matt shrugged. 'Nothing much, he was friendly enough, in the end…I met Susie as well, she seemed nice. I'm surprised that she and King are an item.'

'So that was it!' squealed Andy triumphantly. 'You made a play for Susie. Can't blame you, she's great. Bloody hell, no wonder King was pissed off with you.'

'No, it was nothing like that,' insisted Matt as they passed through the Staff Only door. 'I was just saying that…'

'So you don't fancy her, then?'

'I'm just saying that I don't want you doing any stirring; I've got off to a bad enough start as it is.'

'Oh, so you *do* fancy her but you don't want me telling anyone?'

'Yes, I mean no – Christ, Andy… I mean I don't want King, or Susie or anyone thinking I'm after her!'

They burst through the door into the zoo kitchen.

'Which I'm n—'

Big Al and Jez stood in the kitchen, nudging each other with wide, delighted smirks.

'Don't worry,' whispered Andy with a grin, 'your secret's safe with me.'

Looking around the room Matt was relieved to notice that neither King nor his minions were there. Julian however was, his round face flushed and nervous as he approached.

'Ah, Matthew.' He stopped and cleared his throat stiffly. 'You're here a little err, later than I had hoped.'

'Not his fault, Julian,' chirped Andy, 'seems you told him the wrong start time, nine instead of eight.'

The curator scratched his chin 'Did I?'

'Shite, Julian, you and that memory of yours,' said Big Al, crunching on an apple and winking in Matt's direction.

'Forget your head if it wasn't fixed on, wouldn't you,' said Andy, tossing Matt a banana.

The curator, smiling furtively and visibly relieved, gave Matt a slap on the back. 'Sorry old chap, the lads are right, memory's not my strong suit. Anyhow, no harm done, glad I found out before I ripped into you, wouldn't have been a good start.' His eyes darted around the small gathering and he cleared his throat 'I believe you met all the lads the other night, excellent, no need for introductions, best get straight into it then. Al could you be a dear and take Matt with you today, show him the ropes.'

'No problemo,' boomed Al. He turned to Matt. 'Come on then Rip Van Winkle, we got us some catching up to do.'

Andy gave Matt a sly grin as if to say 'told you it would be okay.'

They left the kitchen and walked around a corner into the recess where the calf had been hanging the day before. The carcass had gone and in its place stood a trolley – a basic but functional design that reminded Matt of a go-cart that he and his brother had made when they were kids. It was littered with lumps of hacked-up meat and a single rabbit, its eyes bulging from the shock of what Matt guessed must have been a gruesome end. Scattered around the meat, like an obscene garnish, was a condiment of yellow day-old chicks and some mice and rats, all of which, judging by the damp sheen that coated their fur and feathers, had only recently been defrosted. As Matt greedily consumed his banana Al liberally shook some powder over the raw feast. 'Vitamin supplement,' he explained, picking up the handle of the trolley and setting off.

As it trundled behind him the wheels squealed reluctantly into obedient life giving the horrible impression that the rodents and chicks had awoken and were pitifully squeaking their innocence as they were being dragged to their doom. He shook out the image, discarded the banana peel into a bin, and followed Al down the corridor and into the walled garden.

'What was all that about?' asked Matt once he was sure he was out of earshot. 'He must have known Andy was lying, you all must have.'

'That's Julian for you,' said Al, 'anything for a quiet life – he'd much rather make a public apology than face a showdown. Shite, didn't you see the relief on his face when Andy gave him a get-out clause, brightened up no end the wet sod. Give him a choice of a confrontation or running away he'll leg it every time...So anyway,' he looked down at Matt, 'what's this about you fancying Susie?'

'What! No, you got it wrong. It's Andy...'

'You fancy Andy?'

'Huh? No. I fancy Susie – I mean Andy was saying I fancy Susie... which I don't. But I was trying to explain that when we came into the kitchen. Trying to stop Andy from–'

'I'm only joshing with you,' said Al, 'I know what a scandal mongering bastard Andy can be. Still, you better hope King doesn't get wind that you fancy her or you'll end up on this trolley with the rest of the dead meat...come on.'

CHAPTER 9

They weaved their way around the paths, stopping occasionally to distribute some chicks or rodents to the expectant servals, ocelots and small jungle cats who would crane their necks and lick their lips in anticipation when the sound of Al's meals on wheels came squealing around each bend.

Al was almost doubled up in the cramped enclosures, cooing over his girls whilst Matt collected the faeces onto a spade and raked over the sandy perimeter, obliterating the mass of stereotypic criss-crossing paw prints.

By the time they reached the lynx exhibit all the snacks and titbits were gone and they were using the larger chunks of meat that spilled over the rim of a bucket.

'So, who's the rabbit for?' asked Matt.

'You'll see soon enough.' Al's eyes sparkled with mystery. 'We'll leave the trolley here. You bring the bucket of meat and I'll take Thumper.' He picked up the rabbit and removed the wire from around its neck. 'Snared it this morning – special bank holiday treat.'

The only other person they had seen on their rounds was Tommy, but he was oblivious to them. Standing inside an enclosure and transfixed by a group of juvenile parakeets that Matt recognised as Red Lori, he flinched and giggled as their little hooked beaks nipped at his nose and earlobes, unaware of the world beyond the mesh.

Continuing under an arch they left the walled garden and came to another path that split in two. They took the right fork that led down the winding path, past the paddocks, over the river, and into a small fenced-in copse.

Al ducked under the plank of wood that hung corral style over the door with the words *Timber Wolf* carved into it in relief. Then after a brief jangle of keys and a click of the padlock they stepped into the safety porch.

'Christ,' said Matt, 'we're not going in with them, are we?'

'Relax, I'll be right behind you – if they get too close they'll feel the sting of this across their arses.'

Matt did a quick head count as Al grabbed the rake that leant in the corner. 'A rake… against twelve wolves? You're kidding!'

Al shoved him forward and into their enclosure. 'Fourteen, unless we've lost a couple. Now hurry the fuck up, Beth's waiting.'

Matt watched nervously as the wolves stretched and yawned into life; two more appeared from the relative cool of the undergrowth and lazily sauntered over towards their bucket of meat, stopping expectantly three yards short of him with their nostrils twitching and flaring in the air. 'They're no different to domestic dogs,' he said, fighting off an urge to say 'sit.'

'Yeah, I s'pose,' said Al, 'as long as you don't start running – triggers the predatory instinct and before you know it they'll be on you like… well, like a pack of fucking wolves. Now scatter the meat for fucksake before they start drowning in their own saliva.'

Matt did as he was told, throwing the meat around and trying to work out from their reactions which were the alpha dogs. Frustratingly, none of them paid much attention to natural order, listlessly flopping back down onto the dusty ground with their easily gotten gains.

'Better get a move on you two,' said a languid voice, the owner of which was obliterated by a bale of straw thrown awkwardly over his back. With a grunt Roger let the bail fall to the floor and sat heavily on it, wiping away the sweat and spitting out bits of husk. He acknowledged Matt with a casual nod. 'Never seen anything like it, cars backed up to the main road, had to abandon the tractor, couldn't get through, gonna have to do the top end by hand.'

'Shite,' replied Al. 'I'm not looking forward to today – you fancy a wee pick-me-up?' He dug into his pocket and brought out a suspicious-looking bottle and rattled it at Roger.

'That's your answer to everything,' he said. 'No, I'm okay thanks, but I wouldn't mind a hand with the camels when you're finished.' He paused, noticing the rabbit in Al's hand, 'That for Beth?'

Al nodded, 'You bet.'

'Shit Al, you're going to be sodding ages messing around with that pet of yours. Can't you let me have Matt for an hour… if that's cool with you, Matt?'

'Sure,' agreed Matt.

'Fine my arse,' said Al. 'Julian gave him to me, and anyway he wants to meet Beth, don't you Matt?'

'I guess…if I knew who Beth was?'

Al ignored his question. 'So, we'll be as quick as we can and join you later, alright.'

It was more of an order than a question and Roger, sighing, conceded.

'There's no arguing with you Al, just try not to be too long, okay.'

He heaved the bale back onto his shoulder; a shower of loose strands cascaded down on him. Matt watched with pity as he staggered off along the path, looking like an ancient scarecrow whose stuffing had burst.

All of a sudden a Tom Jones tune blared out, flooding the park with its distorted cacophony.

'Shite,' said Al, 'must be almost ten. That's the carousel starting up.' Victorious from his conflict with Roger, Al locked the wolves' porch behind them and strode off along the tree-lined path, booming along tunelessly with the carousel, 'What's new pussycat – whoa, whoa, whoa...Pussycat, pussycat, I love you, yes I do, you and your pussycat nose.'

CHAPTER 10

All the resentment that he'd felt by being stamped with 'property of big Al' immediately deserted him as he watched his colossal master's reunion with the leopard. It was at first unbelievable as Al stepped unguarded into the enclosure, and then plainly the most touching thing that Matt had seen – two hugely powerful beings lost in the rapture of each other's company.

The leopard had initially pounced on Al, her two massive front paws, claws tenderly retracted, clamped around Al's bull-like neck. Then a greeting ritual of rubbing and bumping heads against each other commenced. After a few minutes Al got the rabbit out and began playfully taunting Beth who seemed to be relishing the mock hunt. Crouching low and almost motionless, with only the tip of her tail twitching excitedly, blatantly visible in the dusty dried earth but thinking herself suitably camouflaged. Al would play along with her delusion. 'Beth, Beth where are you, where have you gone?' In two giant leaps she'd be on his back and they would be wrestling on the floor.

'I hand-reared her from a wee bairn three years ago,' explained Al, breathing heavily.

Beth had taken to a shady corner of her enclosure, also panting, her furry prize gripped between her paws.

'Her mother killed the other cubs and I only just got to her in time.'

'She's beautiful, it must be amazing playing with her like that…can anyone do it?' Matt longed to touch her.

'I wouldn't recommend it, she could take your head off as soon as look at you. It's just because I'm her Dada that I can get away with it.'

Matt couldn't tell if this was strictly true or whether he was seeing another glimpse of Al's possessive streak. He was about to push the matter when a voice burst from Al's back pocket.

'*Roger to Al, Roger to Al, are you receiving, over.*'

Al pulled out the walkie-talkie, held it to his mouth and depressed a button on its side. 'Yup, receiving you Roger, what you want? Over.'

'*What ya mean what do you want, you great Scots oaf, I've been waiting half an hour for you, just put your pussy down and get your arse down here, over and out.*'

Al, chuckling, replied. '*Roger,* Roger.' He turned to Matt. 'I'll never get bored of saying that. Come on, we best give the soft southern nancy a hand.'

They left Beth busily plucking the rabbit, collected their equipment and made their way down to the camel yard.

Despite the discomfort of the midday heat that bore remorselessly down on them, Matt was having a great time.

Al and Roger, he discovered, had worked together for five years and were clearly good friends. It wasn't hard for him to see why. Al's crass and child-like impulsiveness fed Roger's sardonic attitude. It was, thought Matt, a perfectly symbiotic alliance.

It was close to midday and the heat was inescapable. Clouds of dry husks clung to their sweat-drenched skin and caught in the back of their parched throats as they turned over the straw bedding.

'I used to like the summer, but this is just taking the piss,' groaned Roger, pausing to stretch his back.

'Aye, but it's worth the suffering when lasses wear next to nothing...will you just look at the legs on her.' Al put two fingers between his lips, getting halfway through a shrill wolf whistle before Roger yanked his hand away from his mouth.

'Don't worry about him. He's escaped from the baboon enclosure, but we've got him contained now.'

The girl smiled at Roger's remark, then looked at Al before rolling her eyes with disdain as she walked away.

'What the fuck did you say that for?' said Al, 'reckon I could've scored there.'

'Because, my friend,' replied Roger once the girl was out of earshot, 'you could do *soo* much better.'

'You think?' said Al, then after a pause added, 'Okay...thanks.'

Roger looked over to Matt and shook his head in mock despair.

CHAPTER 11

By the time they had finished mucking out it was close to lunchtime and the park was heaving. They stacked their tools in a corner of the corral and began forcing their way through the steady stream of pedestrians that poured down the path, Al never missing an opportunity to shout abusively at any visitor he caught feeding crisps to the meerkats or taunting a primate with a stick. 'Perk of the job,' he said, grinning, 'you fancy a go?'

He directed Matt's attention to a family whose bald father was leaning precariously over the lynxes' safety barrier and pushing their snarling Jack Russell against the mesh whilst being egged on by two fat, sticky children.

'Go on then,' prompted Al, 'you're the education officer, go fucking educate.'

With a shove of encouragement Matt was catapulted through the crowd towards the family and within earshot of the father and his kids.

'Who wants to chase the pussycats then, huh. D'you, d'you want to chase the big pussycats?'

'Hey, Dad, could Eddie beat 'em in a fight, not both at the same time, but more fair, just one of them?'

Matt swallowed in anticipation of the confrontation and stepped forward, forcing his voice to sound as authoritative as possible. 'Excuse me, could you not do that, please.' He received no response so he tried again, tapping the father on his shoulder. 'Excuse me, could you stop doing that.'

The angry faces of the father and two boys turned to him, whilst the mother shrank back.

'What's it to you, Sunny Jim?'

'Well, I work here and it's my job to–'

'It's your job to leave folk to enjoy themselves in peace,' said the father.

'I don't think your dog is enjoying itself very much and the Lynx certainly aren't, so if you could just…'

'Our dog could 'ave your cats, couldn't he, Dad,' interrupted one of the children.

'Bloody right he could, tough little bugger – the best ratter I ever had.'

Matt glanced at the terrier.

'Now you listen 'ere, I paid good money to get into this place, not to be lectured by some jobsworth on what I can or can't do with my dog.'

'Just leave it, Frank,' pleaded his wife, going through the motions as if reading from a script.

'I'm not doing anything, it's this upstart.'

Al, lunged forward. 'You calling my friend an upstart?'

Everyone in the vicinity stared at the father who began blustering his innocence, too late to appease Al.

'You see, all my friend is trying to explain to you is that if you taunt our wee beasties again with that fucking mutt then I'll personally ram your fat fucking cue ball head through the mesh till your face comes through the other side like fucking minced meat. Is that clear enough for you?'

'Go on, Dad, you could 'ave 'im, don't let 'im talk to you like–'

The father clamped his hand urgently around his son's mouth and edged nervously back into the crowd, muttering something about 'not ending here,' and 'going to speak to your supervisor,' before being swallowed up by the hordes.

'Watch and learn,' said Al, beaming proudly, 'now come on, I'm fucking starving.'

'Education in action, huh?' said Roger, giving Matt a sardonic smile as they followed in the wake of Al's purposeful, path-clearing stride.

'How does he get away with talking to people like that?'

Roger shrugged. 'Who's going to stop him…Julian?'

'Okay,' acknowledged Matt, imagining the curator's round, nervous face, 'perhaps not him. But what about the owner, he can't be happy about it?'

'The boss?' Roger let out a derisive humph. 'He spends his summer posing round the French Riviera on his yacht, won't see him 'til the start of the hunting season, likes to play the landed gentry, so you see, no come-back.'

Finally, they reached the staff room, bundling through the door and up the stairs, parched and sticky from the journey. They were the first ones there.

'Like salmon trying to get back to their breeding ground,' sighed Roger, collapsing into a chair.

'Don't get me going on breeding, shite, just look at the knockers on that!' groaned Al who had gone to the French windows and had managed to pick out a girl in a revealingly tight pink vest top from amongst the vast crowd that swarmed below.

As Al leered studiously out of the window he suddenly craned his neck to the left. 'Fuck me, hey you two, you gotta see this!'

Matt and Roger both went to the window and stared down as two multi-coloured elephants lumbered around the corner, greeted by gasps and applause. Each was led by their young keeper and sitting astride the neck of the lead elephant was King, regally waving his elephant hook like a sceptre in acknowledgement of his public.

'Fuck me!' said Roger, 'I don't know whether to laugh or salute.'

They were still looking out of the window when Andy and Tommy bundled in, closely followed by Jez, grinning widely. 'Hey dudes,' he said, 'whatcha think, busy enough for you? Man, that must be the biggest show I've ever done, standing room only.' He sauntered over to where Matt, Roger and Al were standing. 'Christ, if it was like that for the morning session God knows what the two o'clock's going to be like – still, the sea lions loved it, seems the more applause they get the better they perform. Tommy, make us a coffee, there's a pal. What about you dudes, fancy a drink?' Jez took the orders and shouted them over to Tommy. 'Make that three coffees and two teas. So, what are you lot all gawping at?'

Al grunted in the direction of the elephants and stepped aside to give Jez a better view, blocking Andy's attempts at a curious glimpse.

'Oh yeah, King and his subjects,' said Jez standing next to Matt.

Matt noticed the immediate area filling with a bizarre, although strangely pleasing aromatic mix of chlorine, fish and aftershave.

'Who the hell does he think he is? Hannibal?' Jez gave a dismissive humph that hinted of showmanship envy then turned to Matt. 'Julian gave me a couple of messages to give to you, there's a group of boy scouts coming tomorrow for a talk, wants you to deal with it.'

Matt felt his face crumble; he had not expected his talks to start for at least another week. 'You're kidding, right? I don't even know my own way around yet, and anyway, how can I do a talk when it's like this, even if I don't get lost in the crowds the kids certainly will!'

'Relax,' said Andy, who had finally muscled, or rather slithered his way past Al. 'It won't be anything like this tomorrow, this is the last big day of the year, the place will be deserted after today, even Jez packs up in a week or so, bums around Europe for a couple of months whilst we look after his sea lions, – jammy bastard.'

'Jammy's got nothing to do with it,' said Jez, grinning. 'Life's what you make of it, that's all. Which reminds me, have you told Matt about the party on Saturday night? End of season bash at my place, by the sea lion pool, everyone will be there.'

'Even Susie,' said Andy with a grin.

Matt ignored Andy's taunt, obsessing over what else the curator had told Jez. 'So, what was the other message?'

Jez looked blankly back at him.

'You know, from Julian. You said that there were two messages.'

'Oh yeah, sorry, can't remember it all. I was working on a score at the time so I wasn't giving him my full attention – a cracking blonde, tits like you wouldn't believe.'

'Not wearing a pink vest top!' said Al excitedly.

'That's the one.'

'Shite, you're a canny bugger. I'd picked her out for myself, was gonna invite her to your party.'

'Eey Al,' replied Jez, 'you're a big man but you're nay too quick enough to get laid by the southern lasses.'

'Looks to me like you've both lost your touch.'

They all followed Roger's gaze towards the elephants where the same girl was being chatted up by Colin and Gary.

'Easy come, easy go,' said Jez, shrugging.

'Fucking tart,' added Al.

'So, what *was* the message?' prompted Matt, feeling stressed from the various scenarios that his imagination was throwing at him.

'Oh yeah,' replied Jez,' something to do with picking up this mahout from the airport – I can't remember when, Wednesday or Thursday I think he said, wow, I don't want to be around when him and King meet.'

'You're kidding, I wouldn't miss it for the world,' said Andy with relish. 'I hear these mahouts are raised with elephants, spend their entire life with them, even talk to them telepathically.'

'That's shite.'

'Yeah well, they've got some kind of mystical thing going on, some special understanding, and this one the boss has hired is supposed to be the best in the business – he'll certainly put King in his place.'

'Poor bugger won't get one foot through the elephant house door before King eats him alive,' said Roger. 'Matt, if you're going to collect him you had better let him know the situation, at least give him a fighting chance, warn him to tread lightly, you know.'

'Sure… but…'

'That's crap,' said Andy, 'he's here to sort out Dan – the poor sod's been stuck in that dungeon for over a year now and this mahout is his last chance, so fuck King's feelings.'

'We all know what you feel about King, but like it or not you can't blame him for the way Uddanda is,' said Roger.

'The hell I can't,' replied Andy.

Matt's head was panning from Andy to Roger and back again. The lack of inclusion was resurrecting deeply buried childhood resentments: last to be picked in PE, no one to sit next to on the school trip.

A thought from the previous night popped into his mind. In the Huntersmoon Inn – was it Jez or Roger who said something about ancient history? He couldn't remember – he had been too stoned – something to do with Uddanda…

Frustration and curiosity finally overwhelmed him; he blurted out to no one in particular. 'Is anyone going to tell what the hell I'm missing?'

The question was met by an immediate, awkward silence from the group. They all turned to Roger. The whole room now staring at the paddock keeper, awaiting his decision.

With a purposeful rub of his large, baleful eyes and after a long sigh of resignation he looked at his companions and shrugged. 'Have you ever heard of an elephant going into a trance, just shutting down like that?

'Christ, Roger.' Andy's voice was squeaking, 'You *know* why he's like that. You were there, you told me what King did to Dan after they found Tommy and Jack. *Any* animal's going to act weird after that kind of treatment.'

Matt was about to ask what Andy meant by 'treatment' but Roger was already answering.

'But that's my point. Dan was in that trance when we found them, not after the beating, but before – that's how come Tommy wasn't finished off, why we were able to shackle Dan so easily. He didn't even flinch when King laid into him. Man, King used anything he could lay his hands on, forks, mattock handles, it was like he was possessed, couldn't get near enough to stop him for about ten minutes until his strength finally gave out, and the whole time, I mean, like through the whole beating, Dan didn't even blink, nothing, just blank. He's been like that ever since.'

'Christ, that's awful,' cried Matt. Aware that all eyes were now on him, he shook the image of brutality from his mind and tried focusing on Uddanda's behaviour. 'What was Dan like before all of that happened?'

'A pussy-cat, give or take,' replied Roger. 'Sure, he could be a bit bloody-minded at times but never aggressive. He'd only been here about five years and beyond that we don't know much. I think he was wild caught from young, did the rounds – zoos, circuses – but I guess he just outgrew everywhere he went, then he ended up here. He came with another keeper, a Frenchman, but after a couple of years he got homesick and that's when King started.'

'That's all well and good,' said Andy, 'but it doesn't change the fact that if King hadn't sent them into the enclosure when Dan was coming into *musth* then Dan wouldn't be in his situation. Jack wouldn't be dead and Tommy wouldn't be lobotomised.'

'You can't prove that,' insisted Roger, 'no-one knows why Jack and Tommy went there that night but you sure as hell can't prove King had anything to do with it, why would he?'

'I dunno, but if King didn't send them, why were they there?' Andy left the question hanging, unchallenged in the air before continuing. 'Exactly. And we'll never know if everyone's too scared to confront him.'

'Ahem,' interrupted Jez, nodding in the direction of the kitchenette where Tommy stood with wide, moist eyes, a tray of mugs gently rattled in his trembling hands.

Andy shrugged, and continued with his tirade. 'That's why we should get this mahout on our side, get him to find out what happened, you know, get him to use his telepathy on Dan or something... ouch!'

'Thanks, Tommy,' said Jez, handing out the mugs. 'Ignore Andy, he's just having one of his 'trade union' moments.'

'I'm just saying what everyone here knows but are too gutless to say, that's all.'

'Well, why don't you tell him yourself?' said Jez, 'and looks like here's your chance.'

Matt followed Jez's gaze to the elephants outside, watching King as he slid down from Devi's back, spoke to Colin and Gary who nodded obediently, and then waded through the crowd that parted reverently before him.

'Shit,' cried Jez, 'first he's Hannibal, now he's Moses!'

CHAPTER 12

Two gigantic cheese plants loomed in the corners of the room with insipid, prehistoric-like leaves, half unfurled and reaching out towards the French window as though grasping for sunlight. Placed randomly around the room, three neglected yucca's pushed up against the ceiling, their spiky leaves bent double, and their anaemic roots bursting from their pots, creeping across the vinyl laminate floor like giant, fossilised worms probing the floors accumulated layers of mud and sand for nutrition.

Even the room's seven chairs and double sofa had lost their sense of domesticity. Long, dangling strands of frayed fabric and the clumps of russet coloured horse hair burst from their seams, adding to the lost world effect.

At the sound of King's feet pounding up the stairs all the keepers instinctively leapt into the chairs in an attempt to capture an atmosphere of innocent nonchalance.

All but one. Tommy remained at the window; his narrow, wan face turned towards the growing crowds outside.

'Man, you could boil a bullfrog under that sun,' announced King, swaggering into the staffroom and collapsing into the sofa. He was the colour of a braised boar and his shirt was drenched in sweat. 'Throat's drier than lizard spit on a hot rock.' He pushed his shades up his forehead, his pale blue eyes briefly boring into each keeper with a questioning intensity, finally coming to rest on Andy. 'What's up? Feels like I've walked in on a wake.'

'Nothing, just all a bit knackered,' said Andy, 'let me get you a cold one.' Avoiding the scornful looks from the others he scampered off to the kitchenette.

Tommy continued looking outside, his attention now drawn to the two elephants below, their heads gently, hypnotically, rocking in metronomic unison.

Outside, the crowd had multiplied, becoming a flock that engulfed the picnic area where the two young keepers and their enormous charges stood.

'You think we'd better call up King,' said Gary, his master's orders still ringing in his ears, *Don't split them up, don't let anyone get too close and for fuck sake keep your eyes on the job and off the broads.*

'I dunno,' replied Colin, 'I don't want him to think we can't handle it, but...'

A large faced woman cut him short. 'How much for them to have a ride?'

Colin looked down at the chocolate-stained faces of her brood. 'Sorry love, but we're not doing rides. So, Gary–'

'That's not what I heard, I was told you were doing elephant rides.'

Another voice, male and Manchurian rose from the crowd. 'Hey mate, is that right? You doing rides?'

'I wanna go on the elephants,' wailed a little boy a few feet away.'

Colin tried to ignore them but was forced to respond as the woman began tugging impatiently on his shirt.

'Oi, we were here first.'

'I think you've got confused, Missus. We don't do rides.'

More voices leapt into the air.

'How much to go on the elephant?'

'Where's the queue start?'

'I wanna go on the one with the green flowers on its trunk!'

'Can four people go at the same time?'

With his back to the other keepers, Tommy stared from the window, transfixed by Devi and Joti. Slowly he began rolling his head, matching their rhythmic movements. His fingers began plucking at imaginary pieces of fluff on his T-shirt, jerky little movements that distracted his mind from its sense of déjà vu.

Craning his neck Gary searched for Colin, but the thickening crowd obscured his vision. He could only hear fragments of his friend's voice becoming more distant and desperate with every passing second. He knew he shouldn't leave Devi's side; he had been warned by King about abandoning his post, but loyalty to his best friend trumped his common sense. As he waded into the crowd a surge of people, taking advantage of the freed-up position, flooded into the space, forcing the two elephants further and further apart.

Tommy stopped plucking at his clothes and instead began rubbing his hands, then his arms, trying to rid himself of the itching, tingling sensation that was spreading around his limbs. His focus was now entirely on Devi. He was mesmerised. His head rolling becoming more pronounced, mimicking her back and forth motion.

Devi's trunk was now swaying from side to side like a gigantic pendulum. A shouting, rowdy group had now completely surrounded her. Prodding, probing, sticky hands were stifling her senses, filling her with panic and feelings of resentment towards the wedge of people who were driving Joti away from her.

'Hey Tommy, what's up?'

Devi's ears were fully forward and her whole body was now rocking from side to side, fighting the powerful urge to lunge towards the security of Joti, regardless of the people that stood between them. Low rumbles began to emit from her trunk, noises so different to the human shouts and cries that it became instantly audible, finally drawing Colin and Gary's attention away from the baying crowd and towards the stranded elephant.

Both keepers looked helplessly over the sea of people whose undertow had carried them at least twenty feet from Devi. Close enough to see the rising fear in her eyes but too far to calm her.

'Tommy, what's up?'

Andy watched Tommy's back, curious as to what he found so absorbing. He wondered over to the bird keeper's side and looked out of the window. His eyes immediately widened, greedily absorbing the chaotic scene outside.

Then he turned to Tommy as the boy let out a muffled moan. His feet and hands were twitching and drool dangled from his thin lips.

Gary tried clawing against the current of people who were beginning to back away, at first cautiously but with increasing abandon as they realised their exit was blocked by others. Like a wave racing from the epicentre, panic tore through the crowd, increasing Devi's alarm to unbearable limits as men, women and children shunted and crashed around her.

Colin, seeing Gary swept away in the torrent, reached for his walkie-talkie, just as Devi reared up and bellowed her dismay in a desperate roar.

Tommy fell to the floor, his arms and legs thrashing wildly, his entire body convulsing. Roger ran to Tommy, narrowly missing King who was charging towards the door. He dropped down to Tommy's side, and then looked back up into Andy's horrified eyes. 'Quick, go and get a wooden spoon from the kitchen.' Roger's voice was calm.

'A spoon?' repeated Andy, incredulously.

'For his mouth, he's having a fit. I don't want him biting his sodding tongue off.'

Andy ran past Matt, Al and Jez who approached hesitantly, looking from Tommy's frail, contorted body to Roger, helplessly awaiting instructions.

'It's cool. I've got it. You lot get outside and help King.'

They barely registered Roger's voice as they continued staring at the boy writhing at their feet, his eyeballs rolling over and ivory white spittle foaming from the corners of his mouth.

Kneeling at Tommy's side, Roger looked up at them. 'He'll be fine... Go help King...Now!'

'You heard him!' yelled Al, the orders shaking him from his daze and into action 'Let's go.' He grabbed Matt and Jez roughly by the arms, half dragging them behind him as he pounded down the stairs, the three of them stumbling out of the door and into the blazing heat.

'Shite, it's like a scene from the towering inferno,' shouted Al above the holler of the fear-drenched public which crawled and clambered past. 'Stay close behind me.' He waded into the stampede and towards the chaotic core like Achilles in search of Hector, relishing the challenge and sense of power.

King had already reached the elephants, his physicality being more suited to the charging bull approach, scattering people as though they were skittles in his wake.

He quickly realised that Devi was beyond reason, even after the blows from his hook, so he pushed his way through to Joti whom Colin had managed to keep relatively calm throughout. 'Joti, suno, listen.' He whacked her on the trunk. 'Joti, suno!'

She listened.

'Good girl, now come, aao, aao.'

She tentatively turned herself around

'Walk Joti, chalo, chalo.'

She obediently followed King who tugged her to where Devi now stood, rocking and lashing out randomly at any hint of movement.

73

Her trunk came heavily down on Joti who responded by grasping it with hers and entwining it around her own, its tip seeking out the tip of the other's. Slowly Devi responded to the other's influence, her swaying subsided as she feverously groped and stroked her companion.

'Sorry, King,' said Gary, meekly appearing at King's side just as Al and the others approached through the thinning remains of the crowd.

'Looks like this mahout is getting here just in time,' Al muttered to Matt.

King's hand curled itself into a fist and he stared at Al. Gary continued to grovel. 'Things just got out of control, I couldn't stop her, there were just so many people and—'

King's knuckles slammed into Gary's jaw. The keeper staggered, then dropped to his knees, stunned by the force of the blow, a trickle of blood seeping from his mouth.

'I told you, don't *ever* separate them,' growled King standing over Gary's dazed, cowering body. 'Get them inside, I'll fix Devi later.'

With a quick, cursory glance, like a general assessing the aftermath of a battle, King surveyed the damage. A couple of bloody noses, some minor cuts and grazes, a few kids sobbing into their mothers chests. 'So, who are the first aiders?' he demanded.

'Err, Roger, but he's busy with Tommy,' replied Jez.

'Tommy? What the hell is wrong with him, he was up in the staff room wasn't he?'

'I think one or two memories got the better of him,' said Al sardonically. 'It was some kind of fit,' added

Jez. 'Roger seemed to think that he would be okay, though.'

King looked up at the French windows, his brow momentarily creased with indecision.

'What about Julian, he's a first aider isn't he?' suggested Jez.

'Fuck him!' said King, dragging his eyes away from the window and back to the sea lion trainer, 'I wouldn't trust that useless fag with a plaster, no, we'll sort this mess ourselves, Matt, Jez, you go around those families, sound them out, promise some ice creams, a meal, free tickets if you have to, whatever it takes to keep them happy. Al, you can use your unique charms to disperse the onlookers.'

'My pleasure.' He grinned striding off towards the remaining public, rubbing his hands together in gleeful anticipation. 'Right, you bunch of blood – sucking vultures, you're going to sod off or do you need a wee bit of encouragement.'

Jez raised his eyes in mock despair, 'All the tact of a brick in the face, Hey, King, where the hell are you going?'

King pulled his radio from its pouch, 'I'm gonna check on Tommy.' He called Colin on the walkie-talkie as he walked away.

'Colin Receiving.'

'Are you back at the barn yet? Over.'

'Yeah, just about.'

'Good, I want Devi chained up, front and back, I'll be along once the park closes. And cancel any plans you had for tonight, It's gonna be a long session. King out.'

Matt looked at Jez, 'What did he mean by that?'

'Don't ask,' said Jez, stooping down to a child, 'Hey, kiddie, what's your favourite ice lolly?'

Tommy's eye's flickered open; he looked up at Roger with mild recognition, and shivered. His T. shirt clung to his frail torso and his sopping hair lay flat against his skull.

Roger gently lifted his head out of the small puddle of drool. 'You okay?'

'I guess.' Tommy smiled weakly. 'What happened?'

'Nothing.' With his free hand Roger attempted to spike up Tommy's tufts of hair into its familiar style. 'Nothing for you to worry about.'

CHAPTER 13

By dusk the elephant house was completely drained of colour. The beams of sunlight that had failed all day to penetrate the barn had finally given up, receding from the gloom like an octopus sliding down into the depths.

With the darkness came complete silence, eerie rather than calming, a subterranean stillness where time had lost all meaning.

Devi, Joti and Kali stood with their heads hung low, trunks resting on the floor like a fifth limb. Their anxiety over the earlier events had subsided but the presence of the two young keepers, dozing nearby on a pile of straw, left them feeling uneasy. It was not their normal routine.

Kali suddenly raised her head and gave a long rumble that roused her companions. Devi instinctively attempted to move toward the safety of Joti but her shackles snapped tight around her ankles.

Thirty seconds later and the cause of their alarm appeared in the doorway, flicking a switch and bathing the barn in an orange glow.

King stood in the opening, momentarily taking in his surroundings like a wolf sniffing the air. With a nod of satisfaction he turned to where Gary and Colin lay, shielding their eyes against the fluorescent glow.

'Come on boys, can't have a party without some music. You know what I wanna hear.'

Gary and Colin scrambled off the straw, clambering over each other in their eagerness to appease King. Colin got to the cassette recorder first whilst Gary fumbled for the tape.

'Music for all occasions, eh boys?'

Straightaway they knew King was in a strange mood, one that they hadn't seen before.

'When I punched you, what'd you learn?' said King.

'Huh?' said Gary, brushing the last few bits of straw from his clothes and still dozy from the long wait for King's return; he looked at his watch, eight thirty-five.

'Don't 'huh' me boy. you learned your lesson, right?' Gary nodded. 'That's right, to do as I say. I've just been on the phone to the boss for the last hour and a half. That faggot Julian thought that he should be informed of today's little event and the boss thinks maybe this mahout could help with some of the elephant training, that I could learn a bit from his fucking experience. I'll tell you now, by the time the boss arrives back from poncing around the Med that mahout won't have made a damn's worth of difference to Dan. Meanwhile I'll have Devi juggling chain saws whilst riding a unicycle, then we'll see who has the experience.'

He yanked out his hook and considered it briefly. 'Music for all occasions and the right tool for the job.'

Slamming the hook down on the table he pressed play on the cassette recorder; the mournful opening chord of 'Freebird' by Lynard Skynyrd floated out.

'Colin, get me a mattock handle and the cattle prods. You see Gary, when an elephant goes bad you gotta fix 'em. You can't have four tons of muscle and fat making a fool of you on the busiest day of the year. You let them get away with that you may as well forget it, chuck in the towel and get yourself a poodle. No, you gotta go back to square one, beat some respect into them, then start again with some basic commands.'

Colin came hurrying back with the equipment, a large wooden handle in one hand and in his other a long box with the word 'Hotshot; high voltage' written on its side. King opened the box, removing the cylindrical rod by lifting it by its battery pack and handle, carefully avoiding contact with the rubber- tipped end on which two electrodes protruded. Inspecting both tools, he picked up the mattock handle, taking a couple of practice swipes in the style of a baseball player about to step up to the plate. 'Respect and trust you see, they respect you so then you can trust them.'

As the first blow struck Devi squarely on the base of her trunk her companions shared in her fears and her pain, thrusting their weight against their chains and reaching out to her with their trunks in a futile effort to provide some comfort and protection.

'If I leave here tomorrow, would you still remember me?,' sang King, his voice perfectly suited to the southern twang of the song.

He brought the club firmly down on the more sensitive tip of Devi's trunk. In vain she tried to avoid the following blow, but it caught her in almost exactly the same place and she cringed away until the chains began to cut into her ankles.

Had she been Kali or even Joti, she may have retaliated, taken some swipes back, but she was the most timid of the three, submissive by nature, and all she could do was cower at the brutality.

'*But if I stayed here with you girl...*'
Whack.
'*...things just couldn't be the same...*'
Whack.

King beckoned to the two keepers who were looking on with an expression of guilty voyeuristic pleasure. '*Cause I'm as free as a bird now, and this bird you can't change...* Come on boys, you don't learn nothing by watching, use the cattle prod and get stuck in...*Lord help me I can't cha-ya ya ya ya.*'

The song moved up a gear, and another, the guitar solo gradually heading for the searing climax, carrying all three men along with its ascent.

'Not her flank, you idiots,' King yelled. 'She won't feel a thing there – zap her between the legs.'

There was a brief scuffle as Gary tried snatching the cattle prod away from his friend. 'My turn.'

Colin yanked it forcefully back. 'I ain't done yet... you can go after.'

Sulkily, Gary conceded, relaxing his grip. Colin smirked triumphantly, cradling the prod as they crept wolfishly to Devi's rear, one cautious step after another. Colin edged slightly in front as they approached, holding the prod at arm's length and placing the electrodes just inside the flap of loose, sagging skin. Mischievously, Gary gave Colin's elbow a sudden, hard shove, propelling the electrodes deep inside Devi genitalia just as Colin pulled the trigger.

The current flared into Devi and up her body; she bellowed with pain and confusion. Her heart pounded and echoed around her chest cavity, faster and faster with every current that pulsated through her.

Kali repeatedly threw her head at the bars. Joti rocked with despair as the thumping of Devi's racing heart beat penetrated her thick hide and through the soles of her feet until it felt as if she had two hearts beating within her.

Only Uddanda was still. Yet something unfathomably subtle was changing, an almost unperceivable light of awareness began flickering from deep within, a brightness replacing the unreceptive gaze that had for a year existed behind his vacuous eyes.

King's arms were beginning to tire; he roared to his minions, 'Gary, Colin, come here.'

Suddenly the torture stopped and Devi, so solid, so powerful, crumpled onto her knees. Forcing her eyelids to open she looked longingly over to Joti. In that single glance they seemed to convey all their thoughts: the passionate need they had for each other, the consummate reassurance that each brought. Devi longed to feel Joti's breath, to draw from her power and strength. It wouldn't be long now. Any moment the bolt would be drawn and the chains removed, allowing Joti back into her pen, the pain would be over, the torture would stop.

Her trunk, tender and sore, slowly lifted, reaching out for Joti, but instead found an alien, rod-like object. Instinctively she curled the pink fingertip of her trunk around it, just as Colin pulled the trigger on the cattle prod.

The current tore into her, like an explosion from deep inside. Devi was aware of a terrible noise, a wail of hideous despair from Joti, and the anguish in her consort's cry was even more distressing than the pain that tore into her chest. She made one last attempt to unfurl her trunk and reach out to her companion, wanting more than anything to be able to give her the same comfort and consolation that Joti had provided to her for so many years. She unfurled her trunk just as Joti reached out with hers but the gulf was too great. A moment later Devi's trunk fell limply to the floor.

The heartbeat was gone; Joti felt its absence immediately. For seventeen years it had gently, rhythmically played alongside her own, filling her with a sense of togetherness, a oneness that had made her feel complete. Devi had kept her strong, calm, reliable. It had been the fear of unsettling Devi that had helped keep herself in check… she was as dependent on Devi's weakness as Devi had been for her strength and for the first time in her life she felt lost and fearful.

Joti bellowed again, but this time it was different, lacking the rage and frustration that had accompanied her previous cry, this time it was simply a mournful, pitiful cry of loss. It was a cry born out of utter misery, the tortured cry of Prometheus, an endless, sorrowful call for help that could penetrate the deepest, coldest tomb and wake the dead within.

From the dark recess of the barn Uddanda's eyes, alert and unblinking, stared out.

PART TWO

Nature's great masterpiece, an elephant, the only harmless great thing.

John Donne, The Progress of the Soul

CHAPTER 14

Tuesday 31st

Matt was just finishing his coffee when there was a knock at his door.

'Hey Matt, it's Andy, you ready?'

Throwing back the last dregs Matt sighed, hoping that this wasn't going to become the norm. Andy seemed to be latching onto him, and although he didn't mind his company, he did like to be social on his own terms, and seven fifty in the morning was not one of those times. 'Coming.' He grabbed his keys and stepped outside into what looked like yet another relentlessly hot day. 'Christ Andy, you okay? You look awful.'

'Just had a bad night is all. Lucky was really restless for some reason, I couldn't calm her down, and when I eventually dropped off I kept having these bloody horrible dreams where I was being chased through a forest by Dan. Wherever I went or however high I climbed he could always reach me with his trunk. There was no escape. Pretty freaky, huh.'

'You're kidding, me too, I…I had the same dream, well almost, except mine was in the elephant house. I kept climbing up into the rafters but wherever I hid he always found me.'

Andy looked genuinely scared. 'Bugger me, that *is* pretty freaky!'

'I guess that what happened yesterday must have got to us more than we realised,' suggested Matt. 'How is Tommy by the way?'

'Fine.' Andy was briefly quiet and thoughtful as they carried on through the walled garden that was awash with litter from the previous day's hordes.

'God, this place is a mess,' said Andy finally. 'Bet the bastards wouldn't treat their own homes like that,' He booted away a coke can that lay in his path, 'You'd think that the parents would know better than to let their kids just chuck their stuff on the ground. Trouble is, the parents are just as bad, I mean what do they think bins are for, and who do you think's going to have to clear all this mess up? *Us*, that's who.' He nodded towards the Capuchin enclosure where broken branches and rope lay strewn around the pen. 'Bloody hell, they've even got the animals at it.'

'Christ,' said Matt, 'how the hell did that happen?'

'Monkey see, monkey do I guess. Man, it's going to take forever to sort this mess out. It's alright for you, you're well out of it with that cushy little talk you've got this afternoon.'

Matt had almost forgotten about the tour and his heart sank at the sudden reality of its imminence.

'Maybe Julian can cancel it,' said Matt hopefully. 'You could tell him you need me to help sort all this mess. Or you can do the tour instead, I don't mind. In fact, really I'd…?'

'What, me? No way!' Shielding his eyes from the sun with his hand Andy peered up the path and called out to the figure who appeared a little ahead of them. 'Hey Jez, what about all this mess, huh? You ever seen anything like it?'

Jez stopped briefly, as though deciding whether or not to ignore them, before hesitantly turning. His white teeth were clamped behind tight, pursed lips and his usual cocky, carefree stride was now furtive as he approached.

'I was just saying to Matt about all this sodding rubbish; don't s'pose you're going to lower yourself to help clear…' Andy's sentence tailed off, as he noticed Jez's down-cast eyes. 'What's up, didn't get laid last night?'

'You haven't heard, have you.' Jez paused, clearly reluctant to finish the sentence.

Matt and Andy glanced at each other.

'Are your sea lions alright?' asked Matt.

Jez looked at Matt, making eye contact for the first time. 'They're fine, thanks. It's…it's Devi, she…she died last night.' He flashed a nervous look at Andy.

Matt suddenly understood Jez's reluctance to talk. It wasn't being the messenger of bad news. It wasn't even, Matt suspected, the news itself, it was telling Andy that really concerned him.

'What! What do you mean, died?' exploded Andy.

'Just chill will you,' pleaded Jez. 'I mean just *that*. She died.'

'But how?' Andy was pacing up and down and gesticulating wildly. 'How did it happen…*tell* me.'

Jez sighed. 'Look, I dunno much. King says it was a heart attack. Roger's dragged her up into the woods with the tractor; he's dug a hole already. Susie's with them, she's doing an autopsy so we'll find out soon enough.'

'We don't need a sodding autopsy, we all know already!' Andy looked up at Matt for confirmation but

Matt was staring at the ground, recollecting King's words from yesterday afternoon *'It's going to be a long session.'*

'It was King!' squealed Andy looking back at Jez, 'And those two bastards. You know it was, don't you.'

'I mean that I dunno,' said Jez. 'It could've been her heart, it must have been pretty stressy for her yesterday and this heat...'

'Heat – bollocks!' Protested Andy. 'She's from India, not sodding Siberia. Heat she can do – American psychos and their cronies, she can't,'

Andy turned angrily to Matt. 'I'm right, aren't I, you know I'm right?'

'I don't know, I mean I've only been here a few days.' Matt paused, struck by how long a few days can feel. 'It is a pretty big coincidence though, especially after what he said ...' Matt stopped, but it was too late. Andy pounced on his unfinished words.

'What? What did he say? – I bloody knew it – he said he was going to fix her, didn't he.'

"Calm down, will you,' pleaded Jez. 'He didn't say that.'

'What then?' Andy's voice had reached falsetto. 'Sort her out? Do a bit of re-training? Come on, what did he say?'

Matt shrugged his shoulders. 'Honestly, it was nothing, more of a feeling than anything.'

'Then tell me what the feeling was...tell me!' insisted Andy.

Matt shrugged again so Andy turned to Jez for enlightenment.

'Come on, I can see why Matt wouldn't want to rock the boat in his first week, but you know the deal – if you know something you gotta say.' Andy paused to catch his breath before continuing, his voice now a begging whine. 'This is our chance to get him, shaft the bastard good and proper like he did to Jack and Tommy, and for all the shit he's done in-between.'

'Screw you, Andy,' snapped Jez. 'I've got five more days and then I'm out of here, South of France, Italy, Greece, Turkey wherever there's sun. You ever tried hitching with both of your thumbs busted, 'cause that's what'll happen if I start mouthing off about what I know, or think I know about what happened last night, and if you want my advice you'll keep your head down, and you too Matt, it's all over the park that you've got the hots for Susie.'

'What! 'How the hell...who's been saying that?' balked Matt, watching Jez's eyes fall on Andy

'Doesn't matter,' replied Jez. 'The point is that if you say anything it'll just look like sour grapes. Take my advice and just wait and see what the autopsy digs up.'

'Yeah, well if you can live with your conscience.' said Andy, avoiding Matt's reproachful glare, his voice settling back into its familiar nasally drone.

'Conscience!' Jez grinned. 'Who needs a conscience when you're hung like a Shire horse?

'I know which one I'd prefer,' replied Andy unconvincingly. 'Anyway, it *is* possible to have both you know.'

'True, but I find that one seriously hinders the other.'

Andy sullenly began to pick up a few wrappers and cans that had almost, but not quite, made it into the bins. 'And I s'pose you're going to leave us to clear up all this mess as well?'

'Afraid so, I've got to get my head down for a few hours, didn't get a wink of sleep last night.'

Andy looked up in alarm, missing the bin with the rubbish that he had collected. 'Bugger me, you as well. We had the same dream, didn't we Matt.'

'Dream?' said Jez. 'What the hell are you talking about dreams for?'

'The shared dream – where you're being hunted by Dan. Man, this is so weird.'

'You're the weird one' scoffed Jez. 'You're bloody obsessed by Dan. I didn't even get a chance to sleep, let alone dream. Remember that chick with the tits and the pink vest – seems she got stood up by Colin and Gary – man, she was gagging for it, insatiable, those boys don't know what they missed.' He yawned, flashing his gleaming white teeth. 'Right, I'm off, and don't forget to check the empty fag packets, I found a fiver in one once.'

'I bet you did, you jammy bastard,' muttered Andy. 'Hey Matt, where the hell are you going?'

'Sorry Andy, I've gotta swat up for this scouts' visit, I'll see you later.'

'Tell you what, I'll clean the whole soddin' park up by myself shall I!' Andy scrunched up a discarded Dunhill packet in his hand and launched it angrily at the bin.

CHAPTER 15

In the dark, dank recess of the elephant house stood Joti, hunched and trembling, her mind filled with the scent that still lingered after Devi's death, a hateful smell that hung vegetating in the air, bringing with it desperate, loathsome emotions that Joti could still taste with every inhalation of her breath.

She felt so alone.

She had tried reaching out to Kali but her pleas for contact and comfort were ignored.

It had come as no surprise, this was how Kali coped, or learned to cope, after Uddanda had left her and retreated into the shadows. Like Joti, she also had sought physical assurance, feverishly tugging and prodding at their patriarch, but she never received any response. As the days, then weeks and then months passed so did the frequency of her attempts until finally, and with no conscious decision, she gave up altogether and Uddanda faded into the shadows.

With Devi's death it was different; it was a sudden severing, like an amputation, that left her with no hope, no gradual coming to terms. Devi was there and then she was gone. Now Joti was alone.

She was so distraught that she didn't at first notice the tender pressure that brushed against her flank, but gradually her mind began to register the motion. Automatically she reached around with her trunk to investigate the touch that was distantly familiar to her, strong yet tender. She breathed in deeply, thousands of sensors carrying the information to her brain where it was instantly translated then dismissed as impossible. Slowly she turned her head, adrenalin pumping through her veins and quickening her heartbeat as the object curled itself around her trunk, encouraging her towards it.

A sudden trumpeting mixed with the clanking of chains from the other end of the barn increased her excitement; it was a bellow of joy and frustration from Kali who was straining at her shackles in her need to be with him.

Joti didn't look over to Kali; her gaze was completely mesmerised by the intense walnut brown eyes that looked compassionately down into hers.

Uddanda had returned to them.

CHAPTER 16

Susie collapsed to her knees, exhausted. Her hands and forearms dripping with blood and her face as grey as the huge mound of lifeless flesh that lay slumped next to her. 'No doubt about it, coronary thrombosis.' Her voice was quiet, weakened by the exertion that the autopsy had required.

Even with the kitchen knife ground into scalpel-like sharpness, the process of cutting into the flesh and trimming back great folds of skin and muscle to expose the ribcage had been strenuous. When it came to opening up the ribs she'd readily stood aside, allowing room for King to swing the axe, her eyes flinching with each heavy blow until he finally went through the sternum and breathlessly staggered down from the corpse. He'd given himself a minute to recover before picking up two ropes and, making a slip knot with one, he'd placed the loop over the right side of the ribcage and thrown the other rope to Roger who proceeded to do the same. King took the end of his piece once around a tree and braced himself, leaned back whilst planting a foot firmly against the tree trunk. Roger, lacking the stature and brute strength of King, took his end of the rope and tied it onto the tow bar of his tractor, then, climbing into the cab he'd released the brake and taken it out of gear, allowing the steep gradient on which he'd parked to carry the tractor forward. With man and machine tugging at both sides the gigantic ribcage finally conceded with the crack, laying bare Devi's diaphragm.

King had nodded to Susie, acknowledging her access to examine the elephant.

It was the first time all morning that King had made eye contact with her. In fact, Susie had noticed that he had been uncharacteristically subdued, barely saying a word and leaving the logistics of dragging Devi's body up into the woods to Roger. Then, as she had begun her post mortem his attitude had changed again, he'd become restless and agitated and Susie had wondered if Roger had noticed. She looked over to him but he'd been engrossed in her morbid task, so she continued with the post mortem with a mixture of conflicting emotions, torn between the horror of the event and her undeniable professional fascination at the scale of Devi's anatomy.

'No doubt about it,' said Susie,' a coronary thrombosis, nothing could have been done.'

She cleared her throat, bringing strength back to her voice in an effort to reassure King. 'I don't think it was the first time either, judging by the clots in her arteries I'd say she must have suffered some minor attacks in the past, undetectable to us but a time bomb to her. Could've happened any moment and after a traumatic experience like yesterday... there really was nothing anyone could have done for her... and it would have been quick.' She broke off, unsure what else to say, and began yanking out clumps of grass, wiping her blooded hands on them as a stark silence fell around the wooded copse.

Susie got up from her knees and wandered over to Devi's head. The professional duties that had held her together and helped distance her from the tragedy were complete and she felt a sudden wave of emotion fill her as she looked down at the lifeless face. Pity engulfed her, pity for Devi, pity for Joti who had been her companion for so long. She bent down to stroke Devi's trunk one last time. 'Funny.' she said.

'What is?' King's voice sounded apprehensive.

'These markings on her trunk, I thought I knew Devi's face like the back of my hand, every blemish and line but I never noticed these marks before – they look a bit like bruises.'

King hurried over. 'Oh yeah... must have happened when she was dragged up here, you know, the chains or perhaps stones. What ya reckon Rog?'

Roger shrugged. 'I guess, although I didn't think a body could bruise after death.'

'Abrasions then.' King's voice was dismissive, 'Come on, this ain't doing neither of us no good, let's go get cleaned up and let Rog finish up here.'

'Bye Devi,' she whispered and a tear escaped her eye, followed by another and then another. Looking back over her shoulder one last time she thought she could see Roger squatting down by Devi's head, but her vision was blurred by tears and obscured by the foliage so she let the strong, comforting arm of King remove her from the desolate scene, relieved she didn't have to witness Roger unceremoniously drag Devi into the hole and cover her with dirt – she did not think she could have borne that. The autopsy, that was different, exploratory, it had some purpose, could even have helped in some way, but burying her, it just seemed like a horrible waste.

CHAPTER 17

Good morning, children, and welcome to our wildlife park, no, too formal, hey kids, you wanna see something big and furry? 'Oh Christ, what am I thinking?' muttered Matt as he headed off to meet the scouts.

He had spent the morning attempting to plan his route on the simplistic zoo map, but whichever direction he plotted he found he would always end up at the elephant house or the spot where he first saw Susie, and his thoughts would become a tangled mess of wild conjecture and concern. King's words *'I'll fix Devi later'* kept going round his head. Could it be coincidence?

It was an irrational leap of fancy but still he couldn't prevent his imagination going off on melodramatic tangents. Something dark and unthinkable had directly contributed to Devi's death, something that Susie was unknowingly exploring and may innocently stumble across. He pictured Susie uncovering some kind of proof that King was responsible for Devi's death – confronting him. Then King standing over her, his expression contorted with rage at her accusations – reaching for his ivory goad, his southern drawl oozing menace. 'I fixed Devi and now I gotta fix you.'

Matt shook his head to rid himself of the image, but it only dissipated like mercury, momentarily dividing and subdividing before sliding and tumbling back to become whole again. Remembering Jez saying that

Roger was with them gave him some relief, but still his mind wouldn't let go – at the expense of his planning the scout tour.

Matt sighed, glanced at his watch, pushed the books aside, lit a cigarette and went to meet the group.

'Hi everyone, I'm Matt and it's my job to show you all a good time.' He cringed inside as a loud whisper, 'Matt the Pratt,' circulated around the small, khaki-clad crowd congregated in the reception room.

'Settle down, boys,' instructed the leader, who, despite his years, (Matt guessed he was in his mid-forties, although the shorts and wide-brimmed hat made him difficult to age), was shorter than most of his charges. He turned to Matt and gave him the traditional scout three-fingered salute, exposing a large sweat stain that circled his armpit. Matt reciprocated hesitantly and another snigger started the rounds.

'I said *settle*.'

His voice was like brass. He apparently had no volume control either, addressing Matt as though he were a large crowd.

'Nice bunch of lads, but you can't afford to be too lenient, you know, boys will be boys and if you give them an inch, well you understand...' He leaned confidentially into Matt's chest. 'Between you and me,' he bellowed, 'I'd avoid the Christian name approach, stick with Sir, makes it more formal and helps with discipline. Now, if you can point me in the direction of Julian's office, I'll leave you to it.'

'Aren't you coming with us?' asked Matt anxiously.

'Love to ordinarily, but Jules is expecting me – one of my oldest friends, we were cubs together actually. The stuff Scrapper and I used to get up to, why, there was this one time, (oh he'll hate me for telling you this), but it was typical of our mischief…' He glanced around the room to check that no-one was listening. Everyone was, and blatantly, so he cleared his throat instead.

'Perhaps another time. So, where does the old scallywag lurk?'

Matt rubbed his chin. 'Err, through the doors, turn right and carry on passed the marmoset house until you get to the aviaries – his is the green door before it marked Curator, you can't miss it… specially in your line of work.' Matt's weak laugh echoed in the silent response 'You know, being a scout…'

'Thanks, I'll find it,' replied the man, briskly sweeping Matt's joke aside and turning back to the boys issuing orders. 'Rendezvous back here at 1600 hours, troop dismissed.'

They all watched as he marched out of the door, pausing momentarily, and to the roars of delight from his troop, turned left.

'Old bastard won't find it in a month of Sundays!'

'Have to call out search and rescue like before, remember – on the moors that time?'

'That weren't 'im, that was Birdie.'

'Yeah, but he's just as bad.'

'Worse I reckon.'

They had all seemed to have forgotten that Matt was there, lost in their nostalgic one-upmanship, so he took the opportunity to assess the group.

They consisted of around fourteen eleven to fifteen-year-olds dressed in light khaki shirt and darker shorts, lemon yellow neck scarf complete with toggle. Each had managed to individualise their uniform in a way that conveyed their personality. The boy speaking at that moment had his collar turned up James Dean style, and was clearly the group's leader.

Matt dug into the back pocket of his jeans and tugged out his tobacco. Despite the addition of orange peel, the packet stood little chance against the relentless heat and the powdered consistency made it hard to roll, but experience won, and lighting the cigarette he exhaled the smoke that drifted lazily across the room. The boys' noses twitched in the air and pointed towards to the source.

'Hey Matt, can I have one of them?' said the James Dean boy.

Matt took his time before answering, inhaling greedily and puffing out three little smoke rings, (a trick he'd learned at college); some of the troop gasped in awe. 'Maybe… What's your name?'

'Mickey.'

'And how old are you, Mickey?'

'Fifteen. Sixteen in November.'

'I'll tell you what, you lot pay attention and do as I say and we'll see at the end.'

'And what about me, can I have one too?'

'And me?'

'And me?' clamoured all the boys.

Matt drew in sharply and puffed out another ring, this time much larger, immediately followed by a smaller one that darted from his lips and through the centre of the first.

The boys fell silent.

'What you think, Mickey?' said Matt. 'We could blow a little smoke in their direction.'

'Yeah.' Mickey grinned with pride. 'S'long as they do as we tell 'em.'

They all bustled outside, Mickey muscling his way next to Matt who smiled, inwardly triumphant.

'What we going to look at first?'

'I wanna see the gorillas.'

'Ahh, he wants to visit his family.'

'Sod off, penis breath.'

'Anyway, they ain't got gorillas 'ere, stupid.'

'How about lions then?'

'Lions neither, ain't you read the leaflet?'

'Don't be daft, Si can't read.'

Matt raised a hand, hushing the bickering group. 'Small mammals first,' he announced.

The boys nodded in agreement.

It took them five minutes to reach the otters. There was no sign of Andy, nor of anyone else. Andy had been right when he said that the park would be quiet from now on.

The otters squealed and mewed loudly as they approached, standing on their hind legs and attempting to crane their stubby necks in greedy anticipation of lunch.

Matt cringed at the sound, to him it was tantamount to stereotypic behaviour indicative of lazy husbandry. If Andy made the effort to feed them properly, shutting them away and hiding their food around the enclosure then releasing them to search for it naturally instead of casually tossing the feed over the wall, then this type of begging could be greatly reduced.

However, this did tell him that Andy was late for his round and he scoured the landscape for some sign of him.

Seeing no-one, he turned his attention back to the group, many of whom were leaning precariously over the wall, dangling their fingers teasingly close to the otter's eager jaws.

'Careful you lot or you'll lose your fingers.'

Twenty-six hands were snatched back.

'Could they bite a finger off?' cried one scout.

'Could they kill you?'

'Don't be a nerd, look at the size of them.'

'They could go for your throat.'

'Yeah, or a whole lot could attack at once,' suggested another.

Matt looked down at the first few lines of his notes:

Asian short-clawed otters are the smallest of the otters and come from the carnivore family 'mustelidae' that also include ferrets, weasels and skunks. Their diet usually consists of amphibians, small mammals and crustaceans...

He screwed the paper up in his palm and put it in his pocket. 'To my knowledge, the number of otter-related deaths, be they from individual attacks or gangs is nil.'

'Huh,' responded the boys.

'He means, you bunch of thickos, that they couldn't kill you,' said Mickey looking up at Matt for approval.

Matt nodded. 'But they can give you a nasty nip on your hand.' Seeing the disappointment on their faces, he added, 'that, if not treated, can lead to infection and then gangrene and the need for amputation, or, if no

101

treatment is sought, septicaemia and eventually a horrible, painful death.'

'Told you they could kill you.'

'That's not what he said, penis breath.'

The disputes and abuse continued behind Matt and Mickey as they ambled around the paths, frequently stopping at enclosures where Matt would be bombarded by demands for increasingly elaborate and gory ways in which this or that animal could kill you. Matt was happy to oblige as, although initially feeling guilty for the lack of educational content, the kids were enjoying his tour, (which he thought must count for something), plus it helped take his mind off Susie.

'The Emperor Tamarin is the most psychotic of all the small primates,' he said. 'See how he squats on that branch like a benign old Chinese ruler, the way he rests his hands on his little pot belly, and the way his long white moustache, groomed to majestic perfection, juts pertly out from his face. He may seem the picture of arrogance and indifference but that's just a trick to make you complacent... and you turn your back on him... that's when he attacks!'

'What's it do?'

'I bet it bites your neck, sucks your blood like Dracula.'

'No e' don't, e' goes for the knackers, don't e,' sir?'

Matt smiled. 'I can't tell you, you're too young and it's too horrible.'

The group cawed in unanimous frustration.

'All I can say is, by the next day, a whole team of forensic scientists accompanied by your mother couldn't identify you, okay. Now don't ask me to say anymore.'

At the reptile house Matt found himself briefly redundant. The boys found the snakes, lizards, insects and arachnids so gruesome that there was no need to embellish them with murderous tales.

Whilst they ran from tank to tank, rapping on the panes of glass to illicit some response, groaning if there was none and screaming with exaggerated hysteria if there was, Mickey remained with Matt, mirroring his stance by leaning casually against the wall, and watching his troop with a hint of paternal fondness.

'Have you got any brothers or sisters?' enquired Matt.

'No, well not any more, I had an older brother, seven years older but he died a few years ago – hit by a car.'

'Sorry.' Matt did the sum; he guessed that would make him about Matt's age, had he lived.

Micky looked at the floor. 'Not your fault, not anyone's, just a stupid accident is all.'

For the first time in many months Matt thought of his own family and a pang of regret shot through his body. It had been over three years since he had swanned out of their lives, thrilled by his new-found independence and brimming over with the excitement and optimism that university in a big city had to offer.

He hadn't severed all links and had always spent the obligatory Christmas back home, but these had been reluctant visits, full of resentment for the parties he would miss, and he would always find an excuse to return early, keen not to miss out on any New Year celebrations.

This was by no means a reflection on his family who were, he concluded, as loving as the next and certainly very proud, (at the time Matt thought embarrassingly so), of the first Flynn to get into higher education. It was more about his own selfish enthusiasm. Not, he convinced himself, in a nasty, ungrateful way, just a healthy exuberance in entering a new phase.

The last three years had been easy, joyful, a carefree and careless time that had ill-prepared him for his current situation, and although nothing bad had directly happened to him, the uneasy undercurrent that seemed to enshroud the park had given him a horrible sense of foreboding.

'What about you?' asked Mickey.

'One brother, couple of years younger, but I don't see him much anymore.'

'You should, you know… make the effort.'

'Yeah, I know.' Matt met the boy's eyes. He was staring up at him, unblinking. Matt turned away. 'Come on, let's catch up with the others. I want to show you Bertha, a reticulated python who could, at a push, swallow you whole.'

CHAPTER 18

Ten minutes later the group were pushing their way through the exit doors of the reptile house and outside into the raw gaze of the sun. They followed Matt down the steeply sloping path that wound its way to the paddocks.

'Hey look, deer!' shouted one of the boys. 'Can we stroke them?'

Well,' said Matt, 'it is a walk-through paddock, but I doubt that we'll get close enough to actually touch them, especially with the racket you lot are making.'

Almost immediately the scraping and dragging of boots on gravel faded into a soft march as they all fell into a kind of 'what's the time Mr Wolf' exaggerated stalk.

'How's that?' whispered the same boy, 'pointing proudly to a cloth badge badly sewn onto his breast pocket that depicted a hoof print. 'We did wildlife observation class last week, see.'

'Not bad,' remarked Matt, 'but don't expect too much, they already know we're coming.'

The herd of twelve Sika deer were slumped under the protective shade of a large beech tree within a two-acre field. The access was across a rickety bridge that lay over the dehydrated river.

The scouts squeezed through the gate that creaked lethargically, and stepped into the dry, rutted field. As the last boy entered, the scorched grass seemed to burst into life as thousands of crickets sprung into the air; a loud chorus of chirping followed like a call to arms warning of an invasion.

'Why are those insects doing that?' asked Mickey.

Matt shrugged. 'Not sure, I've never seen crickets so alarmed, I guess we must have spooked them.' He gazed further up the paddock – twenty-four large, alert ears swivelled in their direction. Cautiously the deer watched as Matt and the boys began trudging towards them. Once the group were within about thirty feet of where they stood the deer reluctantly abandoned their shady sanctuary under the tree and wandered a little further up the rutted field with resentful snorts.

'You see that, as long as they keep to that ten-yard distance, although still wary, they'll tolerate our presence,' said Matt, above the ruckus of cricket song. 'Of course, these deer are fairly tame and used to people, in the wild you would be lucky to get within a half a mile of them.'

'What about that one?' piped up one of the younger boys who Matt recognised as the source of the bubble gum popping noises that had been irritating him throughout the tour. 'He don't look scared.'

A large hind had left the main group and was walking hesitantly down towards them; her nostrils flared and her gait implied suspicion.

Suddenly she charged. Covering the small distance in a blink of an eye, she stopped just as abruptly as she had begun, six feet from the scouts. Her doe eyes conveyed a menacing gaze that Matt didn't think was possible in such a gentle, timid creature.

'Bloody hell, that scared me,' cried the boy with the gum.

'Me too,' agreed another, forcing a laugh.

The group gathered and huddled behind Matt, all but Mickey, who remained stoically at his side.

'Why did he do that?'

'He's a she and I don't know.' Matt, stepped forward and clapped his hands. 'Whoa, get out of here.'

The deer flinched slightly then stamped the hard earth with her hoof and uttered a shrill bark.

'Look! The others are coming!'

Matt snapped his head in the direction of the rest of the herd stealthily heading towards them. They were led by a magnificent buck, who must have weighed about 170lbs. His eight-pronged antlers held high in the air were just beginning to lose their velvet which hung down like moss, partially covering an eye in a piratical manner.

Matt clapped his hands again, despite the pleas not to from some of the boys who were convinced it would just make her angrier. Matt ignored them and tried one last time as the main herd loomed within ten feet of them.

'Go on, clear off!' he shouted.

This time it had an effect. Simultaneously the herd raised their heads and, looking over their shoulders, slowly turned and began to meander up the field.

'You did it!' cried Mickey, followed by a cheer from the others that was straight out of an Enid Blyton book.

'Wasn't me,' replied Matt.

The group followed the direction of his gaze to where a tractor had appeared from the top of the paddock, the bales of hay bouncing around in the trailer as it trundled down the slope towards them. It stopped at a hay rack fifteen yards from where they stood and Roger climbed stiffly out of the cab and gave Matt a wave, indicating that he would be over in a minute. Replenishing the empty hay rack he then sauntered down to the group.

'Hi Matt, wondering where you'd got to. How's it going?'

'Good thanks, Roger. I was hoping I'd see you. I wanted to–'

'We almost got killed!' said the boy with the gum.

'Yeah, them deer tried to stampede us,' cried another.

'There was this one who wanted to eat us!'

Roger looked at Matt suspiciously. 'Imaginative lot you've got here.'

This led to cries of indignant outrage. 'It's true, they went all psycho on us, tell him Matt, tell him we ain't making it up.'

Roger turned back to Matt who shrugged.

'I must admit they were acting pretty weird, and this one hind in particular was very agitated… in quite an aggressive way.' Matt was tempted to mention the cricket activity but the incredulous expression from Roger put him off.

'That right?' said Roger with a mocking tone. 'I suppose it's possible she's had a late calf she's protecting which I may have missed, that's the only reason she may have acted like that, but it's not very likely. I'll have a scout around later. Anyway, she certainly wouldn't have harmed any of you, just trying to scare you away – you know, bluffing.' He turned to go.

'Gotta love you and leave you I'm afraid. I'm a bit behind this morning. So long lads, enjoy the rest of your day.'

As he walked back to his tractor, Matt looked anxiously after him, and then at his group, and then to the deer that were still staring suspiciously at the boys.

'Mickey you're in charge, I won't be long. Hey Roger, can I have a word?'

Matt jogged over to where Roger was clambering into the trailer to secure the bales of hay. 'You know, I was beginning to think I was the only one left in the whole park. Where the hell is everybody?'

'Keeping their heads down mainly,' replied Roger, 'all except Andy, he's been hanging around the zoo kitchens most of the day, after the latest news. He almost jumped on me when I got back, but I didn't tell him anything, thought it would do him good to learn a little patience, and the last thing we need is him stirring things up even more with his gossiping.' Roger jumped down, rubbing his knees after landing. 'Twenty-four and already arthritic, gonna be crippled by the time I'm forty. So, what did you want me for?'

Matt shifted his stance.

'Oh, I see,' said Roger, grinning, 'you wanted the latest news as well.'

'Well, not really, I was just wondering. You know, whether…'

'Don't sweat it, your motives are different. I'm guessing you want to know how Susie is, right? Not like Andy, he's just a nosy sod, and he wants ammunition against King. Thing is though…' He paused and Matt felt himself being scrutinised as Roger's large eyes bore into him. 'The thing is, Andy's right, at least I think he is. Look, I think I'm fairly intuitive, comes with working with animals, and from what I've seen I think I can trust you…' Again, he paused as though he was making a decision; he made it. 'I've known King since he came here and I've seen, or thought I'd seen, all his moods. I even worked on eles with him for a while, filling in after Jack died and before Colin and Gary arrived, and I know, probably better than anyone here, what he's like.' He paused to pick up a piece of orange bale twine from the ground and began winding it tightly around his fingers as he continued speaking. 'He isn't that hard to figure out, you know, with King what you see is what you get. He did a pretty rough spell in Vietnam, I don't know if you knew that. He told me a bit about it one night when he'd had a few up the pub, not everything, but enough. I guess that must change your outlook, something like that, killing people, the threat of being killed. If you live through something like that I guess that would make you more prone to telling it like it is, not take any crap. I'm not making excuses for him, I dunno, maybe I'm wrong, maybe he was born that way, the point is that I think I know him, seen all his moods.' Briefly he stared at where the twine was cutting into his hand, the tips of his fingers bulbous with trapped blood. 'When we found Tommy and Jack, I'll never forget the way he looked then, it was as though every emotion that he had kept pent up erupted to the surface: it contorted his face. The way he just walked up to Uddanda, with the bodies of Jack and Tommy barely ten feet away, he just strolled right up to him, got out his hook and walked him back into his enclosure like he was a Golden Retriever or something. Man, that takes balls. Then he shackled him, and then, only then, did he lose control, laid into Dan with a mattock handle, like he was possessed, and not once did he show any fear...

But this morning, while Susie was doing the autopsy I'd swear... he looked scared.'

'Scared of what?' Matt knew the answer before Roger even said it.

'Of what Susie might find, did find, although I don't think she realised it, she was too messed up by then.'

'Messed up!'

'Yeah, by then she was pretty upset. Don't worry, she'll be okay, she's a strong girl.'

'So... what did she find?'

'Bruising around the trunk. She put it down to marks from being dragged, at least that's what King told her, but I've seen them before, like I said, when he beat up Dan with the mattock it left those same marks... and there was something else. After they left I had a good look at her and I'm sure she had burn marks between her legs and on the tip of her trunk. I don't know how, unless...' Roger looked down at his bloated fingers and quickly unwound the twine and massaged his hand, 'Shit, Matt, I think they tortured her.'

'What... but, what did Susie say, I mean about the cause of death?'

'Heart attack. By the look of things her arteries were fucked so that's it, as far as any comeback is concerned.'

They stood in silence. Matt watched Roger wind the twine back around his hand, vaguely aware of some noise, of the ground springing into life.

'Matt.' Mickey's voice cut into his thoughts.

'Just a minute Mickey. So...what are you going to do?'

Roger shrugged, yanking the twine from his fingers, he tossed it into the back of the trailer.

'I don't know, that's why I told you. I've got no one else to ask: Julian's too wet, Susie wouldn't believe me and Jez is looking after number one. Al may be interested if it means a fight, but I don't want that, and besides, I don't think even Al would seriously want to mess with King, and as for Andy and–'

he gazed down at the crickets that bounced around his feet. 'What the fuck, it's like someone poured hot coal over them!'

'Matt!' Mickey's voice again, followed immediately by the others. 'Sir, Sir, they're coming back again!'

They both looked over to where the boys stood huddled on the path, staring in terror at the herd that was stealthily creeping toward them.

'I'd better go down,' said Matt.

'I'll come with you, I'm so behind on the feeds a few more minutes won't make much difference... and I want to see what a killer deer looks like.'

CHAPTER 19

Andy stomped truculently through the walled garden, grumbling angrily to his rat. 'I'm always the last to know anything, it's not bloody right, Roger's such a self-righteousness bastard sometimes.'

He had waited all morning for Roger, and was now so behind in his chores that he had decided to abandon his usual routine of cleaning out the enclosures whilst he fed and, instead, carried only a bucket containing various feeds which he scattered carelessly into each enclosure, hardly noticing the animals or the subtle change in their behaviour, the lack of interest in the food that rained down on them as he passed, the beady eyes that stared after him and showed none of the usual recognition for the daily ritual.

'What's the matter Lucky, do you need the toilet?'

The rat had suddenly become agitated, spinning around beneath Andy's shirt. He reached down into his collar and pulled the writhing animal out. 'It's alright Lucky, you can go just here.'

He placed the rat on the ground, and then jumped, startled by the noises that suddenly erupted, deafening cries that reverberated all over the walled garden. He watched, bewildered, as the gibbons bounced off their mesh walls and tossed their dishes in the air with a metallic clatter.

A Macaw's squawk resonated in Andy's head and he spun around in time to see the pinioned bird launch itself from its perch and spiral to the floor like a sycamore seed, landing with a heavy thud.

The capuchins clung to the bars, stretching their arms out to Andy, beseeching him to come closer, their black lips curled back over their savage canines, eager to sink them into Andy's flesh.

Andy looked back down at Lucky, and then gawped in horror, – she wasn't there. Spinning three hundred and sixty degrees he scanned the immediate area then looked further up the path. A flash of movement darted around the corner and he broke into a sprint, his calls for her return drowned out by the noise of the animals.

Rounding the corner Andy stopped abruptly. Lucky was squatting, hunched and breathless next to a wire mesh gate. On the other side two otters clambered over each other, screaming hysterically. 'Lucky, you gave me such a scare.' He took a step towards her and her hackles rose, doubling her size. She looked at the gate.

'Lucky no, don't!' He lunged towards her but didn't cover even half the distance before she scampered up the gate. Andy let out a desperate cry, just as Lucky, to the otters fevered delight, tumbled into their enclosure.

CHAPTER 20

Matt looked in the direction of the walled garden. 'Christ, what's going on up there?'

'God knows,' replied Roger. 'Probably Andy pissing the animals off by feeding them so late.'

The scouts clambered around Matt and Roger the moment they reached them, still alarmed by the close proximity of the herd. Matt didn't feel too relaxed either. He looked at the deer – was it his imagination or was there something different about them? Their usual timid trepidation had been replaced by something more provocative. Deciding distraction was the best course Matt turned back to the scouts. 'So, has anyone got any questions?' he asked.

'Yeah,' answered the boy with the gum, 'can we go now please?'

The others laughed nervously.

'Come on you lot,' prompted Matt,' it's not every day you get this close to deer.'

'That's what's bothering me!' replied the same boy.

Matt scanned the group. '*Someone* must have a question?'

Mickey dutifully raised his hand; a few of the others groaned. 'Shut it you lot, I got a question, alright?'

They instantly fell silent.

'Why are some of their ears torn up?' continued Mickey.

'Thanks Mickey.' Matt looked over to Roger, but the paddock keeper wasn't listening, distracted by the herd.

'Roger?'

'Huh?

'Mickey wants to know why some of the deer's ears are tatty.'

Sure...right.' He turned to the group. 'That's where they had tags which have come out.'

'How d'ya mean, come out?' said Mickey.

'Well, when they are a few days old, before they get too agile, we catch them up, sex them, check they're healthy and then put in an ear tag with their own number on it so we can identify them. The problem is that as they get older and...'

'Does 'urt em?' piped up one of the older boys, 'when you put the tags in?'

'No, well, just for a second, the same as getting your ears pierced. Anyway, as they get older and start fighting, a lot of the ear tags end up getting ripped out which...'

'Does *that* hurt?' he called out again, but another boy answered.

'Course it bloody hurts, what ya think!'

'Is there lots of blood? I bet there is, gotta be.'

'Is deer blood red?'

Matt caught Roger's eye and shook his head in despair.

'Cause it's red, you idiot. What colour did you think it was?' snapped Mickey.

'I dunno, just thought it might be different is all.'

A small, ginger-haired boy spoke. 'It could be green, they eat grass and that's green.'

'S'pose you just eat carrots then,' said the boy with the gum in-between pops.

'You're all a bunch of idiots.' Mickey looked at Matt apologetically. 'What the bloody hell's what you eat got to do with the colour of your blood?'

'What I mean,' continued the ginger boy, 'is that a boy in my class at school, he cut himself in Biology last term and his blood was red.'

'Well yeah…and?'

'Well, his mum always gives him beetroot sandwiches for lunch.'

Matt grimaced and turned to Roger who shrugged his shoulders and looked at his watch.

'I think I've done all I can here educationally and so, if no one has any further questions I'll be—'

Matt didn't even have time to call out. The stag just appeared, slamming into the paddock keeper and lurching his entire body forward towards the startled boys.

Roger's eyes bulged with a mixture of confusion and pain. His hand slid down his torso and fell on to something that was protruding through his side, his fingers groping at the hard, bone-like shaft, rutted and pointed at the end.

The others watched horrified as Roger's body began rocking from side to side then shake violently as the stag attempted to dislodge him from his antlers. He lowered his neck, pushing Roger's face down into the baked earth and forcing the prongs of his antlers deeper into his body, then, with a deep bellow, he flicked his head back up again. Roger flew into the air like a doll thrown from a pram and landed in a twisted heap on the ground.

The stag bellowed again, inciting all the others to join in a chorus of pulsing, resonant barks, which savaged the senses of the group that stood petrified before them.

The earth around Roger's discarded body was thirstily quenching itself on the blood that oozed from his wound, but Matt could see from the occasional twitch and the steady rise and fall of his chest that he was still alive.

'Everyone get behind me!' shouted Matt.

Cautiously the boys obeyed as the deer crept ever closer.

'Keep looking at the deer and walk slowly backwards towards the trailer.' Matt peered over his shoulder, the trailer was at least fifteen yards away and the deer were only five, growing in confidence with each step.

'How about if we try shouting at them, ain't deer supposed to be afraid of stuff like that?' Mickey's voice trembled as he whispered into Matt's ear.

'I don't know...' Matt glanced back to the trailer, it seemed no closer than the last time he had looked, 'Okay, let's try.'

Matt and Mickey began to shout, encouraging some of the older boys to join in.

'Whoa'

'Sod off'

'Go away'

The deer hesitated, snorting with hostile distrust, then continued their stalk, bolder than before.

'Well, it gave us a couple of yards,' Matt muttered, 'Christ!'

One of the doe's charged at the group, stopping just a few feet short. The boys, many now sobbing, cringed back into a tighter huddle. Then another doe charged, then another, each onslaught, Matt realised, getting more audacious. He chanced another look over to the trailer, fifteen more feet, now sixteen, seventeen; Panic flooded Matt's senses, the deer had circled above them and were now herding them away from the sanctuary of the trailer.

Suddenly Matt felt a terrible blow to his chest. He staggered back, winded, but managing to keep his balance, and looked into the belligerent eyes of his attacker, an immature buck who had yet to develop antlers. Many had solid, sharp horns that jutted from their skulls. Matt shuddered. He had to do something, and quickly…

CHAPTER 21

Andy scrambled into the enclosure, swearing and kicking out at the otters that were tearing at his legs and shredding his trainers with their needle-like teeth.

Their eagerness to attack Andy gave Lucky the opportunity to shimmy up a tall, spindly tree where she now clung precariously, just out of reach of Andy's outstretched, trembling hand.

Tears and sweat merged and ran down his cheek as his frustration boiled over, and he lashed out at the otters who dodged his feet with ease and then made a counter assault, becoming a blur of fur, teeth and claws that tore mercilessly at his legs, forcing him away from their prey.

The futility and pain was too much for Andy and he retreated, hurdling the low wall of the enclosure back onto the path where he looked back helplessly at the victors. Insolently they returned his gaze, their muzzles soaked in blood and saliva, before scampering back to the base of the tree and baying relentlessly for their quarry to fall.

Andy scooped up a handful of gravel and hurled it at them. 'Eat that, you bastards!' he screamed, scooping up a second handful then pausing, his words triggering an idea.

He sprinted back to where he had left the bucket, grabbed it and charged back, relieved to see that the scene hadn't deteriorated.

In a single bailing motion, he launched the contents of the bucket into the enclosure, showering the otters in a cocktail of day-old chicks, mice, eggs and mealworms, hoping that the feast would distract them from Lucky. It didn't, in fact they barely noticed and continued with their persecution.

In a fit of frustration he hurled the bucket, missing the otters, but striking the tree, which shook violently on its impact.

Andy watched in horror as the rat lost her purchase and began tumbling down the branches. The otter's greedy mews of anticipation changing into embittered cries as Lucky, hanging by her forepaws, managed to hoist herself back up onto the safety of the thin branch.

'Screw this!' said Andy. He dug into his back pocket, pulled out the walkie-talkie and raising it to his mouth he firmly pressed down the button on its side. 'Andy to anyone over... Andy to anyone... come on you bastards answer, I need help. Anyone...'

CHAPTER 22

Matt could just make out the sound of Roger's walkie-talkie.

The voice was distorted and the words muffled from beneath his body. *'Andy to anyone over... Andy to anyone... come on you bastards answer, I need help.' Anyone...'*

'He's saying something!' cried Mickey.

'It's not Roger, it's his radio,' said Matt.

'Radio?' Mickey thought for a second. 'If we can get to it we can call for help.'

'Yeah, but that's a big *if*. No, we're better off trying to get to the trailer, hold out until someone comes looking for—Hey, what you doing?'

Mickey had bent down and picked up a large stone, which he launched in the direction of the tractor. It was a good shot, the instinctive skill of a fifteen-year-old guiding it onto the rusty tin roof with a loud clang, not loud enough to frighten the deer, but enough to momentarily divert their attention. And that was all Mickey needed, he darted through a gap between two hinds, breaking through the circle and back into the open paddock and towards Roger, the cheers from his comrades filling the air.

'Mickey, get back here!' Matt looked desperately at the boy and then to the large stag, which immediately lowered his head and bounded after him.

The cheers from the boys turned to screams as the thundering of hooves gained on their friend. The troughs, ditches and dried out tussocks twisted and bent Mickey's posture, upsetting his balance and twice Matt thought he would trip, but somehow the boy regained his balance and hurtled on towards Roger. A wave of relief hit Matt, Mickey was going to make it, ten more feet, then eight...then five...then...

Matt gasped in horror as Mickey's foot caught awkwardly in one of the ruts, turning his ankle at right angles and sending him sprawling to the ground.

Unable to watch Matt looked away, imagining the full weight of the stag driving his antlers down into Mickey's chest. A few of the other boys followed his example but most couldn't tear their eyes away and continued to watch in morbid horror; even the deer looked on in studied fascination at their patriarch's relentless savagery as he gored deeply into the baked earth.

'He's alright... Mickey's alright... the deer ain't got him, it missed... Look!'

Matt turned to the boy at his side who was shouting excitedly and jumping up and down, gesturing wildly, then followed the boy's gaze to where the mauling was taking place.

Mickey was pinned down by the antlers which lay either side of his slight frame and, although he was battered and in obvious pain, the spread of the spurs had formed a bridge over his body preventing them from piercing his flesh.

Matt seized his chance and, scooping up two of the smaller boys under each arm, screamed for the others to follow him as he burst through the blockade and towards the tractor. Before the deer could react, the group were scrambling into the trailer like rats in a flood pouring onto a makeshift raft.

'Wait there!' ordered Matt. Grabbing a bale of hay by its twine he launched himself back to where Mickey and Roger lay. The deer pounced clear in shock and surprise as Matt howled through them with his battering ram pulled tight into his chest, all but the stag who, in response to this new challenge, abandoned interest in Mickey and turned to face the pretender to his crown. Snorting with contempt he charged.

Nothing could have prepared Matt for that impact. The stag didn't falter from the collision but drove his antlers deep into the shield of hay.

Matt's jaws snapped together and air mixed with mucus exploded from his nostrils as the blow whipped him backwards. Losing his grip on the bail Matt slid to the ground and felt a sharp kick to his thigh and then his shoulder as the stag ran over him. A constellation of lights danced in front of his eyes and he swallowed back the taste of vomit that instantly burnt his throat.

Defenceless against a further onslaught, Matt looked urgently over to where the stag now stood furiously battering his head side-to-side trying to dislodge the bail that was still attached to his antlers. Its anger and frustration began to spread to the rest of the herd who mimicked his vexation by leaping and prancing around him.

Crawling commando style, forearm over forearm, Matt quickly reached where Mickey was lying.

'You okay?' he whispered.

Mickey nodded. 'But I think my ankle's broken.'

'Do you think you can crawl?'

Again, the boy nodded.

'Come with me then.'

Tentatively they covered the short distance to where Roger lay. His conscious, almost inaudible moans gave Matt some relief. 'Hey Roger, you're still with us!'

His groans became louder as Matt slid his arm underneath him and began rummaging through his pockets.

'Sorry Roger, just got to find your radio and then we can get out of here, get you to a hospital'

He dug deeper,

'Got it!'

Clutching the walkie-talkie in his hand he was about to speak when a scream rang out. Whirling around, Matt could see the boys standing in the trailer pointing wildly beyond where Matt, Mickey and Roger lay. Following the direction of their out-stretched arms he saw the whole herd, led by the stag, clumps of hay scruffily adorning his antlers, thundering towards them.

'Christ, they're going to stampede us!'

He looked around frantically, searching for some inspiration, a weapon, protection, but there was nothing. Matt wrestled against his instinct to run; the urge towards self-preservation boiled up inside him at the image of the pain he was about to experience. He blinked, almost here, the hollow pounding of hoof against baked earth became deafening: he couldn't escape now...he had waited too long.

He looked down at Mickey. His eyes were closed tight, like a child cowering away from a nightmare. Matt threw himself over the boy and waited. Waited for the sharp hooves to shred his back, lacerate his legs, puncture his skull, he waited but it never came...just silence. A nothingness that precedes death. Calm, still. Mute. Even the crickets fell quiet.

After what felt like an eternity Matt turned his head and looked straight into the timid eyes of the stag. It jumped back. The look of trance-like malice that had been present was now replaced by a startled, scared expression and Matt was overcome by an uncontrollable urge.

He stared right into the stag's eyes. 'Boo!'

The stag scattered, joining the rest of the herd who, in perfect formation, tacked their way up the paddock until they reached a tolerably safe distance and slowed to a standstill, staring back nervously at the scouts.

'What happened, why did they change like that, why didn't they kill us?' Mickey's voice was unsteady.

'I don't know,' replied Matt, 'I really don't know.'

CHAPTER 23

Susie sat in King's flat, her fingers idly caressing Shadow's head which rested contentedly on her lap. The dog let out a long sigh and Susie looked into her half-closed hazel eyes, then over to the body lying slumped on the couch. An empty bottle of whiskey lay on the floor next to it.

'Been quite a day, hasn't it Shadow – still, at least you seem okay now.'

Her gaze fell on the clock on the wall and absently she calculated how long she'd been sitting there. They had finished the post-mortem at eleven – got back to King's flat at twenty past. She had wept, for how long? That part was vague – then he had suggested a 'strong one'. She had refused, watching instead as he took the bottle to the couch and one long swig followed another until he eventually passed out.

'God,' she thought, 'must be at least five hours.'

King let out a single, rasping snore, rolled onto his side, and was still again.

The age gap hadn't bothered her at all, at first. He was good-looking, tall and powerful, not just in his stature but in his manner. And he was mysterious, *'you don't do what I've done, see what I've seen, and just walk away….'* He would never elaborate further, just left it hanging. It wasn't even meant as an excuse or an apology, it was just fact, – who he was.

Looking at him now, the flecks of grey peppering his sandy hair, the fold of loose skin where his face met the couch, the angry creases in his brow that seemed a permanent fixture of late, she felt uncertain of the relationship. This wasn't a sudden revelation, she had been feeling this increasingly for the last few days – since...

'Christ,' she groaned, then looked at Shadow, 'come on, I think we need some fresh air.'

As they stepped out of the flat a low growl from the dog alerted her to a figure sitting on the wall a little way down the path.

'Hi Susie.' Andy flashed a nervous look and clutched his rat protectively to his chest as the dog crept towards him. 'Maybe you should put her on a lead?'

'Shadow, come.' The dog obediently slunk back to Susie's side. 'Don't worry, she had a funny turn earlier that's left her a bit out of sorts,' she patted the dogs side, 'feeling much better now, aren't you Shadow.'

Andy stood up abruptly, 'What, like a kind of fit – about one-ish, yeah I bet it was...I bet it was the same thing that got into all the animals today!'

'How...how do you mean?' With a sudden sense of unease Susie hurried over to Andy,

'What! Don't you know what happened? Didn't you hear it on the zoo grapevine?'

'Andy, you *are* the zoo grapevine – tell me what happened!'

'Well... it started all of a sudden,' Andy sat back down, pausing to give Lucky a gentle scratch behind her ear.

'Andy?'

'Sorry – well, all the animals, and I mean *all* of them,' he pointed a scolding finger at his rat who sniffed the tip curiously, 'they all went crazy, psychotic, Lucky almost got killed!'

'Andy, this better not be one of your stories?' She looked from Andy to the rat. 'She looks fine to me.'

'Of course she is… she's Lucky.' He looked down at the rat, pride shining from his narrow eyes, adding, 'Roger's not so good though, probably lost a kidney, and he'll be in hospital for at least a month.'

'Roger! Hospital, why…what happened?' Susie stood in alarm.

'I told you, the animals went mad – one of the deer gored him.'

'A deer?'

'Yeah, one of the Sika; they attacked Matt and his group of scouts as well. One of the boys was hurt – broke his ankle. It's cool though 'cause Julian's friend is the scout leader so there's not gonna be any police or legal stuff involved.'

'And Roger…' Susie felt her head spinning, 'Roger – is he definitely going to be okay?'

'That's what Al said. He went to the hospital with him, got back about an hour ago.'

'And what about Matt?'

'Hero of the hour… apparently. Saved Roger and the scouts by all accounts. But the point is, why did the animals behave like that? It's really weird.'

'No Andy, the point is that everyone's okay,' said Susie, imagining Matt in a heroic role.

'I guess…' Andy shrugged, gave Lucky a kiss and nuzzled her to his chest. 'But you got to admit it's pretty strange.'

Susie gave herself a minute to digest all the information, half watching Shadow who was sniffing around the shrubs.

'Strange yes, but not necessarily weird.' She sat back down next to Andy and stroked his rat. 'I mean, there's bound to be an explanation for it.'

Andy raised his eyebrows. 'Yeah…like what?'

'I don't know, maybe some kind of animal mass hysteria.' Susie was feeling a little more relaxed as the logical part of her brain began to kick in. 'Could have been a panic, starting at one source and spreading from enclosure to enclosure. That sounds possible.'

'Okay, so what caused the panic in the first place?'

'I don't know – could've been anything: sudden noise, smell of a fire…' Susie's analytical mind was beginning to relish the challenge as she quickly formulated a theory. '…or the smell of death?'

'Death! What d'ya mean? Squealed Andy.

'Calm down Andy, I only mean that if you do an autopsy on something the size of an elephant then the other animals are likely to pick up on it, the smell of blood, of death, it travels, and we were only up in the copse.' She nodded towards the far side of the valley.' Not exactly far, and I bet the breeze was in this direction.'

'So, you think that's what happened today?' Andy sounded unconvinced.

'I'm sure of it.'

Shadow padded over from where she had been investigating the bushes and sat at Susie's side. She ran her hand up the dog's muzzle, reminding her of something from her childhood.

'When I was young, there was this old man who lived a few doors down from me.' She paused and petted Shadow. 'He had this dog called Bobby who would refuse to walk past the local abattoir. As soon as they got as far as the building he would start shaking and growling, straining on his lead in the opposite direction. If the old man tried to pick him up Bobby would snap at him, and he was *never* aggressive – I used to play with him sometimes and he was soft as anything. It just wasn't in his nature to be nasty. But there was something that he sensed in that building that made him go crazy. The smell of fear, the old man said.'

'The smell of fear,' repeated Andy, his eyes widening 'yeah, I s'pose that could explain it.'

They both sat in thought, Andy stroking his rat, Susie stroking the dog.

'So, do you know where everyone else is? asked Susie, as much to break the silence as out of any real interest.

'I think Al's taking some of Roger's things back to the hospital, your brother's gone with him and I guess Jez's still shacked up with that bird he met on Monday – he'll be walking like John Wayne by the time she's finished with him. I don't know about Colin and Gary,' he paused to think about it, 'I did hear some chain-sawing up in the woods so they might be collecting branches for the eles' breakfast. Oh, and Matt's gone to bed early, said that he's going to leave at five tomorrow morning—'

'Matt's leaving? Susie quickly checked the disappointment in her voice. 'I mean... I suppose I shouldn't be surprised, as a first week in a new job goes, his has been rather eventful. I just thought that...'

'Relax, he's not *leaving* leaving.' He smirked. 'He's got to go and collect the mahout from the airport, remember, he arrives tomorrow.'

Susie gave an involuntary shudder, which seemed to amuse Andy. 'Yeah,' he said, 'going to be interesting when he arri–' Andy was cut short by a distant shout from the direction of King's flat.

'Sorry,' said Susie, avoiding Andy's eyes, 'I'd better go back. If you see Tommy, can you tell him that I probably won't be home tonight? Come on Shadow.'

CHAPTER 24

Susie re-entered the flat and, realising how dark it had become, flicked on the light switch, illuminating King who lay sprawled but awake on the sofa.

'Where the hell were you?' he growled.

'Just needed some air.'

'Well, I need a drink. Get me a bottle.'

'Maybe we should call it a night?' suggested Susie tentatively. 'It's been a horrible day – I'm exhausted.'

King stared at her, long and hard. 'Should be a fresh bottle in there.' He nodded towards the cabinet in the corner.

With a sigh, Susie went and got it. 'I met Andy outside, Roger was badly hurt today, gored by one of the deer.' She put a glass next to him and attempted to open the seal but her hand was unsteady.

'Andy? That snivelling piece of weasel piss.' King snatched the bottle from her, tearing off the seal and snapping open the lid with an impatient twist. 'I wouldn't believe him if he told me the earth was round, always lyin' like a no-legged dog, can't help himself.' He took a long gulp straight from the bottle.

'Even so, he's gone to hospital. Apparently all the animals went crazy today. I think it must have started the same time that Shadow had her fit. I remember hearing a lot of noise outside. I guess you didn't notice… with all your drinking.'

King smiled, at least his lips smiled but his eyes were cold and Susie saw no signs of mirth.

'I think maybe they sensed Devi's death,' continued Susie, 'you know, perhaps the smell of blood unsettled them.'

'That's your problem, baby. You think too much.' Carelessly, King poured the whiskey into his glass, watching with a detached expression as the liquid overflowed and ran down his finger. 'You know what an animal thinks when he smells blood, nothing, that's what. An animal reacts, that's all.' He placed the bottle on the floor – it teetered before settling upright – and took a long swig from the glass, wiping away the dribbles on his forearm. 'A coyote smells blood it means fresh food, an easy meal – an antelope smells it then it gets the hell away coz it could be him next. No thinking, no analysis, just a reaction, instinct.'

'Yes, but…'

Yes, but nothing. I weigh sixteen stone, an elephant over four tons, and yet it does what I tell it. You know what it would do to me if it could think, if it could reason things out?' He picked up the glass and hurled it across the room. It exploded against the wall showering the carpet with shards of glass. 'That's what it would do to me.'

Susie jumped back. 'King…please don't…'

'Then you get some bleeding-heart animal rights asshole crying like a pine knot in a sawmill *'cause animals having feelings'.*' King took a quick belt, let out a mocking laugh then took a longer slurp. 'You think a pride of lions worries about a zebra's feelings before they rip it apart? Nature don't work that way, if it did there wouldn't be no animals left. You give things a conscience then doubt creeps in. God knew that, that's why he didn't give animals no soul, without that you can't rationalise.' He grabbed at the bottle and put it to his lips, draining the last of the liquid then peered back at Susie; his eyes were half closed like he was struggling to bring her into focus. 'A deer – a fucking deer sees some movement in the grass, he don't stand there pondering on the fucking reason or he'll find himself being eaten from the arse end up. Thinking and feelings, they ain't no use to animals, gets them killed.' He paused, perspiration oozed out of him like a squeezed sponge and he raised the bottle to his mouth, looking bemused as nothing came out. He then tipped it upside down and gave it a shake as if in disbelief. 'What the fuck. Bottle...another.'

Susie said nothing as she took a nervous step away from him.

'Fuck y...get it myself.' He stood abruptly and lurched forward. Staggering to the right he careered into the cabinet and crashed to the floor, his huge chest rising and falling steadily, forcing out rippling moans from his parted lips

Susie watched as Shadow skulked out of the room with her tail between her legs, then she looked back down at King.

Finally, with a long sigh, she crossed the room, turned off the light and collapsed exhausted into the chair.

She woke abruptly.

Screams and wails had wrenched her from sleep and now seemed to surround her. Cries, not only from outside, but inside the flat as well.

She could hear Shadow howling in the bedroom as if in pain. And another noise – closer, much closer – something wild, feral in the room with her.

She leapt off the chair, groping and crashing her way across the room, grabbing for the light switch. Thrown into sudden glare she was momentarily dazzled, but her eyes quickly adjusted and she stared at King who was thrashing around on the floor, his arms and legs jerking awkwardly and his face wet with tears.

'Leave me alone,' he cried. 'Please leave me alone!'

Spots of red dappled his shirt as he rolled over the broken pieces of glass, but most alarming were his eyes, wide open and staring into some other world as though petrified by what they saw.

Susie squatted down beside him, grasped his huge shoulders and shook him with all of her strength. 'King...wake up, wake up, it's a drea–

He lashed out, knocking her to the floor, then began clawing at the air as if he were trying to scale a wall.

And then it stopped.

The animals outside, Shadow, King, everything became still, as if a massive surge of electricity had tripped a switch.

Shakily, she got to her feet and stepped cautiously back towards King. His chest rose and fell with the steady rhythm of untroubled sleep. His eyes were shut tight, not even a flicker of his eyelids; his face was relaxed and peaceful.

She knew that she should wake him, bathe his cuts, but she needed a moment to work things out so she headed back to the chair and fell into it, allowing the security of its cushioned arms to envelop her.

Shadow appeared cautiously from the other room and padded softly across the floor. She rested her muzzle on Susie's lap and looked searchingly up at her. 'It's okay,' said Susie, placing her hand on the dog's head, feeling suddenly self-aware as her voice cut through the silence. 'It's okay.'

What she wanted more than anything was reason, common practical reason to take her hand and lead her to a satisfactory explanation of what had happened, but her mind was foggy and uncooperative, allowing the snippets of previous conversations to randomly clutter her thoughts...*The animals all went crazy, psychotic... Roger's in hospital...the smell of fear... Could've been anything, sudden noise, smell of a fire... an animal reacts that's all...'*

Susie sat bolt upright, trying to recall Andy's words. *'Said that he's going to leave at five tomorrow morning.*

She looked at her watch – five-thirty. 'That's it!' she cried, her mind clear and unfettered as the scenario unfolded in front of her: Matt fumbling around the zoo's mini estate in the darkness, slamming the door, the exhaust backfiring, or blasting the horn as he groped for the headlights, a Lemur calling in alarm, triggering cries from the other animals in the park and finally entering King's subconscious, distorting and twisting his drink-induced dreams into nightmares, magnified by the alcohol. She laughed out loud with relief and ruffled the dog's head, 'You see Shadow, there's nothing to worry about.'

CHAPTER 25

Wednesday 1st September

'I believe that you may be waiting for me?'

Matt looked down and straight into the dark twinkling eyes of an Indian man who, having taken Matt's free hand, was shaking it vigorously.

'My name is Gajadhar' he said. 'It is so kind of you to meet me like this. I trust that it has not been too much of a bother?'

Matt tried not to grimace as his fingers were crushed by Gajadhar's enthusiastic grip, its power belying his short stature. 'I'm Matt, and it's no problem, I hope you had a good journey. Here, let me take your bag.'

Prising his hand free Matt tossed the hastily written 'Lankin Moors Wildlife park' sign that he had been holding up into a bin and stooped down for the bag, underestimating its weight and dropping it back to the floor with a grunt. *'Christ,'* thought Matt, *'did he bring his own elephant?'*

'I am very sorry,' said the mahout, taking the backpack from Matt. 'It was so very difficult to know what I should need that I may have brought a little too much. I do hope that you have not hurt yourself.'

'No, I'm fine, I just wasn't expecting it to be so heavy – caught me a bit off balance.' Matt watched as Gajadhar nimbly hoisted the backpack onto his shoulder with such ease that he felt compelled to reassess the Indian as they set off out of the airport and towards the car park. Certainly he was short, the pack obliterating his entire form so that, from behind, all that could be seen were two sandaled feet, but he was also powerfully built, not artificially like a body-builder, but like a man who has never known a moment's idleness, a body designed for and created by a lifetime of manual labour.

'So, is this your first time in Britain?' It was the bland opener question that Matt had decided upon during his long drive. Not knowing how much English the mahout understood had been increasingly bothering him with every mile and although it was now apparent that this would not be an issue, (he spoke almost too fluently, with each word pronounced with clipped perfection), he decided it was still a useful ice-breaker.

'Oh yes, as a matter of fact I have never even been on an aeroplane before, and I must say how truly delighted I am that my first visit out of India should be to your beautiful country. And your climate is a wonderful surprise, not at all foggy and wet as I was informed. I feel more foolish now than ever for bringing so many jumpers.'

'Don't be, your informant was right, it's just been an unusually hot summer, hottest on record apparently, ahh...here we are.' Matt dug into his pocket for the keys, unlocked the two front doors and then opened the double doors at the back for the mahout's bag, 'If you want to put your backpack in there...' He looked behind him but Gajadhar was not there, he had stopped five yards back and was beaming at the car.

'Oh, this is perfect, a mini I believe, just like in the Italian Job, but a van version. Is it yours?'

Matt briefly scanned the vehicle – painted from front to rear in black and white stripes. The zoo emblem (a transfer on both sides of the car) was scuffed and peeling off at the corners, and the passenger side wing was badly dented, but once again Matt could detect no hint of insincerity from Gajadhar's tone. 'Eh…no it belongs to the park, but if you want to put your bag in the back, it's a five-hour drive, so we should get going.'

They climbed in and the car spluttered into life, ground into gear and lurched out of the car park, all the while with Gajadhar paying homage to its beauty, elegance and practicality until an explosion from the exhaust backfiring caused him to leave his seat in alarm. This was followed swiftly by a burst of laughter. 'You were only supposed to blow the bloody doors off!' he said, and then he giggled, sending little ripples around his body.

The genial atmosphere was contagious and Matt found himself chuckling along with him. He was beginning to feel very much at ease with his companion, almost paternal, (although, for all he knew Gajadhar could have been twenty, even thirty years his senior),

His skin was without a line or a blemish and his face so simplistically open that it could have been drawn by a child. His beaming mouth seemingly incapable of a frown and his two large sparkling eyes somehow managed to convey both innocence and wisdom in equal measures. Even his hair defied ageing, long, thick and fluffy like a blackbird after shaking off the morning dew, and dark with a bluish sheen.

'Your English is remarkably good.' The moment he said it Matt realised how patronising it sounded.

'Thank you, although all credit must be given to my tutor, a very patient and learned man.'

Matt checked in the wing mirror and pulled onto the road. 'A tutor, that sounds expensive.'

'Yes, you would imagine so, but I beg of you not to think that I am a wealthy man, more a very fortunate one. You see, for many generations my family has been lucky enough to be in the employment of an extremely generous and important man. He and my father played as boys together, as did I with Amish, his son, and as a result we have become very close, almost like brothers, and their kindness to me has exceeded that which you could usually expect from a master and servant, to the point that I was given the opportunity, no, that is not the right word, the privilege, that is more suitable, the privilege to have lessons alongside Amish. So you see, here I am, a humble mahout granted a fine education and now driving around England in a Mini, Om shri Ganesháya namah.'

Matt glanced over at Gajadhar, whose eyes were twinkling brighter than ever.

'Oh, I beg your pardon, I was giving salutations to the illustrious Ganesha, remover of obstacles, who has blessed my life in such a generous way.'

'Ganesha, isn't he an elephant god?'

Gajadhar began giggling again.

'Please, you will have to excuse me, it is not you that I am laughing at, but your interpretation of our beliefs. Amish warned me that westerners found the concept of our religions hard to grasp.'

Matt simply smiled. 'And was it also Amish who warned you about our weather?'

'Oh yes, and the food. Amish has come to England on many occasions, in fact he has visited most of Europe and America, as I mentioned, his family is very important.'

'So, are you going to enlighten my un-enlightenable western mind?'

'I can try if you wish,' chuckled Gajadhar, 'although I fear that I may be wasting your time.'

Matt looked out at the endless road that stretched ahead of him.

'Don't worry about that, I'm very interested.'

'Well... put simply, Lord Ganesha isn't an elephant god.' He chuckled again at the idea. 'He is a God with an elephant's head.'

'That's a bit pedantic isn't it?'

'Amish was right,' sighed Gajadhar. 'There is all the difference in the world. You see Ganesha is the son of Shiva and Parvathi, born out of the very dirt from her body when she needed to bathe but had no-one to guard her door, and so she created Ganesha. But whilst she was in the bath Lord Shiva returned and Ganesha, not knowing who he was, refused him entry, angering him so much that in fury he decapitated the young guard. So, when Parvathi discovered what her husband had done she was furious with him, and to placate her he instructed his guards to bring him the head of the first sleeping creature that they found. This turned out to be an elephant's, which Lord Shiva placed on the young Ganesha's shoulders and, as further compensation, he declared that everyone would worship him before commencing any work.'

'And this is what you believe?'

'Naturally, I am Ganapatyas, that is, my sect worships Lord Ganesha as the supreme deity, and in his benevolence he grants us success, prosperity and the education and wisdom to protect us from adversity.'

'But what about Shiva? If he is Ganesha's father surely he is the supreme god...' Matt paused, fumbling for the lever to the windscreen washer, the trickle of water and squealing wipers smearing the screen. He sensed Gajadhar tense as they briefly hurtled down the motorway completely blind until the washer finally spluttered out a jet of water that cleared the grime.

'Sorry about that, what was I saying...so don't you risk his wrath – you know, Shiva's wrath – by claiming that his son is the true god?'

'You see, already you are struggling to understand,' replied the mahout, relaxing again into the discussion, 'I did not say that he was the true god, only that we revere him specifically, which is still complementary with the worship of other deities. Do you understand?'

'I'm starting to,' lied Matt. 'So, you work with elephants, you worship an elephant, sorry, an elephant-headed god, basically your life revolves around elephants.'

Gajadhar laughed, 'You are yet to meet my family.' He reached into his shoulder bag and pulled out a purse from which he produced two passport-sized photographs.

Matt checked his mirrors and took his foot off the accelerator, risking a lingering look. The first one, in sepia, was a picture of an elephant, presumably a mother as next to her was a calf and leaning against that was a boy of about twelve who was unmistakably Gajadhar, (for other than filling out, he looked exactly the same).

'This is Lalite, it means beautiful lady, and she was, if you will excuse the sentiment, like a mother to me. I was riding her before I had learnt to walk, she was I believe the most gentle creature that ever lived.'

'So does that make her calf your sibling?'

Gajadhar missed Matt's flippancy. 'I like to think that I have that honour. Here, this is a more recent photograph.' He held a colour print out for Matt to glance at. It was Gajadhar, chunky and topless sitting on board an elephant, presumably the calf now fully grown, 'She has the grace and beauty of her mother, do you not think. Her name is Ananda, joyful one.'

Matt detected a more subdued tone to his voice.

'I only pray that she is missing me with nothing like the intensity that I am missing her. I tried to explain to her that I had to leave, that I had no option, that I would return as quickly as possible, but I do not think that she could understand…'

He left the sentence hanging and in his peripheral vision Matt noticed a look of grim determination in his bright eyes as though trying to will his thoughts across sea and land and to his home. Matt left him in this state for as long as he could bear. 'So why have you…come?'

'I am sorry, what did you say?'

'Well, it's just that you obviously haven't come here for financial reasons, and you seem unhappy leaving Ananda, so I was wondering why you did come. I can understand why you would want to help, elephants are very important to you, that's obvious, but Uddanda can't be the only one with behavioural problems. There must be many elephants in captivity around the world in a similar predicament.'

'Sadly, I am sure that you are right, a cage is no place for such an animal, but you see Uddanda is not just any elephant.'

Matt sensed Gajadhar's gaze in his direction.

'I...We the Ganapatyas, we believe Uddanda *is* Lord Ganesha.'

CHAPTER 26

As was often his habit, Andy had sloped off for an early lunch. Convinced he worked far harder than any of his colleagues and was the only one who genuinely cared about the animals that he was entitled to a longer break.

His flat was part of the converted coach house that overlooked the sea lions' enclosure and which, over the years, had been divided and sub-divided into dwellings that housed most of the keepers.

His initial feeling about moving from his old flat (now inhabited by Matt), to this block had been one of hope for acceptance, that he was now one of the 'gang'. Also, there was the luxury of much more space which made it an appealing swap. But now the novelty had worn off and he was regretting his decision. The attitude towards him from the others seemed, if anything, even more thoughtless. Jez, who was in the flat directly underneath, was particularly selfish, his lousy record player blaring out all the time, and a procession of girls who traipsed in and out day and night. His husbandry with the sea lions was also abysmal, with bins of fish guts left rotting for days beneath Andy's window, and the sea lions themselves often not released from their night pens until almost ten in the morning. He picked up his pen and made a note of it in his scrapbook to show the boss when he returned. No point in taking it to Julian.

He had been compiling data on and off for over a year, a way to vent his frustration and gripes, to right the wrongs. Then came the greatest of all the wrongs, his friend Jack's death and the purpose of his scrapbook took on a whole new focus. He turned now to the thickest chapter simply headed 'King' and almost immediately his palms began to sweat as he looked over the photos stuck scruffily down with dates and times scrawled underneath. He wondered whether he dared to take anymore. King was suspicious; a hunter's sixth sense that he had become the hunted had made him wary, and he had warned Andy off, said what he would do to him if he caught him poking into his affairs.

Often, when Andy looked through his book, his mind wandered into gratifying thoughts of revenge. King would splutter out denials, accuse Andy of lying, then, just as the boss was about to side with King, Andy would triumphantly slam his book on the table. His daydreams would quickly digress into more fanciful plans, fantasies that re-wrote his character, He would become Andy the warrior, thrusting aside anyone who got in his way, Andy the activist, bolt croppers in his muscular hands, cracking open the padlocks, Andy the hero, releasing all the animals and marching them to freedom over the corpse of King.

He closed the book and lent back in his chair; his thin lips curled into a self-satisfied smirk. He had no need to fantasise, no need for any more photos, his plan was clear. The mahout was coming, and with him came the end to King's reign.

CHAPTER 27

'I'm sorry…' Matt strained to hear Gajadhar's words as he battled to steady the mini from the slipstream of an articulated lorry that rumbled past them. 'Did you say Uddanda is Ganesha?'

'Perhaps that is not quite the right way to put it.' Gajadhar paused. 'Incarnation may be a better word, or spirit, yes, we believe that the spirit of Lord Ganesha lives in Uddanda, would that make more sense to you?'

'To be honest, I'm not really a very spiritual person,' said Matt, 'I believe in evolution rather than the err… creationist point of view.'

'An atheist, how wonderful! I hope that we can look forward to many stimulating discussions on the subject.'

Matt laughed nervously.

'Do not worry, it is not my wish to convert you, although I must admit to feeling a bit sorry for those who have never, as a child, sat sleepily on their grandmother's lap, their thoughts and dreams filled with the wondrous stories of Lord Brahma laying in his bed of lotus petals and breathing life into all the plants and animals.'

Matt thought of his own grandmother, the rank, stale odour of cod liver oil and sherry on her breath, the large hairy mole on her top lip. 'Trust me, missing out was no hardship.'

'Ah, another point on which we differ, and yet, if you will excuse the impudence, I cannot help thinking that in many ways we are also very much alike. I sense in you a great sensitivity and empathy towards animals that I also humbly strive for.'

Matt balked. Anyway...you were saying about Uddanda.'

'Yes. Uddanda. Tell me, how much do you know of his history.'

Matt thought for a few seconds, trying to recall what Roger had told him. 'Well, not much – I believe he's been around a bit, Europe I think, started off in a circus before he got too big, oh, and I was told he was wild caught.'

'You were told correctly,' Gajadhar lowered his voice, 'he *was* wild caught and his entire herd massacred. It was a truly horrible thing – I was a young man when it happened and yet a day has not passed when I have not wept for that moment. I can still hardly bear to imagine how terrifying it must have been...' He gave a long sigh before continuing. 'They would have been chased from the forest and into the open, Uddanda desperately trying to keep up with his family, the smells and sounds of fear disorientating his senses, the herd finally exhausted and turning on their attackers, the matriarchs fruitlessly gathering their young and surrounding them in a futile attempt to protect them against the bullets that tore into their flesh...and little Uddanda not even given the opportunity to mourn before the ropes would have fallen around his neck, dragging him away from his world.' Gajadhar stopped and cleared his throat. 'I am sorry, it is a very emotive subject for me.'

Matt peered across at Gajadhar as the Indian tugged a handkerchief from his shirt pocket and dabbed his eyes.

'Did they ever catch them, the people who did it?'

'The poachers? No... It was several weeks before the slaughtered herd was found and the trail had long since vanished. Even so every effort was made to discover the perpetrators and return Uddanda to us, for, as I have said, he is an extremely important elephant to our sect – his family has been revered for several centuries and there are many legends surrounding them and linking them to Lord Ganesha himself, and Uddanda, he is the last of their blood line.'

'I'm sorry but I'm still not quite clear why you think he is our elephant. You said that you'd found no sign of him and his captors since the bodies were found.'

'That is true, yes, but we had never stopped looking, and perhaps never would have had any success had your boss not put an advert in an Indian newspaper for an expert handler for a difficult bull elephant whose age and circumstances fitted those of Uddanda. Often it is far easier to start at the end of a puzzle and work back, and so it was in this case. Amish contacted your boss and discovered that he had purchased the elephant from a zoo in France, then they told him that they had got him from a zoo in Holland, and so on. His life after his capture began to fit together like pieces of a jigsaw, until finally he was traced to an Italian circus. That was the most difficult part...excuse me.' He blew his nose loudly. 'Where was I – yes, Italy. So Amish is as resourceful and powerful as his dear father was and eventually he was able track the circus owner down. He was unable to tell us who sold him the elephant but we discovered that he was shipped from India just three months after the killings. Once we had discovered that,

Amish once again contacted your boss and offered him my services.'

'Well okay, if it's not the same elephant then that's a pretty big coincidence but...'

'Ah, coincidences,' said Gajadhar, his voice lifting, 'that is something I do *not* believe in. Destiny is pre-ordained and that leads me to my final point, we do not know at what point of his journey Uddanda was given this name but it is of great relevance. You see our deity go by many names. Lord Ganesha himself has over a hundred, and one of them, you may be surprised to know is Uddanda...Nemesis of evil and vices.'

Gajadhar paused. Matt suspected for affect.

'So, do you still think that this is merely coincidence or can even an atheist detect an element of divine intervention?'

Matt wiped off a drop of sweat that was trickling down his forehead. 'Sorry, I'm not converted yet, but it is a fascinating story. So, what happens now? Will you take Uddanda back?'

'That, I am sad to say, would be extremely difficult. He has, I am told, killed a man.'

Matt nodded; another droplet of sweat fell from his brow.

'That isn't surprising considering his past,' said Gajadhar. 'No, I am instructed simply to help you and your team in any way that I can in the shared hope of improving his quality of life.'

Matt was momentarily confused. 'I'm sorry, I never introduced myself properly. I'm not an elephant keeper; I'm the education officer. Well, when it's properly set up I will be – at the moment I'm just kind of helping out, learning the routines, collecting mahouts from airports, that sort of thing. I only started on Saturday, so we're both new boys.'

Gajadhar laughed, 'You see, I told you that we had a lot in common. I am only disappointed that our professional relationship will not extend beyond that of taxi driving. So, what can you tell me about the people I will be working with?'

Matt wiped his forearm across his forehead leaving a glistening sheen of perspiration that flattened the hairs on his arm. It was the question that he had been dreading.

He had told himself on the journey to the airport that if the mahout didn't speak English then he'd be spared any difficult questions. But now the question had been asked, in perfect English, by someone who, despite the shortness of their acquaintance, he had a real fondness and respect for.

He unwound the window, suddenly aware of how unbearably hot it had become, but the fresh air just rushed past the opening, unable to penetrate inside the car.

Reaching down to a panel on the dashboard Gajadhar began fiddling with the knobs and sliding levers, and then he finally gave the underside of the controls a tentative thump. A loud whirring noise cranked into action as a blast of cool air flooded into the car and onto their faces.

'Sometimes these things just need a little encouragement,' said the mahout.

'Thanks,' said Matt, winding the window back up, 'I can hear myself think now.'

Matt sensed Gajadhar looking at him.

'I do hope that my question was not indiscreet. It is one thing to learn another language, but to learn a culture, to understand all those little rules that evolve from within a society, I am afraid I am completely ignorant and so if I have caused any offence then I can only beg your forgiveness.'

'No, you've said nothing wrong, it's just…it's like what you just said about societies – the park is like a micro-society in itself; it seems to exist in a separate place—no, that's not right.' It was the first time he had really analysed his impressions and suddenly he felt grateful for the opportunity. 'It's more like when you're in the park there *is* no other place; it's completely shut off, like an island. I wouldn't be surprised if it had its own climate. Sure, there's visitors, but they are faceless, nameless entities and almost unreal because of that, drifting around from ten 'til six and then they're gone leaving the people who really exist, those who live in the park, leaving them to continue with their insular lives. It's like a secret, subdued kingdom.' Matt laughed bitterly. 'It even has a King.'

'I think that I understand. It does not surprise me that it is like that; it must be very strange living in a place that is continually enshrouded in such barely contained despair, an unperceivable madness if you like.'

'Unperceivable madness?' Matt frowned. 'How do you mean?'

'It is only my belief and I trust that you will not take offence but, for example, if we take the elephant, to deprive such an animal of all but its most basic needs, to deny it access to its most primal instincts, to provide a life so constrained and contrary to its wild state, this will surely lead to madness, a madness born out of despondency and despair, not necessarily detectable to us, but there all the same.'

'Despair, surely that's a human emotion?'

'I would suggest that the only emotion that humans do have a monopoly on is that of arrogance, the arrogance to believe that they are the only animals capable of such feelings. Why is it so difficult to bestow other species with emotions, certainly they might manifest themselves in different ways but that is only because they live in such a different environment. When a domestic cat purrs we readily accept it as a sign of contentment, as though the mere process of domestication endows in it an inclination towards humanisation, but if a wild cat, say a leopard...if a leopard were to purr then it would be assumed that it was merely for some practical function.'

'Leopards can't purr,' said Matt.

'I am sorry?'

'They can't,' insisted Matt, 'it's one of the things that defines large and small felines. Small cats can't roar and the big cats...leopards, lions, jaguar, tigers...they can't purr.'

'Or is it...' said Gajadhar, 'that no-one has ever heard them? Perhaps, in captivity, they have not the inclination.'

'Yeah...and if a tree falls in a forest and no one hears it...'

'Hmm...it appears that I should begin with a different example,' said the mahout. 'If a tigress does not feel an irrationally strong bond for her cubs then she would never protect them at great personal risk, and what is this irrational bond if it is not love? I have seen dogs waste away from the loss of their master; I have seen animals in uncontrollable rapture at the return of a loved one that they thought lost. Love, sadness, joy, they exist in all things living, they are life. Surely even a spider must feel some kind of emotion when rushing out in response to vibrations of an insect struggling on its web.'

Matt felt cornered. He had never considered Gajadhar's theories in quite that way and ideally he would like to have the time to give them proper thought. But he had studied Animal Science, he had a degree, and his pride insisted he took a stand. 'But the elephants in your charge, aren't they captive, aren't they deprived of their freedom to roam?'

'That is true, and indeed some in my profession treat their animals very badly. They are the 'Balwan' and they use cruelty to control their elephants, then there are the 'Yucthiman' who prefer ingenuity; however, I have always regarded myself a 'Reghawan', that is to say that I like to train through–'

'Kindness?'

'Thank you, yes. But I have strayed from your excellent point. I believe that captivity is as much a mental state as it is physical. Simply because an animal propagates and feeds in that environment does not automatically make it a suitable one: a canary caged on a windowsill will still sing. In a zoo, just because an elephant no longer needs to roam and forage for food, does not diminish the instinct to roam or for the mental stimulation that a nomadic lifestyle provides.'

'But your elephants, the ones at your plantation, they're not free to roam, are they.'

'That is true,' acknowledged the mahout, 'but they do get to experience the smells and sounds of the forest. It is an integral part of them; it is what makes them whole, that opportunity to embrace all of their senses. Particularly that of communication. For an elephant it is paramount that they can communicate with one another, their trunks are capable of calls that can be detected and answered by other herds over a great distance. But when an elephant in a zoo tries to communicate what does it receive in return? – nothing. Just emptiness, isolation; the sound of the forest is absent.'

Matt said nothing. Although he was still not convinced, he knew that he couldn't simply dismiss Gajadhar's point, which, if correct, left him as an education officer at what was tantamount to a creature concentration camp. But he wasn't convinced. He had fallen under Gajadhar's ideological spell but it was based on personal thoughts and on instinct, and, he acknowledged, kindness, but they were not based on science. He shuddered, again thinking of the mahout's and King's opposing philosophies and he knew that he would have to deal with it at some point, but the easier option was to put it, if not out of his mind, certainly to the back of it, and Gajadhar's discussion was just the way to achieve this.

'I agree that, if not done right, a zoo can be little more than a prison for an animal and certainly a wild caught one is going to find adjustment to captivity much more difficult, but those instances aside, I can't go along with your 'unperceivable madness' theory.

Firstly, most animals live in the present, the here and now–'

'But–'

'Before you say it, I know some primates and, yes elephants as well, do use tools and yes, that does indicate abstract thought, but it's not proof that they will suffer in a zoo environment, if anything, it can make it better. It's not just about the size of enclosure, but more how it's used. Given the choice between a hundred acres of fenced-in bare paddock or a thirty foot enclosure with trees and branches a primate will choose the cage every time, that's been proved, then add to that some environment enrichment...' Matt paused to swerve past an ancient-looking Morris minor that was blocking his lane '...and I don't just mean scatter feeds but straw-filled hessian sacks with hidden tit-bits, hanging feed stations, that sort of thing, then that animal will be just as content as its wild counterpart, more so, 'cause they can exist without the threat of predation. Did you know that an animal's longevity doubles in captivity?'

'I think you will find that, in the case of the elephant, quite the opposite is true,' said Gajadhar.

'How can you say that?' Matt almost wailed. 'Where is the scientific proof?'

He glanced over to the mahout who was smiling like a cat that had got the cream.

'Ah Matt, your effervescent passion is truly a joy to hear. Living as I do, day in and day out with the same people that I have grown up with, people of the same opinions as myself, it is easy to forget what a simple and stimulating pleasure a debate can be.' He began chuckling with delight.

Matt couldn't help but join in. Suddenly he felt like it was time. 'Look Gajadhar, you asked about the elephant keepers, well, I don't want to embarrass you by my own bias so I'll tell you just the facts and allow you to make up your own mind, but this much you should know, the head keeper, a man called King, I don't think that he has much time for spirited debates or spiritual beliefs. I believe that he is, what did you call them, Belwand?'

'Balwan', corrected the mahout. 'Thank you for your candour, but please do not worry about me, once Mr King realises that we both only want what is best for Uddanda I am sure we will become great friends.'

Matt forced a smile. *Christ*, he thought, *King's going to murder him.* Then he began relating the events of the last few days as impartially as he could.

It was five o'clock when they turned into the lane that twisted its way down to the zoo.

The car park was almost deserted and Matt couldn't help but harbour a slight concern that some other dreadful event may have occurred in his absence. However, his worries were quickly quashed as the khaki-clad curator appeared from his office and marched towards them, a welcoming grin firmly fixed on his face.

'You must be Gajadhar, delighted to finally meet you – I'm Julian. So sorry not to be able to meet you in person but a curator's work is never done. Anyway, glad to have you on board, I trust Matthew has been treating you well.'

Matt took a slightly sadistic pleasure watching small tears pop from Julian's eyes as Gajadhar mangled his hand warmly.

'Oh yes, we have had a lovely journey, although I must admit to being happy to have finally arrived and to have the opportunity to see Uddanda.'

Julian shuffled his feet. 'Let's not jump straight into business, plenty of time for all that, anyway I'm sure you must be exhausted.'

'No, not at all, well, perhaps a little, but I am sure that the sight of Uddanda would invigorate me better than anything else could.'

'Nonsense,' insisted Julian, 'anyway, I believe that our elephant team are a little busy at the moment, probably making sure everything is spick and span for your arrival.' He laughed nervously. 'So perhaps it's best we don't disturb them quite yet. Let's go to my office and sort out your keys and what-not and then Matt can take you to your accommodation.'

Gajadhar tried to object but Julian talked over him. 'Matt, could you be a darling and take our guest's bag over to your flat.'

'My flat?'

'That's right. I thought it would be nice for you both to bunk up together, now that you are acquainted,' He turned to Gajadhar. 'It's not the roomiest but it should be adequate. I quite envy you, takes me back to my scouting days. Do they have boy scouts in India? Wonderful organisation, happiest time of my life, I remember once when I was…'

The curator's voice faded as he and Gajadhar walked off to his office, leaving Matt alone by the car. Sighing, he grappled with Gajadhar's bag and staggered towards his flat.

CHAPTER 28

'Matt...Matt...are you awake?'

Matt groaned, rolled over for the umpteenth time, and squinted at the fluorescent glow of his alarm clock; it was almost midnight.

'I am truly sorry to impose on you. I had hoped that perhaps, like myself, you were also having problems sleeping, and if that were so then I had a proposition for you.'

Matt rubbed his eyes and opened them fully; the blurred features of Gajadhar came slowly into focus. 'Go on then,' he sighed, 'what have you decided is so exciting that it can't wait until morning?'

Gajadhar's face immediately brightened 'I knew that I could count on your help,' he gushed, 'It is simply that I have come such a long way...waited so long, and now that I am so close, not to be able to see him is... it's unbearable.'

Matt sat bolt upright. 'You're thinking of going to the elephant house...right now...that's crazy, you're talking as if you're visiting some long-lost friend, not an elephant...a killer elephant, in the middle of the night. At best it's breaking and entering, at worst it's suicide!'

'I assure you that it would not be breaking and entering,' he replied, dangling a large bunch of keys in front of Matt's eyes, 'I would never dream of involving you, or indeed myself in any illegal activity. Julian gave me the keys this afternoon, with his blessing.'

'Yes, but I don't think that he meant for you to go gallivanting about in the middle of the night.'

'Possibly you are correct,' said Gajadhar. 'You are a very astute young man, I have seen that. Even your comment about visiting a friend was, whether or not you realised, startlingly perceptive. I could not have suggested a more suitable analogy if I tried.'

For the first time since their acquaintance began Matt doubted the Indian's sincerity. It was, he thought, Gajadhar who was the astute one.

Again, Matt sighed. 'Okay, okay. Let me find my shoes.'

The park was not completely unfamiliar to Gajadhar. After dinner they had gone for a stroll just before sunset, bumping into Al and Tommy, where Matt was able to get an up-date on Roger's condition (which although still serious, was no longer life-threatening). They were both either stoned or drunk, and Gajadhar was visibly relieved when he finally worked out that neither were involved with caring for the elephants.

Matt had watched amused as Gajadhar, clearly struggling to make sense of Big Al's dialect, had asked if he were a genuine Cockney, to the delight of Tommy who fell to the floor clutching his stomach as the giant spluttered and boomed that he could 'fucking trace his fucking ancestor back to Robert the fucking Bruce!' But the mahout's agreeable aura worked its magic and Al knocked him flying with an affectionate pat declaring 'shite, there's not many who could walk away after calling Big Al a fucking Cockney.'

Now, six hours later, the paths were lit by an eerie silver moonlight and the park had become alive with nocturnal menace: a forlorn howl from a wolf, a cry of a deer, a screech of an owl, a scream of a leveret – the minutia stories of life and death.

'The heat, the sounds, it is as though I am still in India,' mused Gajadhar as they crept their way towards the elephant house.

Matt grunted in agreement; he felt like a hundred eyes were glaring hatefully at them from behind the mesh of their enclosures. A Serval spat and slunk away, her form swallowed up into the black recess of her cage. In the distance they could hear the rasping, sawing call of a leopard. He looked over to Gajadhar who appeared un-characteristically uneasy.

'That's Beth,' said Matt, 'she's like a big kitten. I'm sure Al will introduce you sometime, she's his pride and joy.'

'And she is also in a cage?'

As Matt nodded in reply it occurred to him that, for an Indian, the sound of a nearby leopard must be a very real concern.

In the distance they heard a low rumble of thunder.

'I fear that there may be a storm on its way,' suggested Gajadhar.

'I hope so, it's so bloody oppressive; we could do with something to clear the air.'

They both looked up at the clear, twinkling sky.

'I don't know, I can't see any clouds up there,' added Matt wistfully.

They entered the zoo yard, passed the kitchens and approached the elephant house. Silhouetted against the moonlight the building looked imposing. Like some kind of ancient rural cathedral, it had a strange sense of foreboding.

'This is a very unhappy place,' said Gajadhar simply.

'Night time can have that effect you know. It would probably feel a lot less gloomy if we came back in the morning,' hinted Matt.

Gajadhar didn't answer, he was focused on the gate, looking for the padlock. Unable to find it he fumbled for the bolt instead, located it and slid it across. Pushing gently, the door swung easily open.

'That's strange,' said Matt. 'I would've expected King to be pretty hot on security, maybe it was–'

A pleading look from Gajadhar stopped Matt abruptly in mid-sentence. It was a look that required no explanation – this was the mahout's big moment, something that he had been waiting many years for.

'Sorry,' Matt said, 'I'll be quiet.'

Gajadhar nodded gratefully and groped his way to the inner door that he discovered was also unlocked. It creaked and groaned as he eased it open and stepped inside.

Despite the two small skylights, it was too dark to make anything out, and considering that there was accumulatively fourteen tons of animal in there with them Matt thought it was also uncannily quiet. He felt his way along the circuit board that he remembered being on the right side of the door and found a row of switches. Deciding to risk just one he flicked it down. A tube light flickered and stuttered, and then burst into life with a buzz, illuminating the far end of the barn where the massive bulk that was Uddanda stood. Slowly he turned his head to face them.

Gajadhar let out a small gasp of deference, dropped to his knees and began chanting.

'Agajananapadmarkam gajananamaharnisam
Anekadam tam bhaktanamekadantamupasmahe.'

163

He continued for a minute, and then raised his eyes and gazed in awe at the elephant. 'You did not mention that he only has one tusk.'

'I didn't know, it was dark and...his right side was against the wall.' Matt was aware that there was something else different and was struggling to put his finger on it. 'Why, is it important?'

'It is, I suppose, what you would call one of those coincidences, but for myself it is the final corroboration of many truths. You see, Lord Ganesha has only one tusk.'

Matt knew that this was not the moment for a theological discussion, and besides, he was still distracted by another thought, something that disturbed him. He looked at the bull elephant, who returned his stare.

'Something's changed,' he whispered. 'The dead look in his eyes, that trance-like state I told you about, it's gone. He seems... aware.'

'He is magnificent,' said Gajadhar. He got off his knees and walked towards the elephant like a child taking its first cautious steps towards its mother. 'Just look at his size,' he murmured, 'his dignified posture. He is the most perfect thing that I have ever seen.'

As the mahout approached, Uddanda's huge ears fanned and flapped, slapping loudly against the side of his head.

'Careful, he looks agitated,' said Matt.

'Do not be concerned, it is a friendly greeting. That is right isn't it dear one. Can you smell your home on me, do you remember?'

Uddanda's trunk reached out for Gajadhar.

'Even so, I'd be happier if you didn't get too close.' Matt looked to his left where Kali had begun weaving her head from side to side and tugging at the chain around her leg. On his right Joti was partially obscured, but the repetitive jerking, rocking movements of her body suggested something was making her nervous. Matt felt an urge to look behind him, suddenly convinced that other dangers were lurking in the shadows but he quickly dismissed the idea and looked back to Gajadhar.

The mahout now stood next to Uddanda and was showering him with praise and salutations, caressing his trunk with a circular motion of his hands. Matt could hear him muttering some kind of mantra under his breath. 'I think we should go now,' he said.

Once again he sensed that he was being watched. He stole a glance over his shoulder, peering into the dark corner used to store bales of hay, then froze. Two figures, man and dog, emerged from the gloom.

Matt looked directly into the man's piercing watery, blue eyes, feeling they contained more malignance than any of the creatures that had cautiously watched him and Gajadhar as they had crossed the walled garden that night.

King issued an inaudible order to Shadow who growled quietly, halting her stalk whilst her master slowly approached. His head swaying slowly from side to side, like a shark seeking out prey in the bleakest depths of the ocean, looking from the mahout, then Matt then back to the mahout.

Look out!' he roared.

Matt wheeled around just in time to see Gajadhar roll to the floor a second before the full force of the bull's trunk swung past him.

Fearing a second attack Matt leapt to Gajadhar's side, hoisting him clear of the Uddanda's reach. 'Christ! Are you ok?'

'I believe so,' said the mahout, brushing strands of straw from his shirt. They both turned as King stepped fully into the light. A click of his finger and Shadow was at his side.

'Well, well. First I save you from Kali and now your little friend here from Dan. Seems like I'm a real fucking Samaritan these days.'

Matt looked up. 'Christ, King! What the hell are you doing here?'

'What am I doing in my own elephant house? Hell boy, you got some gumption to ask me that.' His teeth were clenched, his thin lips fixed in a reptilian grin.

Gajadhar finished brushing himself down and stepped forward, his hand held out towards King. 'You must be Mr King, I am so glad to make your acquaintance. I am Gajadhar, and I am truly indebted to you for your timely warning.'

King looked dubiously at the mahout's outstretched hand and then at his smiling face. Shadow began to growl. King snapped a glance at her and she dropped onto her haunches. Then, taking Gajadhar's hand he squeezed it until the tendons on his arms bulged.

Matt watched them, unsure whether to intervene. Having been on the receiving end of both men's grips he knew that they must be feeling some pain by now, but their faces expressed no discomfort, just the mahout's warm and open smile and King's icy snarl.

'Everyone here calls me King,' he said.

The men released their clasp, their hands dropped to their sides; both discretely stretched and massaged their fingers.

'Please do not blame Matt for my own act of imprudence,' said Gajadhar. 'He came at my insistence, and to prevent me from getting into any trouble.'

'Well, you sure ballsed that up, hey Matt?' said King.

Matt smiled weakly. 'So how come you're here?'

'Just doing a bit of homework for the boy here.' He looked down at Gajadhar then back to Matt. 'It's like you said back there, some change has come over Dan and I figured to watch him for a bit, see what's making him tick, still, seems to me he's still the same o' psycho out to kill anyone foolish enough to get too close.'

'I am afraid that I do not agree,' said the mahout.

'You don't huh, and I s'pose it was my imagination that you almost got squished like a grape.'

'I admit that I made a mistake,' said Gajadhar. 'I was certainly a little overawed and therefore distracted by the beauty of Uddanda, caught up in the moment you might say, but why he behaved in that way I do not know. I honestly sensed no malice, at least not towards myself.' Gajadhar's eyes twinkled mischievously.

'What the fuck! 'Sensed no malice,' you say.' King barked another gravelly laugh. 'What kinda elephant expert are you? What the fuck d'ya think he was trying to do, give you a hug? Shit, I can't believe the boss fell for this mahout bollocks, – you're gonna be as much use as tits on a boar hog. He'd been better off slapping a bit of black paint on a dwarf and giving him the job...'

'Hang on, King...'

167

King swung around to Matt, his thick, stubby finger poking just short of Matt's face. 'Never, and I mean n…e…v…e…r,' his finger jabbed Matt's forehead as he pronounced each letter, 'never interrupt King when he's talking, you got that, college boy?'

Matt stepped back; he clenched his fists. 'King you basta–'

'I fear that I have got off to a bad start,' Gajadhar quickly interjected, his face a picture of serenity. 'It was never my intention to cause any bad feeling towards yourself and certainly not towards others. My objective, as I'm sure is yours, is merely to help this poor elephant in any capacity that I can, and any advice that you can offer me to achieve this end would be extremely gratefully received. As you have already observed, this is not an environment that I am altogether familiar with.'

'You want my advice,' said King, 'stick a bullet between his eyes and get on the next plane back to where you came from. You're right, this ain't your kinda environment, you're not leading some domesticated cow around some paddy field. Dan, he's a bad elephant, beyond reach, you try and analyse him and he'll kill you, no doubt about it.' He began walking towards the door, Shadow glued to his heel.

'Thank you Mr. King, I will certainly consider what you have said.'

'That's King, drop the Mister, oh and Matt…' King picked up a shovel and launched it at Matt.

He caught it. 'What's this for?' he asked.

'For scraping your boy off the floor next time he gets too close to Dan.' He gave a final laugh and swaggered out of the barn whistling 'Sweet Home Alabama'.

'Thanks for stepping in back then,' said Matt, once the whistling had faded into the dark. 'I don't know what I was thinking of – he just really...I don't know... he really gets to me.'

'He is certainly an interesting character,' said Gajadhar, scratching his chin thoughtfully. 'I cannot seem to think of the word to describe him.'

'A Balwan?' said Matt.

'That,' said Gajadhar, smiling, 'would be the word that I am looking for.'

CHAPTER 29

Thursday 2nd

The gap that Roger's absence had left was apparent to everyone. His relaxed, laid-back manner had had a subtle effect on the others, calming the underlying tension that simmered between the other keepers. Al's brazen attitude, Andy's shifty paranoia, King's menacing machoism, all had been diluted or at least contained out of some unspoken respect for Roger. His easy, effortlessly manner encouraged loyalty and admiration, dissipating minor feuds and petty quarrels with humour, logic and self-assured charm.

Julian was missing Roger's input more than most. Standing hunched and helpless as Al hurled abuse at him; his eyes darted nervously around the zoo kitchen automatically seeking interjection and protection, but the lack of Roger meant that none was forthcoming.

It was supposed to be an opportunity for Julian to formally introduce Gajadhar to the 'troops' but when the issue of who was to cover the paddocks section arose it soon degenerated into a shouting match, led by Al.

'Let me get this straight, you expect me to do all my rounds and then the fucking paddocks. Shite, you must be taking the piss.'

'Al, calm down.' Julian tried to sound assertive but came across pleading rather than stern 'It's only a temporary measure until you can train up Matt to take over.'

'So I've gotta educate the fucking education officer as well – now I've heard every-fucking-thing, why the fuck can't Andy do it. Lazy little shite spends half the day playing with his fucking rat anyway.'

'I do not, no more than you spend messing around with Beth. Anyway, since Tuesday all the enclosures are such a mess in the mornings, branches and food scattered all over the place, that it takes twice as long to clean up.'

'I could do it,' said Tommy, his quiet voice obliterated by the brash entrance of Jez, sauntering casually into the kitchens, his baseball cap sat cocked on his head.

He breezed up to Gajadhar and gave him a warm slap on the shoulder.

'You must be the mahout, good to see you. I'm Jez – sea lions.' After grabbing a large bunch of grapes, he slumped over a table and started tossing each grape into the air and catching them in his mouth. 'So, what's happening with you dudes? I could hear the wrath of Al from the other side of the park'

'What about him,' growled Al, pointing an accusing finger at Jez, 'He could do with a bit of honest work, lose some of that puppy fat.'

'Puppy fat!' The grape bounced off Jez's head as he looked urgently down at his stomach. 'What d'ya mean, puppy fat? You couldn't pinch an inch on this baby.' He stroked his stomach lovingly. 'Anyway, what you talking about honest work, who do you think is slogging his arse off trying to sort out the end of season party for you bunch of ingrates.'

'It's Julian; he needs someone to cover Roger's section,' said Andy.

'*I* could do it,' insisted Tommy.

Julian forced a dismissive smile in Tommy's direction then looked imploringly at Jez.

'Sorry, dudes, but no can do, I'm contract not salary remember, and my contract says that come Saturday I'm free as a bird,' Jez thought for a second, 'What sort of dosh are we talking about here, anyway?'

'That's a fucking good point, if you want me to do the work of two keepers then you can pay me two fucking wages,' said Al.

'Hang on, I never said I wouldn't do it,' interrupted Andy, 'just that it would be difficult, but given a bit of financial incentive…'

Julian cleared his throat. 'Look here, chaps, I've always looked at our little set-up more as a family than a work force, and it is the nature of families that they help out in times of need, not for any individual gain but for the good of the–'

'Shite, not the fucking family speech,' groaned Al.

'So, can you pay any extra or not?' asked Andy.

'I'm sorry, but there just isn't enough in the pot to justify the expense, not now that we have two extra wages to pay – the boss simply wouldn't go for it.'

Andy and Al flashed accusing glances at Matt and Gajadhar.

'Well, you're the fucking curator,' said Al, 'you're just gonna have to convince him.'

'Curator, hah, that's some joke.' King stepped away from the wall that he had been leaning on. Up until this point he had been staring fixedly at Gajadhar whilst sucking noisily and messily on an orange. He dropped the peel to the floor, summoned Colin and Gary to follow with a click of his fingers, and strode towards Julian, the curator visibly cowering as he approached. 'You ain't supposed to plead with this rabble. Show a bit of leadership, tell 'em how it is and if they don't like it show 'em the door, or your boot. Hell, Jules, show 'em both, kick the fuckers out.' King's voice dropped and with a hint of relish he added, 'unless you want me to do it for you, thin out some of the dead wood, huh?'

'Err…no thanks King, I don't think that will be necessary, just joshing with me, weren't you lads?'

Sighs of resignation escaped Al and Andy's lips.

'As you wish,' King shrugged, 'the offers there if you need it, come on boys.'

With his minions at his heal, King swaggered out of the kitchen.

Julian looking nervously after him and then to the mahout. 'Just a minute King, aren't you forgetting Gajadhar?'

King stopped at the door and looked back. 'Not today Jules, ain't got the time for no babysitting duties.'

'Oh…err…okay, right then, Andy perhaps you could take Gajadhar along with you, give him the grand tour, a chance to really get to jolly-well know the place, Al, Matt, I'll leave paddocks in your capable hands.'

Al was about to object but the curator had already scurried out through the door and was heading as fast as he could back to the sanctuary of his office.

'Looks like you got the short straw, Al,' said Andy, grinning smugly at the prospect of having the mahout all to himself.

'Shite, I don't mind really, it's just the principle.'

'Well Andy,' said Matt with a wink directed to Al, 'if you're giving Gajadhar the tour you may as well introduce yourself properly.'

'Yeah…of course. Hi, I'm Andy.' He held out his hand, which Gajadhar warmly grabbed.

Grip like a mangle,' whispered Matt with a grin as he and Al left the kitchen.

CHAPTER 30

The anticipated storm had yet to materialise and the air was oppressive, thick and sluggishly uncomfortable.

Matt had long since discarded his T-shirt, putting it to more practical use by wiping the deluge of sweat from his forehead. Meanwhile, Al's skin, with his Celtic completion, was already raw. His neck and throat were crimson and not wishing to add to his discomfort he opted to keep his shirt on, the same shirt, (Matt could tell by the cigarette singe mark that was on its breast pocket and by the stale, rank odour that occasionally wafted over him), that he had worn the last three consecutive days.

'Shite, we've missed lunch,' grumbled Al looking at his watch, 'come on Matt, down tools, I've had it.'

'You're kidding, it'll take us fifteen minutes to walk up to the staff room, then another fifteen back again,' Matt curled the hosepipe into the water trough and turned on the tap, 'and we've almost finished, haven't we? Just the zebras left to do.'

'Yeah, but their corral is always the fucking worst, and this heat is fucking killing me.'

A sudden, irrepressibly impish desire consumed Matt. 'Well, if that's the problem...' Picking up the hose and placing his thumb over the end he aimed it at Al.

What the fuck!' The cold water struck him like a thousand tiny icicle arrows penetrating his blistering skin and sent a tingling shockwave around his body.

Matt laughed, delighted by Al's cringing reaction, then his jaw fell as the Scotsman bounded towards him. In a single, fluid motion Al scooped up the water from the trough into his bucket and launched the contents at Matt, catching him full in the face. It was a perfect shot, Matt hadn't even time to close his mouth. He gargled and spat the water out, wiping the excess from his eyes in time to see Al's lunge. He tried to duck but Al was deceptively quick and briefly they wrestled, the hose randomly soaking them both, then Matt felt his feet leave the ground and he flew backwards, losing his grip on the hosepipe.

The two Tapir emerged from their dust bath and ambled up their paddock to investigate, watching with bemused intensity the two men who were grinning with childish enthusiasm whilst eying each other up with suspicion.

At that moment Al's walkie-talkie, poking from his jacket pocket that hung from the enclosure gate, burst into life. From where they stood it initially made no sense, just a long crackly monologue. Only when they put down their weapons and approached did they recognise the whining voice of Andy, and with growing horror they listened to his rant.

'The fucking idiot,' cried Al, 'he must be leaning on his radio, the little shite is broadcasting to the whole fucking zoo!'

CHAPTER 31

Andy had Gajadhar cornered in the reptile house. He'd been waiting for this opportunity, planning it, since he first heard of the mahout's arrival. It was his chance, finally he would have an ally. And Gajadhar was proving to be a polite and attentive audience.

'If you want my opinion, hell, what am I saying, it's fact as far as I'm concerned, he's a murderer.' Andy paused, letting the weight of the word sink in, before continuing. 'It must have been him. And now Jack's dead and Tommy might as well be, not much more than a vegetable. But as usual he bullshits his way out of it, that's the thing about King, he's one hundred percent bullshit. I'd say it to his face as well if he didn't always surround himself with Colin and Gary. He knows people are out to get him, that's why he makes sure he's never on his own,'

'But he was on his own last night when–'

It was the second time that morning that Gajadhar had attempted to speak, and once again Andy cut him short.

'Bravado, that's all, I bet he threatened you didn't he. That's what he does, bully and threaten, some kind of insecurity issue, probably a latent queer.' Andy laughed at his comment, releasing his feelings and thoughts like this was cathartic, liberating, and he was loving every moment. 'He's really insecure about you, that's kinda why I'm telling you all this, warning you. I knew Matt wouldn't, he's a nice bloke but he's new – hasn't got the balls like me. Honestly, sometimes I think I'm the only one prepared to stand up to him.' He paused, giving Lucky a little scratch behind her ear before continuing. 'It's not that I'm particularly brave, and I know I'm not the hardest person – that's not to say I can't look after myself – it's just sometimes you've got to stand up to bullies, you know, stick to your principles. That's why I'm telling you this, he's got it in for you, thinks that you'll undermine his empire – and you could too, you know how? By proving that he's responsible, that's how.'

Gajadhar shifted awkwardly; he recognised Andy's type, a rabbit scared of his own inconsequentiality and he pitied him, but at the same time he felt uncomfortable with the discussion, the bias, the thinly disguised envy, the hate portrayed as piety; he was not enjoying Andy's conversation or company.

Andy noticed his companion looking uneasy and immediately he miss-read him. 'Don't be worried, I'll be with you every step of the way...mostly... I don't want you to...'

'Andy, if I may just stop you there.' Gajadhar had had enough. 'You have generously filled my head with more information than a simple man like myself would normally receive in a year, if not a lifetime, and so, begging your forgiveness, I will leave you now in the hope of finding somewhere quiet to digest all that you have told me.'

Before Andy could open his mouth the mahout had bowed his head and briskly drifted through the doors and out of sight.

Andy remained where he was, his arms folded, cradling his rat.

'Well Lucky, what'ya think… me too, I think he's on our side.'

King stood in the Elephant house; his knuckles were white as he twisted his hands around the ivory handle of his goad as though he were wringing the neck of a chicken. He slammed the goad down on the table and snatched up the walkie-talkie, hurling it across the barn where it shattered against the wall in between Colin and Gary's heads. 'You two come with me, we're gonna catch us a vermin.'

Colin and Gary followed, licking their lips like hungry lion cubs being led to a fresh kill.

'How can we make him shut up,' cried Matt, fumbling with the walkie-talkie's button for the umpteenth time. 'Christ – why won't it work?'

'I keep telling you, none of the radios can reply if the talk button stays pressed down, why the fuck do you think we bother with all that 'over and out' shite.'

'Then we've got to find him, before King does!'

They tore up the path, scattering the Tapirs in their wake.

CHAPTER 32

King burst through the double doors of the tropical house, his forehead and cheeks the colour of molten lava. He glared around, scouring the foliage, looking for any signs.

'He's not here,' said Gary as the two boys caught up with him.

'I can see that you fuckwit.'

The plop of a Koi carp feeding drew his attention to the pond. He went over and bending down to it, raked his hand through the water and scooped out a smattering of small brown pellets. 'Some food left, he can't have fed 'em too long ago, where ain't we looked yet?'

'Err, Small Primates and Reptile House,' replied Colin, smugly looking at his rebuked cohort.

'Primates is closest,' added Gary, keen to win back some brownie points.

The sprint had become a jog and now, ten minutes later, it was barely a fast walk as Al and Matt staggered through the gates into the walled garden.

'Shite, I've got to cut down on the cigs,' panted Al.

Matt agreed, he was regretting not bringing his T-shirt to wipe off the sweat that was pouring freely down his face and stinging his eyes; he shook his head like a dog emerging from a river.

'Oi, cut that out, I'm wet enough already!'

Matt ignored him and read the sign at the junction in front of them.

'Carnivores and Reptiles or Monkeys and Aviaries?'

'It's alright,' sighed Al, rising to his full height and shielding his eyes from the sun, 'I can see the little shite, over there.'

Matt squinted in the same direction. 'Does he look okay, is he on his own?'

Al craned his neck, 'Well he's standing – so I guess King can't have found him.'

'Maybe he didn't hear the radio after all?' suggested Matt.

They began strolling towards the Tropical House.

'Maybe so, still I'm almost disappointed that he didn't. I just half killed myself for no fucking reason.' Al cupped his hands either side of his mouth and called to the figure thirty yards ahead of them, 'Hey Andy, you southern twat, have you got some kind of a death wish or what?'

The figure turned to face them, even silhouetted against the glare of the sun it was immediately obvious, the gaunt, hunched posture the patchy tufts of hair.

'Shite…it's not him!'

Andy jumped back in surprise as the door to the Reptile House flew open, the outside world obliterated by the stocky frame that filled the opening.

'King… Man, you gave me a fright.'

King took a step towards him, his jaw line tensed as he spat through his snarled lips. 'I should've thought to come here first, most likely place when you're looking for a snake.'

'Huh – what … what do you mean, what's wrong?' Andy was backing away, heading for the door at the other end of the corridor.

King ignored the question. 'Still, I guess us murdering bullshitters ain't none too bright, what d'ya reckon?'

Andy's heart pounded as he looked down at his walkie-talkie and the sudden realisation of what he had done filled his throat with bile.

Petrified, he looked back at King and he felt his legs buckling beneath him, then he began trembling uncontrollably, fighting against the urge to throw-up. Then the doors behind him were flung open and Colin and Gary appeared, grinning savagely like ferrets cornering a rabbit in its burrow.

Tommy's eyes were red, his cheeks wet and below his nose ran two silver trails.

'Tommy, have you seen Andy – have you seen him?' cried Matt.

Tommy didn't answer; fresh snot bubbled from his nostrils that he wiped away with the side of his wrist.

'Look Tommy,' continued Matt, 'Andy's in trouble, we really need to find him, quickly.'

'Did you hear,' whimpered Tommy, 'on the radio… Andy said things, horrible things.'

'Yeah I know,' replied Matt, 'we heard – that's why we've got to find him, before King does.'

'He said stuff about me as well, said I was a vegeta–' He sniffed hard; a fresh tear sprung from the corner of his eye.

'Shite, Tommy,' Al reached over and gave Tommy's arm a reassuring squeeze. 'Andy's a twat, says all kinds of bollocks, you know that, he can't help himself, but he doesn't mean it, you know that too.'

'So, you think its bollocks then, the stuff he said about me being better off dead?' Tommy looked hopefully up at Al.

'Course it is, and when I find him I'll give him a slap, he fucking deserves that, but not the beating that King will give him if he gets there first.'

'I haven't seen him.'

'Fuck.' groaned Al, flashing a helpless glance at Matt.

'But I did see King, and Colin and Gary.' added Tommy.

'Fucking wank fuck! Did you see where they went?'

'The Tropical House, but they came out again pretty quick, I don't know after that.'

'Shite, thanks Tommy. Hey Matt – wait up.'

Matt was already sprinting up the path in the direction of the Tropical House. He paused impatiently whilst Al lumbered after him.

'Can I help?' called Tommy after them.

'No thanks,' Matt shouted back.

'Yes,' called Al, 'go look for your sister, tell her what's happened…' He looked at Matt. 'She might come in handy with King.'

Beneath their laughter Andy could just make out the plaintive squeaks of Lucky.

King squinted at the sign above the vivarium.

'Cuban boa huh, shame we couldn't have found a King cobra, that'd be more fitting, hey boys?'

In their respective lives the Cuban Boa had never hunted live prey and Lucky had never seen a snake, but instinct made both aware of their roles.

183

The snake was cautious, aware of the risk to herself should the prey retaliate, yet she could have no comprehension that the rat had spent her entire existence pampered, hand-fed, groomed, hugged and kissed, and that she was desperately under-equipped to understand or react to her situation. Even the glass door to the vivarium baffled her, she could see Andy but neither reach him nor smell him; all she could smell was the overwhelming scent of danger.

She ran up and down the invisible barrier, stopping at the end of each run to scrabble piteously at the glass with her paws. On the other side of the glass was Andy, pinned down by Colin and Gary, a fistful of his hair in Gary's hand. They were forcing his head up to the glass so that he couldn't avoid the scene.

'Please, I'll do anything…anything you want, just let her out, she doesn't understand!'

'Hell, boy, it's you that don't understand, this is something you got to see, a lesson in respect.'

'King… please, break my arms, my legs, do what you want but get her out of there.' He tried wriggling free but the little strength that he had left was ineffectual against King's minions who merely tightened their hold.

King coughed out a laugh. 'You presumptuous little shit, you really think a dead rat makes up for what you said, hell no, this is just my little appetiser, get you in the right frame of mind. What was it you said, that you were the only one prepared to stand up to me, to tell me that I was a – what was it – a bully and a murderer?'

He walked over to Andy, squatted down next to him and pulled out a huge knife from the sheaf tied to his thigh. Absentmindedly he began using the tip to pick at the calluses on his left hand as he continued talking. 'I've done my share of killing, for the good of my country, and sure I'll bully those that need it, and there ain't many that couldn't do with a firecracker up their ass from time to time, and if you were to tell me this, man to man, respectful-like – then, you know, I would have shaken you by the hand, admired your integrity and gumption.'

His voice changed into in a hoarse whisper as he leaned in close to Andy's ear. 'But no... a snivelling, parasitic, gutless piece of shit like you ain't considerate like that, you prefer to bitch behind my back, accusing me of bullying, of murder,' He leaned in even closer until Andy could feel the hot breath on his neck, 'of being a fucking faggot.' He stood up abruptly, 'and you think a dead rat can make up for all that?'

'She's not a rat she's my friend, my best friend,' wailed Andy

'All the better, then perhaps you'll find the spirit to stand up to me, hey look, seems like your best friend's got the same spineless traits as you.'

With a nod from King, Gary pushed Andy's head in the direction of Lucky. Her snout was pressed up against a small air gap in the corner. As she scrabbled at it, little beads of blood sprung from the quick of her broken claws. The snake loomed up from behind, its tongue flicking in and out, excited by the fresh new taste in the air.

'It's going for it; look it's rearing up!' said Colin with a blood lust to rival the snake.

'You bastards, I'll kill you bastards,' howled Andy lamely, weeping uncontrollably. He looked up into the cold eyes of the boa, its mouth gapped in readiness, waiting for the right moment to strike. Andy made one last futile effort to escape – he kicked and pushed against his captors with his light frame, trying to get close enough to the glass, to bang on it, somehow distract the snake. An arm brushed across his face and without thinking he bit down on it, whipping his head from side to side like a dog with a rag.

'Ow! You fucker, get him off,' cried Gary.

A fist burst into Andy's gut, winding him; involuntarily his mouth opened, sending a gasp of air wafting over to the little vent where Lucky stood. Her nose twitched eagerly as she sucked in Andy's scent, filling her tiny lungs with his breath. She knew he was close and so she heightened her attack on the little gap, feverously scrabbling, trying to increase its size, it was her only focus.

The Boa's patience had paid off; it had chosen its moment well. It struck, and a single squeal of terror merged with Andy's scream of despair.

Andy collapsed to the floor; his hands clasped to his face.

'Get him on his feet.' King's voice sounded like dry gravel in a cement mixer. He took three steps, stopping just short of Andy, 'Hey boy, you about ready to sort me out now?'

'Leave him alone.' Shouted Matt.

Andy's head turned slowly to where Matt and Al stood in the doorway.

Matt felt all his trepidation leave him as he was gripped by a sudden rage – Andy's eyes were red and swollen and bright red drops of blood oozed from his trembling lower lip.

'I said, leave him alone.'

King's thin lips curled into a snarl as he faced Matt and Al. 'Sure we will, just as soon as we've taught him a little lesson – you understand the importance of lessons, don't you college boy?' His tone was light, contrasting grimly with the raw hate that glared from his half squinting eyes.

Al took a step forward, locked his fingers together and stretched them until they clicked. 'Do as Matt says,' he boomed.

Colin and Gary looked nervously from the giant form of Al to King, who shook his head.

'Why don't you come and get him?'

Al glanced down at the long, glistening blade in King's hand.

'Lose the knife first,' growled Al.

King feigned surprise. 'This little thing? Hell, it ain't much more than a toy, still if it bothers you.' He tossed it onto the tiled floor with a clatter that echoed through the corridor.

Fists clenched, Matt marched towards Colin and Gary. 'Now…let him go!'

They released their hold and Andy slumped to the floor. Matt knelt down to him, lifting his head clear of the cold hard tiles, cradling his trembling body. 'You bastards.' Hissed Matt but Colin and Gary didn't hear, their attention fixed on the clash between King and Al.

Al strode towards King and without hesitation swung with his right arm. His reach was such that no one ever expected and rarely recovered from the premature blow, and if they did then his follow through move, bringing up his right knee to meet the head of his victim as they crumpled down, always finished them off. It was a technique that he had used many times, honed over the years until it had become a naturally flowing movement, his 'double whammy' as he proudly called it.

His fist made perfect contact, slamming into King's temple, like a hammer striking an anvil. King staggered. Al brought up his right knee, but it met no obstruction. Shocked, he looked up to see King still standing erect, grinning with a mixture of masochistic pleasure and sadistic anticipation.

'Not bad,' King rubbed the side of his head.

Al swung his arm around again but it never reached its target, as a searing pain shot up his left leg and he dropped to the floor. It was an old injury, a biking accident that had left his kneecap prone to dislocation. Even through the pain he understood immediately that this was no fluke, no lucky kick on the part of King. He must have mentioned it once, and King, with assassin-like efficiency, had filed it away.

Al reached down to the lump that lay at right angles to where it should. Knowing that King would take full advantage and finish him off, he urgently wrenched it back into position. Briefly the pain was worse than its displacement and he screamed in agony before a click and a dull throb replaced the burning. Bracing himself against the next onslaught, Al looked up into King's wild, glazed eyes and, too late, he realised the vast gulf between King and himself.

For Al a fight was for the thrill, the perfect way to end a night out.

He hadn't always felt like this but had found that the bigger he grew the more people would seek him out, lads with reputations to make, eager to take on a colossus and enhance their own status. It soon became a way of life, a natural part of him, and he took to the role enthusiastically, meeting each new challenger with relish.

There was no such joy or thrill in King's eyes, only savage, uncontrollable determination. He was a killer, a professional, and once in that zone there was little that would stop him. Al raised his forearm over his head, insufficient protection against the sharp, heavy goad that was about to drive into him.

'King stop!'

Susie's cry broke the scene like a spell. King froze; his arm still raised.

Andy also reacted to her voice. He pointed to the vivarium before breaking down again, choking out a few almost unintelligible words between sobs. 'Susie... they've.... they've killed Lucky.'

Glancing over to where Andy's trembling hand indicated Susie glimpsed a tail and hind paw dangling from the snake's mouth. Brushing coldly past King she laid a hand on Andy's shoulder, gave it a squeeze, then bent down and picked up King's knife. 'I'll do what I can.'

She stepped over to the glass door and slid it open, paused for a moment and taking a deep breath, she swiftly grasped the snake below the bulge in its throat.

'I'm sorry,' she whispered, and with veterinary precision she sliced. The remaining five feet of snake sagged to the ground as lifeless as a length of hosepipe and, in silence, she prised and stretched at the remaining orifice, delicately widening the opening with the blade of the knife until Lucky appeared, blinking and shivering, her fur rank with mucus and blood.

'Here,' she said, passing the rat to Andy, 'dry her with your top while I get my kit, she'll need a course of antibiotics.'

She turned to face King, her green eyes bright with rage, but he was gone, along with Colin and Gary – only the stunned faces of Al and Matt remained, looking at her with their mouths agape.

'Fuck me!' declared Al, standing tentatively and rubbing his knee.

Matt walked over to Andy. 'You okay?'

Andy didn't reply, he was dabbing the cradled rat with the sleeve of his shirt whilst gently rocking it, like a parent soothing a child out of a nightmare.

Matt tried again. 'You were right, she really is Lucky.' Still he received no answer. Under his breath Matt could just make out Andy's murmur.

'I'll kill them Lucky, I promise, I'll kill them for you.'

'He's in shock,' said Susie in an overly brisk and workmanlike voice, 'don't worry, I can deal with it.' She ran a hand over Andy's clammy forehead.

'Can I help?' asked Matt, kneeling next to Susie.

She turned away; her features obscured by the thick, red curls that fell over her face. 'I said I'll deal with it!' she snapped – a tear splashed onto the porcelain floor.

'Okay... if you're sure.' He beckoned to Al who limped over and together they began to leave.

'It's not because of King,' said Susie.

'Huh?' Matt looked back to her.

'Why I'm a bit... upset; it's nothing to do with King, we're finished, it was having to kill that snake, that's what bothers me, but I had no choice, it was either the rat or the snake.' She hesitated analysing her thoughts as though they were laboratory results, before reluctantly adding, 'I had no choice... the rat has a name.'

CHAPTER 33

Matt longed for his bed. It was now late in the evening and he just wanted to forget about the day's events, but the mahout's insatiable appetite for debate, and (bizarrely Matt thought) baked beans, meant this wasn't going to happen any time soon.

'I'm sorry,' said Matt as he entered the living room and poured the steaming beans over the toast on Gajadhar's plate, 'what was it you said?'

'Ah, delicious,' complemented the mahout. 'I was just saying that I am not surprised. It must have been extremely traumatic, and especially for her.'

Matt looked at him wearily and sat down on an upturned box.

'So why do you say her in particular?' sighed Matt.

'Simply because of her vocation – as a veterinary doctor she is obliged to help alleviate suffering.'

'Yes. Well, she did; she saved the rat didn't she.'

'Well yes,' replied Gajadhar, pausing to shovel in a mouthful of beans (Matt noted with surprise that someone so preoccupied with etiquette could have such poor table manners).

'But,' continued the mahout, 'it was at the expense of killing another which was guilty of nothing but doing what comes naturally, a very difficult dilemma for someone who cares for animals. I must admit to greatly looking forward to meeting her, she sounds like an exceptional young woman.'

'She is.' replied Matt, immediately aware that he had agreed too readily.

'And you say that she is romantically involved with Mr King?' Gajadhar's eyes twinkled.

'Yes well, not any more. I think she's finished with him, after what she saw I guess.' Matt was feeling self-conscious and keen to change the subject. 'So, what happened to you after you left Andy?'

'I went to spend some time with the elephants.'

'You did what! Are you crazy?' exclaimed Matt.

'Do not be concerned, I saw Mr King and his two companions in the walled garden so I knew that it was safe. Of course,' he added with a hint of remorse, 'had I known what they were going to do I should have returned to the reptile house, maybe I could have helped calm things down in some way.' He forced another huge forkful of food into his mouth then continued. 'But I must admit, having now found out what he is capable of, I do think of myself as somewhat fortunate that I was not discovered, but still, the urge to go was, considering what I had discovered, a necessary risk.'

'What you discovered? Replied Matt incredulously, 'You don't mean the stuff that Andy told you? Surely you realise that half of what he says is from his own paranoid imagination.'

'Ah yes,' said the mahout, nodding, 'certainly he is a very foolish young man, and as you say, suffers more than most from the usual paranoia that often afflicts us, but sometimes paranoia can be an attribute, it makes one more astute to the little things that may otherwise be ignored. Take, for instance, Andy's observations on all the unusual events connected to the death of Devi.'

'Which unusual events?' asked Matt, wary of where this was going?

Gajadhar crammed in more beans, and then carried on between chews. 'You see, my case in point. You are far more intelligent than our young friend, and yet the common sense that feeds your intellect also restrains your mind to the significance of the little details that create the whole picture.'

Matt frowned, trying to work out if he had just received a compliment or insult.

'Let me put these little events in order and context for you,' continued Gajadhar with patience. 'You did, I am told, experience a shared dream in which you were pursued by an elephant.'

'Yes...but under the circumstances there's nothing unusual in that, we had just witnessed the elepha—'

'Please, if you would allow me to finish, it will help with the clarity if you do not interrupt again,' said the mahout, smiling benignly. 'So, all the animals begin to act very oddly, including the deer, usually the most passive and gentle of creatures. They attacked your party and wounded your colleague. But this is not an isolated incident; Andy tells me that every animal in the park has been behaving in an untypical manner and that each morning the enclosures have been ransacked by animals that have previously never been destructive. All of these points may individually be of little consequence, but put together, and including the fact that all this unrest only started after the death of Devi, it is impossible to conclude anything other than that the source of these occurrences lies beyond the door to the elephant house.'

Gajadhar put the last forkful of beans and toast into his mouth and pushed the empty plate into the middle of the box. Sitting back and grinning triumphantly he waited for Matt's opinion.

'So that's why you risked your neck to go to the elephant house, to catch a bunch of elephants in a conspirators' huddle?'

Gajadhar looked at him pityingly. 'You misunderstand. The other night you said you had noticed a difference in Uddanda since the death of Devi, you thought that you could see a subtle change in him. Do you remember on our journey here, I told you what Uddanda's name meant?'

Matt shrugged, picked up his tobacco and began rolling a cigarette. 'If I remember correctly, you said that it means Nemesis of evil and vices… but what has that got to do with Roger's accident? There was nothing evil about him.'

'Perhaps it is captivity itself that Uddanda is exacting his wrath against. We believe that elephants can curse those who bring them misery, but there is no reason why this could not extend to an environment. To me it makes perfect sense, if one wanted to destroy a Kingdom then the most effective way is to turn its subjects against the King. If you relate that to a zoo, then eliciting the help of all the beasts is the logical equivalent.'

'You think that Uddanda is inciting some kind of animal insurrection, that's crazy!'

'Do you think so? I find the concept quite believable, considering the delicate state of mind that captivity evokes in animals and humans alike. It damages the soul and makes them more susceptible to external forces, such as the will of Ganesha.'

Matt's tolerance was wearing thin. He scooped up Gajadhar's empty plate and took it to the kitchen, lit his roll-up from the stove and, after a long drag, returned to the mahout.

'Look, isn't it possible that the animals are merely reacting to the weather? There's been a storm threatening for the last few days now, the air is thick with electrical charges. Can you honestly say that your theory is more plausible than simply the weather being the reason for the unrest? Christ, it's certainly unsettling me'

'I admit that there is the possibility that the weather is a factor,' said the mahout, grinning, 'but I maintain that mine is the more romantic solution.'

Matt, giving in to a wide yawn, smiled apologetically at the mahout. 'I'm sorry, today has really taken it out of me – put me out of sorts. I'm sure after a good night's sleep…' He looked longingly at the couch.

'No, it is I who should apologise,' cried Gajadhar, his voice bursting with remorse.' I should have realised – I have been a most ungracious guest and you have been so kind. You must allow me to help with the chores.' The mahout began fluffing up the cushions on the sofa 'And tomorrow *I* will cook, our favourite – beans on toast.'

CHAPTER 34

Friday 3rd

The next morning Matt and Gajadhar strolled into the zoo kitchen to find Al dissecting a mound of fruit. It was meant to be finely chopped, but in the giant hands of Al was more mashed than diced. He was currently working on a banana that was obstinately avoiding its dissection by sliding around in the juice that covered the chopping board.

'Thank fuck you're here,' he said. 'I thought I was going to be the only one left at this rate. Ouch, fuck! Not again.' Tearing off a piece of tissue he stuck it to the nick on his finger.

Matt noticed six or seven pieces of tissue stuck in a similar fashion all over the fingers on Al's left hand. 'That fruit's for the bird section, isn't it?' he said. 'What are you doing that for?'

Al gestured towards the blackboard. 'Message from our esteemed fucking leader.'

Matt and Gajadhar read the note.

Dear all, I'm afraid that Tommy had another fit yesterday evening. It's not too serious but Susie felt he would be better off recuperating with his grandparents in Hertfordshire.

Fortuitously, it appears that I have to go to a family funeral in Norfolk so I can drop him off en route.

Sorry to abandon you at such short notice but I know the park will be safe in your capable hands.

Any problems then King's in charge.
Julian

'Useless twat,' said Al, 'must've caught wind of yesterday's antics and couldn't hack the tension and… Ouch! That's the tenth fucking time.'

'Please, allow me to help,' insisted Gajadhar, taking the knife from Al, 'You are bleeding all over the poor animals' breakfast.'

'Yeah, thanks – anyway, he's decided to leg it before he gets involved, and left us in the shite in the process.'

'Has King seen the note?'

'I guess – he was coming out of the kitchen as I arrived, looking like the cat that got the fucking cream, cheeky fucker even asked me how my knee was, so I asked him how Susie was. That soon wiped the smile off his face.'

'How about Andy, have you seen him yet?'

'No, not since we left him with Susie. The wee shite better not use yesterday as an excuse not to come in, you and I got enough to do as it is.'

'Well, Gajadhar can help us; we decided this morning that, in the current er… climate, it's probably best if he avoids the elephants and stays with us.'

'That'd certainly help,' agreed Al, enviably watching the blur of the mahout's hands as he sliced his way through the fruit, 'Shite, how d'you do that so fucking quick?'

'It is a question of focus,' replied Gajadhar simply.

'Right…focus.' He turned back to Matt. 'Anyway, you prepare the primate feed while I get the meat ready.

197

If Andy hasn't turned up by then we'll go get him on our way round.'

Halfway along the bird section they abandoned their trolleys and buckets and took the right-hand fork that led down to the sea lions and staff flats. The two sea lions, along with Jez, (in the tightest pair of denim shorts that Matt had ever seen), were flat out on the decking.

'Hey Jez, you seen Andy?' boomed Al, startling the sea lions who leapt up, knocking Jez out of his hammock in their ungainly haste to get to the safety of the water. Once in, their heads bobbed up inquisitively from the middle of the pool.

'Shit, Al, give a guy some warning before shouting at him like that!'

He picked himself up and readjusted his sunglasses. 'What d'ya want anyway?'

'Andy. Have you seen him?'

'No, I haven't seen anyone.' He climbed back into the hammock., 'Come to think of it, I didn't hear him last night either. Why? What'ya want him for?'

'To do his fucking section, that's what. Can we cut through your place?'

'Sure, bring us an ice lolly from the freezer on your way back, and one for yourselves if you want.'

The three of them walked into the sea lion enclosure and through the French doors that opened directly into Jez's flat.

'Fucking slob,' moaned Al, stepping around the clothes, cushions and piles of porn magazines, (one of which he picked up and stuffed into his back pocket), that were scattered around the floor.

At the top of the stairs they reached a door with a sign that read, *'Guard rat on patrol, enter at your own risk.'*

Al tried the handle, but it was locked. 'Andy, get your arse out here.'

There was no reply so Al repeated his command, banging loudly with his fist. 'Andy, you lazy-arsed southern fucking twat, get out here now!'

Still there was no response.

'I do not believe anyone is in,' suggested Gajadhar.

'Yeah, otherwise who could resist opening the door to Al's persuasive charms,' added Matt. He crouched down and peered through the keyhole. 'Andy, its Matt, you okay?'

'Think I should break the door down?' asked Al hopefully.

'I don't think it'll do any good,' said Matt. 'He obviously isn't there.'

They trudged back down the stairs and back into Jez's flat, where Al rummaged through the freezer, then back out through the French doors and into the sea lion enclosure.

'Here you go,' said Al, tossing an ice lolly onto Jez's bare torso.

Jez screamed and tumbled off the hammock again. 'Al, you wanker, that's cold!'

'Yeah well, seeing as you're up now, how about giving us a hand with the animals.' Al gripped his lolly wrapper between his teeth and ripped off the top, spitting the paper into the pool. 'Seems we've got to do Andy's section along with Tommy's and Roger's now. Fuck, it's going to take forever, and I promised Beth I'd spend some time with her today.' He handed out the remaining lollies to Matt and Gajadhar.

'Bloody hell, Al!' Jez leaned into the water and fished out the piece of wrapper, 'don't spit that into the pool, it's bad for the girls. Anyway, you know I can't help, I've got shitloads to do for the party tonight.' He turned to Matt and Gajadhar. 'You two coming?'

Matt felt surprised. After the events of the last couple of days even the idea of a party felt incongruous to him. 'I assumed it was cancelled, what with Roger and everything else that's happened.'

'Even more reason if you ask me,' replied Jez. 'Cheer us all up – so What'ya reckon – you up for it?'

Al didn't give them a chance to reply. 'What the fuck you talking about *shitloads to do*? You're just lying around on your fucking arse is all.'

'Lying around on my...!' cried Jez. 'It's like I've always said, you lot have got no appreciation of what goes into my parties. Firstly, I've got to catch up on my sleep – how would it be if the host had to kick everyone out by eleven 'cause he was too tired? Then I've got all the tidying to do, sort out all the music, the ambience doesn't just create itself you know.' He clambered back into the hammock. 'And anyway, I'm not just lying around, I'm trying to decide if the weather's going to break, it's been rumbling away all morning and I don't want to set everything up outside and then have to move it all inside if a storm comes.'

Al looked up at the sky, shielding his eyes against the glare, despite the sea of pale blue and wisps of white there was something heavy and foreboding in the air.

'Okay, okay,' conceded Al, 'you'll probably be more of a fucking hindrance than help anyway. Just tell Andy if you see him that he better get his fucking self over to us as soon as possible.'

'Uh huh, will do,' said Jez wriggling himself back into the canvas cocoon.

'Come on then, lads, we'd better get cracking. I'm not working past five-fucking-thirty tonight.' As Al passed, he reached out to the rope that dangled provocatively from one of the hammock supports. With a wink to the mahout and Matt he gave it a yank, sending Jez tumbling to the ground.

'What the fuck! Al, you tosser!'

'And remember your promise.' Al bent down conspiratorially to Gajadhar's ear. 'He said I could be the DJ.'

'I reckon Jez may be right about the weather,' declared Matt filling up a dish with water and pouring it over his head. With a moan of satisfaction, he rubbed the water over his face, wiping his eyes clear with a paper towel, 'you know – about the storm finally breaking?'

'I think I'd eat my left bollock for a storm right now. I can't take this fucking heat much longer, especially now we're doing the whole zoo.' Al peered at the clock that hung crookedly on the zoo kitchen wall, 'Shite, six thirty, I'm on fucking overtime. If I don't get extra pay for this I'll tell them where to stick their Job.' Al, sweat-stained and angry, barged Matt away from the sink and submerged his head under the tap.

'Personally, I have had a fascinating time,' said Gajadhar with the same joyful enthusiasm that he had maintained for the entire day and which, Matt suspected, had played a part in Al's increasingly ill humour. 'I am only sorry that we did not have the time to properly meet your beautiful leopard.'

Matt knew that this was not true. He felt that he understood Gajadhar well enough now to be able to read and understand his mannerisms, and his reaction to Beth had been both cautious and guarded.

'She is a beauty, isn't she?' said Al perking up.

'Without doubt the prettiest that I have ever seen,' agreed Gajadhar, 'and you have done an exceptional job in rearing her.'

'Thanks.' Al blushed, the extra rouge adding to the sunburn and turning his face scarlet. 'I've got photos in my flat of when she was a bairn, if you want to come and look–'

A sound like a tower block being demolished stopped him mid-sentence, sending vibrations that shook the metallic tables in the Zoo kitchen and rattled the windows.

'Jesus fucking H Christ, what the fuck!'

Matt grinned. 'Looks like your testicles are on the menu.'

'Yeah, and I guess Jez's party's going to be inside. Come on, best get out of here before the rain starts – looks like we're in for a real fucking monsoon.'

CHAPTER 35

'Just think how sweet the air will taste in the morning,' shouted Gajadhar into Matt's ear.

Matt could barely hear the mahout above the din of the rain hammering down on the cars that had squeezed into the small, cobbled quadrant that served as the keeper's carpark.

'It is always my favourite time,' persevered Gajadhar, 'waking up after such a storm as this, everything is so fresh and clear, it is almost as though the world has been reborn.'

'Yeah – I guess,' Matt yelled back, then groaned with frustration as they came to another dead end. 'Christ! Where did all these cars come from? It's like a bloody maze.'

He could see the fuzzy forms of people silhouetted against Jez's window, barely twenty yards away, but every attempt to reach the flat had been blocked by a vehicle. Single file would have made it simpler, but giving up the protection of the Gajadhar's umbrella would be tantamount to stepping through a waterfall. The task was further complicated by the darkness that had suddenly descended, almost from the moment that they had heard the first clap of thunder in the zoo kitchens almost three hours earlier.

Another flash of fork lightning only increased Matt's sense of desperation, surrounded by metal vehicles and standing in what had now become a shallow lake.

'Christ, we're like sitting ducks out here,' Matt hollered, trying to remember whether his shoes were rubber-soled.

A tremendous crash and instantaneous flash momentarily illuminated Gajadhar's unconcerned, placid face.

'Let's try this way,' Matt beckoned and they squeezed through more cars.

'Christ, it's no good,' Matt shouted in despair. 'This way's too bloody narrow as well! How the hell did everyone else manage it?'

His answer came noisily in the form of a group of teenagers that bounded merrily and recklessly over the roofs and bonnets and into the safety of Jez's porch.

'I do not think that I could be so disrespectful towards another's property,' shouted the mahout.

'It's not about respect, it's about survival,' Matt called back, climbing onto a bonnet and offering his hand to Gajadhar. 'We can't spend the evening standing here like a couple of lightening conductors.'

A few precarious moments later and they stood under the porch, rapping hard on the door like shipwrecked sailors coming across the sanctuary of an inn.

They were greeted by Jez, still in the tight shorts and sunglasses. 'Hi ya dudes, glad you could make it, humdinger of a storm huh?'

'Yeah' agreed Matt, attempting to step inside past Jez. 'So can we come in or what?'

'Sure – but if you don't mind just...' Jez produced a large tin with the words *Drinks Kitty* scrawled on the side and shook it at them, '...most people like to make a small donation, you know, towards the booze, best to do it now in case you forget later.'

'Oh…Okay,' Matt pulled a soggy, crumpled ten-pound note from his pocket, 'can you change this?'

'No need,' replied Jez, snatching the note and stuffing it into the tin, 'that should cover you both nicely.'

'But…hang on, that was a tenner, and Gajadhar doesn't even drink… do you?'

The mahout shook his head. 'It is true that I am fortunate enough to receive stimulation from a more spiritual source.'

'No problem,' said Jez with a wink, 'got shitloads of dope as well… Hey Tessa, Louise, you made it! Great.'

Matt moved aside, making way for the two girls who squeezed past them whilst Gajadhar shook out his umbrella and carefully folded it.

Inside, the flat was unrecognisable compared to Matt's earlier visit. Thick smoke swirled around the various coloured light bulbs, agitated by the vibrant movements of the dancers, most of whom were naked from the waist up.

Gajadhar joined Matt at his side, his bright eyes opening wide in shock.

'It is traditional for English parties to contain such er, nakedness?'

Matt shook his head slowly. 'It's a first for me.'

'I suppose it is sensible, their clothes must be drenched,' suggested Gajadhar charitably.

Matt shrugged and scanned the room in search of a familiar face.

'There's Al, come on.'

They plunged into the crowd, trying to force a path through the sea of bare torsos.

'I think that we should try a different approach,' said Gajadhar after a few minutes of battling against the tide of people.

Matt looked down into the blushing face of the mahout. His eye level was directly in line with the multitude of breasts that flattened and squished against his cheeks as he tried to pass, murmuring long, muffled apologies.

'Perhaps you're right,' yelled Matt, 'let's try this way.'

Reversing out and skirting around the perimeter of the room they finally reached Al, who was standing territorially over the music centre, an enormous joint gripped between his lips.

'Nice tits, huh?' grinned Al, removing the joint and offering it to Matt.

Matt declined, noticing the end dripping with Al's drool. 'I didn't expect it to be so busy. Who are they all?'

'Fuck knows. Jez hand-picks them throughout the summer. Only the gorgeous and the goers get an invite, and some blokes as well, for the sake of balance, don't want to be too greedy.'

'And are these things always a striptease?' The last half of his sentence rang out across the room just as the record ended abruptly. Matt looked self-consciously around but no one noticed and with relief he adjusted his voice to a more suitable volume: he'd been shouting since he and Gajadhar had left his flat.

'Shite no,' Al bent over the record collection and rummaged through it, 'least not this early on. I reckon it's the storm, made everyone a bit frisky... ah, fucking perfect.' Pulling out a Bob Marley album he tipped the record from its sleeve, and placed it lovingly on the turntable. 'A bit of kinky reggae should do it.' He released the needle that bounced noisily before finding the groove and the music blared out.

Matt resumed shouting. 'So how come you're not playing *Silver Machine* over and over?' He grinned.

'Shite, Matt, I'll tell you, it's tearing me apart playing this crap, but as self-proclaimed DJ extraordinaire I have to show a wee bit of consideration for other tastes,' He leaned closer to Matt and after a deep drag on the spliff added, '...and this reggae shite makes the lasses' tits bounce better.' He gave Gajadhar a knowing nudge. The mahout, purposefully fixing his gaze on a spot on the floor, smiled politely.

'So, who else is here?' asked Matt in what he hoped was a casual manner.

Al seemed to read the true meaning and take sadistic pleasure in not answering it. 'Well, I'll tell you who's not fucking here, Andy, that's who. Not too surprising though, after dropping us in it today.'

'Yeah... right, so who *is* here?' urged Matt.

'Well, King's skulking in the corner over there, had some busty brunette on his lap last I saw, probably figures to make Susie jealous.'

'Susie? Oh, I didn't know she was coming.'

Al grinned. 'She's in the kitchen, but you can get any crazy ideas about hitting on her out of your mind, at least while King's about, my fucking knee's only just settled back down.'

'What do you mean? No one's hitting on anyone,' protested Matt, 'It's just I know that Gajadhar would like to meet her. Christ Al, we're not all sex obsessed!'

'Hey – where the fuck are you going?' called Al.

'To the kitchen, I need a drink!'

'Is that her?' asked the mahout, quickly catching up with Matt and looking in from the kitchen door. Matt shot a glance in the direction that Gajadhar was looking.

Susie stood in profile, talking to, or rather, Matt decided with relief after noticing her body language, being talked at, by a serious-looking man with a ponytail and goatee.

She must have got caught in the rain and her blouse and skirt clung to her body. Matt sighed inwardly; she looked stunning. He was surprised at how the sight of her affected him, caused his heart rate to increase, his palms to sweat; he needed to calm down; he needed to get a drink.

Whilst he was tacking his way through the guests and towards the tall pyramid of beer cans Susie looked around and saw him. Her face brightened as she beckoned Matt to come over. With the mahout loyally at his side he had no choice other than to obey.

'Are you feeling unwell?' asked Gajadhar, 'you are looking rather flushed.'

'Shh, she'll hear,' replied Matt through the corner of his clenched mouth. 'I'm fine.'

As they approached, the man with the goatee gave an irritated shrug and turned leerily to another girl to his left.

'Hi Susie, glad to see you've kept your top on – I mean... not that you wouldn't look lovely with it off, it's just…' Matt swallowed, his Adam's apple; it felt like a dry lump of mud, 'It's just that you're… wet.'

'Thanks…I think,' said Susie. She turned to the mahout. 'And you must be Gajadhar.'

Gajadhar beamed widely. 'And you are Susie, I have heard much about you.'

'Nice things I hope?'

'Naturally, one hears only nice things about a lotus blossom.'

Matt double took, looking at the mahout with astonished envy as Susie laughed.

'I'm getting a drink; would you like one?' suggested Matt, in an attempt to break the mahout's spell.

Susie glanced briefly over to him. 'No thanks, I've got one.'

'If you do not mind, I would like an orange juice.' said Gajadhar before continuing to Susie. '…So, Matt informs me that you would like to specialise in elephant veterinary medicine, have you ever thought about…'

Matt turned and trudged to the other side of the kitchen. After flicking open a can, he drank greedily, suddenly intent on getting his tenner's worth. Halfway through his second can, he was beginning to feel some confidence return. Over the heads he could see Susie nodding and smiling and he yearned to be a part of the conversation. He poured out Gajadhar's orange juice and began to make his way back. Al was sticking with his reggae theme; Matt knew the singer, Jimmy Cliff, but was struggling to remember the title. *'I'd rather be a free man in my grave…Than living like a puppet or a slave',* when a chorus of voices belted out the answer, *'The harder they come… the harder they fall… one and all,* followed by loud cheer. Inquisitive, Matt peered into the living room.

Heads and shoulders continually bobbed up and down in front of him, but on tiptoe Matt was able to make out King, standing within a chanting circle consisting mainly of the dancers. Draped over him was the girl that Al had mentioned. The crowd was roaring encouragement as King worked the small crowd with a circus master's verve.

'Come on, you lot wanna see it? You wanna see what it takes to be an elephant keeper, then you gotta do better than that, come on ten, nine, eight, let me hear you, seven, six…'

On the count of one there was a hesitation, followed by a gasp and then a cheer of delight as two pairs of jeans were hurled into the air.

Matt's view was blocked as the crowd jostled for better positioning, then a gap appeared and he had a brief, un-obscured view of Colin and Gary's naked groins, shaved bald and with elephant ears tattooed on either side, their penises hanging wrinkled and trunk-like in between.

'Christ,' Matt muttered, 'they're insane.'

CHAPTER 36

'What was all that about?' asked Susie as Matt returned, passing Gajadhar his drink.

'Don't ask, just some macho stuff I guess, Colin and Gary showing off some new tattoos.'

'Oh God, not the elephant ears! I heard them discussing it last week but I thought that they were joking.'

'Afraid not, they just showed them in all their dangly glory, egged on by King and his busty queen ... oh sorry, I forgot, I mean...'

'Don't worry, he's already flaunted her past me three times, it's really not a problem. I can't believe I got involved with him in the first place–'

'So, how's Andy?' asked Matt, quick to avoid an awkward silence. 'You know he didn't turn up for work today.'

'Didn't he?' Susie's eyes widened, briefly she scanned the immediate area as though looking for confirmation of his absence, 'I didn't know. He was still quite a mess when I left him but he insisted that he wanted to be on his own with Lucky, and then, with Tommy, you know, having another fit, I just didn't get a chance to check up on him.'

'Is he okay?... Tommy.'

'Oh yeah, he'll be fine. Julian offered to take him to Granny and Granddad's. He had to go to a conference anyway and said that he could drop him off on the way – really kind of him.'

'Not necessarily that kind – the note he left for us said that he had to go to a funeral. I guess he couldn't wait to get away from here, at least, that's what Al reckons.'

'Maybe Al's right, I can't blame him though. I'm just relieved to have got Tommy away. It's the worst possible place for him with all that's been going on lately. We were talking about it just now while you were getting the drinks, Gajadhar's got some very interesting theories about all that's been happening here, did you know that Uddanda means...'

'Yeah, I know, Nemesis of evil and vices,' said Matt, 'we've already discussed the more *spiritual* causes.' Susie flashed a shocked look in his direction.

'Sorry,' added Matt quickly, 'I didn't mean to sound rude, it's only I've been over this already...at length.' He smiled.

'Matt is a little cynical about my beliefs,' said Gajadhar.

'Pragmatic is a better word,' said Matt, 'surely you're a realist – you can't really believe this stuff?'

Susie looked from Matt to Gajadhar. 'I'm a scientist, which means I don't like to dismiss anything without considering all points of view.' She said with a hint of piety.

'Very wise,' agreed Gajadhar. 'What was it that the wonderful Sherlock Holmes says, 'when you have eliminated the impossible, whatever remains, however improbable, must be the truth.'

'But Sherlock Holmes is fiction,' said Matt. We're talking about fact, and the fact is that there's not some elephant god going around the zoo controlling the minds of other animals.'

'But you forget,' said Gajadhar, 'that within all fiction exists an element of fact.'

'That's just crap!'

'Matt!' cried Susie, frowning.

'Huh...what? No, it's all right, Gajadhar enjoys an argument, don't you.'

'A debate,' corrected the mahout. 'Most certainly, there is nothing more terrible than to allow one's mind to become corrupted by complacency and stagnate through lack of use, however, there is a thin line between discussion and abuse.'

'Okay, sorry, but that's the point, you have to have some common ground and if we can't even agree on the difference between fact and fiction...' Matt paused to collect his thoughts, draining the rest of his beer, 'Okay, Winnie the Pooh, are you telling me that there is an element of fact to Winnie the Pooh.'

'To many thousands of children, yes. You see, it all depends on your perspective, what is true to a child may not be so to an adult, but that does not make it any less right.'

'What...but...Susie, help me out here.'

Susie had been listening intently and her brow was creased with thought as she considered all the alternatives.

'Well... I guess it comes down to an elephant's potential for controlling in some way, the actions of other species through communication.' She paused to take a long drink, the furrows in her brow deepening. 'Telepathy is one consideration – there has been very little research in that field and it would help to explain certain behaviours.'

Matt shook his head vehemently.

'You mean It would *conveniently* explain a behaviour. You know as well as I do that telepathy is an idea reserved for spiritualists and nuts.'

'Personally, I have always found telepathy in elephants quite feasible,' said Gajadhar.

'You see what I mean,' replied Matt. 'Seriously Susie, I thought that you'd be on my side instead of feeding him more mumbo jumbo.'

'It's not about sides,' said Susie, even more piously.

'And it is not mumbo jumbo simply because it lies outside of your experience,' insisted Gajadhar.

'And it's not plausible simply because it is an explanation.' Matt's head spun from Gajadhar to Susie, 'Why can't you accept the possibility that a combination of the heatwave and coincidence is the most rational cause instead of always looking for mystical reasons?'

'We have heat waves and storms in India, but I have never seen animal behaviour such as this.'

Matt flung his hands in the air. 'That's it – I give up!'

'Even so, that does sort of tie in with another theory that I have.' Susie took another sip of her drink before continuing. 'Well, more of an observation actually, it's kind of hard to explain but…you know when elephants communicate, with the low rumbling from their trunk, you can actually see it vibrating as they produce the noise, it gives you a strange sensation in your stomach, a bit like when a tractor or lorry drives past too close, do you know what I mean?'

Gajadhar nodded enthusiastically.

'Well, sometimes I get that same sensation even when I can't hear anything at all, but – and this is what first made me wonder – I can still see the trunk vibrate, and that started me thinking, what if elephants can communicate at an infrasonic level, below human frequency, it would explain how they can locate each other over vast distances.' She looked down at her drink and knocked back the last mouthful. 'Anyway, it just seems likely that if an elephant was in some kind of discomfort or suffering or...I don't know, even in a dreaming state, they might communicate their pain like that, undetectable to us but not to the other animals.' She looked expectantly over to Matt.

'So,' Matt replied, you're saying that Uddanda is transmitting his nightmares around the zoo?'

'No, not that exactly. I doubt other species could interpret images of what Dan's actually thinking or saying but maybe they could detect the torment... or perhaps it would be like a kind of white noise. I don't know much about it but didn't they use sound during the war for interrogation, you know, sensory deprivation, that kind of stuff, to drive people mad?'

'So how come Kali and Joti aren't affected?' said Matt.

'I don't know, maybe they are, or maybe because to them it makes sense, it's not just random sound, maybe they even join in and it's like Gajadhar says, that there're contriving some kind of revenge. As I said, it's only a theory.'

'And an extremely interesting one,' said Gajadhar.

Susie's face flushed.

'Hmm, it's better than telepathy, but I still think the weather has got something to do with it.' Matt, tipped back the can forgetting that it was empty. 'I'm out, anyone else want anything while I'm up there?'

'Please allow me,' offered Gajadhar, 'you got the last ones.' He collected his orders and sidled, squeezed and apologised his way towards the drinks.

'He's nice – easy to talk to,' said Susie once Gajadhar was out of earshot. 'It must be quite difficult for him, with the way that things are, you know, arriving in the middle of all this…stuff.'

'Yeah, I guess this isn't quite what he expected, but it's pretty weird for all of us too.'

Susie smiled. 'I forget, you've only been here a little while as well, somehow it seems longer, like you're part of us…' She paused and looked away.

'Thanks,' said Matt, 'it feels like it to me as well.'

They fell into an awkward silence that was broken by the coarse Celtic cry of Al coming from the other room.

'That's enough shite, time for some proper fucking music!' Followed by the swirling intro of Silver Machine.

They peered around the door in time to see Al bound across the floor, scattering the bewildered dancers like bowling pins as the giant convulsed and head-banged to the music.

'Looks like the DJ's finally cracked,' said Matt, relieved by the timely interruption, 'bizarre choice to put him in charge of the music.'

Susie winced. 'Same every year; Al wouldn't have it any other way. I think he thinks the role gives him rock star sex appeal, although I've never seen him get a girlfriend as a result. Still, it gives him a chance to ogle the girls and frees up Jez to work on his choice of conquest for his end of party dip.'

Matt looked puzzled.

'Another fine tradition. Jez always takes his *chosen one* to the pool when the party's over, his end of the season shag, as he calls it.'

Matt rolled his eyes, mirroring Susie's expression of disdain in the hope of concealing his own slight arousal at the idea. 'Think I'll see what's taking Gajadhar so long with those drinks.'

He spotted the mahout standing beside a couple of the topless girls who appeared to be cooing over him as though he were some kind of captive pet. Gajadhar, catching Matt's eye, waved helplessly. Grinning, Matt waved back and returned to Susie, via the bar, with their drinks.

'Thank you,' said Susie as Matt passed her the glass of wine. 'Where's Gajadhar?'

'He's, err – making some new friends. I doubt that we'll see him for a while.'

Susie frowned. 'Oh, that's a shame, I was hoping to talk to him about job opportunities in India.'

'Job opportunities?' Matt said, shocked, 'I thought you liked being a vet.'

'I do, that's what I mean, vet work, I'm just…it's just this place has become a bit… claustrophobic. I'd like to branch out more I guess, see more before I settle down.'

'So, what would it be, your dream job?' asked Matt, taking his tobacco pouch from his pocket.

'How do you mean dream job? Dream realistic or dream fantasy?'

'Dream fantasy, otherwise what's the point.'

'Like I said before, elephants, definitely, ideally a refuge, or an orphanage, or both…' She took a long sip on her wine, 'Can you make me one of those?'

'Sure.' The alcohol and churning dope-filled atmosphere was inducing a flirty confidence in Matt who dexterously rolled two cigarettes, lit one, and puffed out a smoke ring before passing it to her.

Susie laughed. 'Corny, but thanks.'

'No problem, so tell me more about your elephant rescue centre.'

He listened, animated by Susie's exuberance, and felt all his earlier inhibitions dissolve as they chatted, and accepting, almost embracing the natural pleasure that they were experiencing from each other's company.

The occasional intrusion from Al, passing at regular intervals to replenish his drink and drug supply and complaining bitterly that even the fucking mahout was getting more fucking girly attention than him, was the only mild and irrelevant reminder of the passing time.

'I am sorry to interrupt,' said Gajadhar, 'but if you do not object then I think that I will be leaving now.'

'What, already, but it's only...' Matt looked at his watch, 'Christ, it's half past one, how the hell did that happen?'

'Exactly, I would not have interrupted but I was not sure whether you would like me to leave you my umbrella. Unlike myself the storm does not seem to be tiring.'

'Er...no thanks, I'll be fine.' A sudden thought crossed Matt's mind and he peered cautiously around the door to where King had been lounging. Relieved, he saw that he had left. 'Will you be okay?'

'Absolutely,' replied the mahout with a twinkle in his eye. 'Do not give me another thought and enjoy the rest of the party.' He bowed to Susie and left with an enthusiasm contrary to his alleged tiredness.

'I should go with him, I'm not sure where King is.'

'I'm sure he'll be alright.' She ran her hand down Matt's arm. 'King never stays late to these things – come on.'

Back in the main room the mood had changed. Tightly clenched couples swayed with intimate insularity.

'Oh…the Faces… *Love Lived Here*, do you know it?' asked Susie.

Matt shook his head.

'You'll love it.' She smiled up at him. 'It's one of my favourites.'

Susie closed her eyes, gently rocking to the music, leaving Matt to consider the implication that he would love what she loved. Up until that moment, that comment, he hadn't been sure. His heart had leapt at the signs, the little touches on his arm, the way she fixed her gaze deeply onto him as he spoke. Self-consciously he looked around – sensing King's eye's watching from some dimly lit corner of the room – but there was no one.

'Let's dance.'

Susie's voice cut into his thoughts. He looked down into her eyes, green and imploring, and took her hands, gently drawing her towards him, his chest thumping with the thrill of what was happening, of what might happen.

Slowly they turned on the spot, holding each other tighter with each rotation. After the song ended there was a moment's awkwardness – should they separate or remain in clenched anticipation of another slow song? Not Hawkwind, thought Matt, please Al, don't screw this up with Hawkwind.

The plaintive strings of The Moody Blues *Nights in white Satin* poured from the speakers, spiralling around them, and Susie sighed contentedly, burying her face into Matt's shoulder.

A new sensation, warm, soft, wet, lightly brushing his throat – her lips, tenderly working their way up to his until, with a slight hesitation, they kissed.

Songs ended, new ones began, people got up, collected their belongings, and still they embraced, intent that nothing else should matter but that moment, and if nothing disturbed them, then that moment need never end.

CHAPTER 37

'Come on girls, kicking out time.'

With great effort Matt and Susie separated and turned grudgingly to their assailant. Paul Simon was singing *Still Crazy After All These Years* on the turntable.

'Sorry you two,' said Jez, 'but me and Rebecca–'

'Rachael!' said the girl at Jez's side. 'It's Rachael.'

'Yeah, Rachael. We need the place to ourselves.'

Matt and Susie looked around. Except for Al slumped in an ungainly heap on a beanbag, the room was empty.

'And you'd be doing me a favour if you could take him with you,' added Jez.

'I'll try,' said Matt giving Al a nudge with his foot.

'Fuck off,' Al murmured, trying to focus his bloodshot, drug-soaked gaze on the four people who stood over him. 'Ah shite, is it over? I didn't even get a fucking shag!'

'You never get a shag,' said Jez. 'Now get up you great lump of doped- up haggis, me and Rebec... Rachael have stuff to do.'

'Okay, no need to twist the fucking knife.' He dragged himself upright against the wall and then staggered forward.

'Steady on there,' said Matt as he and Susie stabilised him on either side.

'Thanks Matt...Hey, Susie, lovely Susie... *If you knew Susie like I know Susie, oh oh oh what a gal*...hey

221

Susie, you'll fuck me won't you, you won't let big Al go home un-fucking-fucked will you?'

'Course not,' soothed Susie, 'we'll have a lovely shag just as soon as you're tucked up in bed.'

'Aw, you're just saying that, you're just like all the other lasses, leading big Al on, I can nay trust none of you. Beth, she's the only gal I can trust. You know why?' Because we're friends, that's why. We trust each other, none of this sex shite to fuck things up, just a man and his leopard, hey…where we going?'

'Taking you home,' said Susie.

'Fuck no! I'm gonna see Beth, hardly seen her at all these last few days, I wanna see Beth.' He swung around, snatched up his leather jacket from the floor and headed towards the French doors dragging Matt and Susie with him.

'I don't think that's a good idea, you're pretty out of it.' Matt tried to turn him back but he was immovable in his determination.

'Don't worry,' said Susie. 'It's not the first time he's gone in this condition. Once we found him the next morning asleep in her enclosure, kind of sweet really.' She ducked out from under Al's arm. 'Time to stand on your own two feet, we're not carrying you all the way to Beth. She turned to the sea lion keeper. 'Thanks Jez,' she added as she reclaimed her place at Matt's side, 'it was a great party, best ever.'

'It's not over yet,' replied Jez with a conspiratorial wink, 'Wow! Look at that.' He opened the doors, stepped out under the plump, warm raindrops and shouted excitedly as the lightening flashed white across the sky. 'Man, that's invigorating… shit…look!' He tugged at Rachael, 'Come on babe, this feels great.'

'No, I'll get my jeans all wet.' She tried resisting his outstretched hand, squealing as he grabbed her arm and yanked her to him.

'Then let's take them off.' He grinned, running his hand down her front and undoing the button with a single well-practised flick of his fingers.

'Come on, we'd better get going,' said Susie, leading Matt past the pool and up the grass bank that acted as an amphitheatre for the sea lion show. 'You too Al, it's not a spectator sport.'

'Okay, okay, I'm coming,' grumbled Al as he slid and stumbled his way up the slippery hillock.

'Shite! Are you two a fucking item now?' he exclaimed, peering up at Matt and Susie's intertwined hands. 'Has this just happened? Are you going to shag her al fresco? Always makes me fucking horny, rain like this.'

'Goodnight Al,' said Susie.

'Why don't you take her to the Tapir paddock, you know, under the oak tree on the top of the hill, that's a perfect wee spot for a first shag, very fucking romantic.'

'Goodnight Al,' they both repeated firmly.

'Okay, okay – Al the wee fucking gooseberry – I get it. At least Beth will be pleased to see me.'

They watched as he weaved and tottered up the path, his booming chorus of *'what's new pussy cat whoa whoa whooa'* quickly becoming swallowed up by the relentless rain that hammered down around them.

Matt turned his face up to the sky and breathed in deeply. Gajadhar had been right about the freshness, what had he said? *Like the earth was reborn*, and Matt felt that he was re-born with it, the smell, the feeling, even the taste of the drops of water that ran down his face and into his mouth. It felt like a new start and yet – he still couldn't shake off a sense of foreboding – an idea that something menacing was lurking out there, somewhere.

He jerked his head back down, startled by a shard of lightening that burst across the sky, illuminating the naked forms of Jez and the girl as they launched themselves into the pool. His eyes followed the splash of water as it leapt into the air, then something else drew his attention, a face staring from the window in the flat above. Matt wiped the water from his eyes and looked again, but the face was gone.

'Hey, I'm right here.' Susie placed a hand on the back of Matt's head, pulling his face to hers and running her cheek against his until her lips met his ear. 'So where to?' she whispered, nibbling at his lobe.

Matt sighed; his hands ran down her saturated body, exploring her contours and lingering on the small of her back. 'I don't know. Do you want to get out of the rain?'

'Not particularly, it feels good, kinda sexy.'

'Hmm…I suppose we could take a stroll along the paddock walk.'

'And if…' continued Susie… 'If we should happen upon the Tapir paddock.'

'Well, if we should find ourselves there,' added Matt, 'then there's this oak tree that I know about.'

CHAPTER 38

'That was Matt and Susie, wasn't it Lucky,' said Andy. 'Did you see them? They're our friends, they saved you.'

The rat buried her face deeper into Andy's lap.

'I'm sorry, you don't want to think about it, but we've got to remember, keep our hate alive if we're going to get our own back.' He watched as the two tightly huddling forms disappeared through the curtain of rain. 'It looks as though Matt and Susie are together now. That's nice, don't you think? They look right together, like we do, well not quite as close, not soul mates like us.'

He lifted Lucky to his face and kissed her nose and drew her closer, allowing her to nibble at his neck until another flash of light sent her scurrying down the inside of his T-shirt. 'Did that scare you baby?'

A second flash drew his attention down to the pool below and Andy swallowed at the brief sight of a naked girl floating outstretched on her back, her legs wrapped around the shoulders of Jez who had his face buried between her legs.

'They probably think that I'm jealous, but I'm not, not in the least. They've got nothing, a quick screw and it's over: no friendship, no companionship, nothing. If King hurt *her*, took *her* away from him, Jez wouldn't care one little bit, probably wouldn't do a thing about it. Because he doesn't care and because he's scared...

scared of *him*. Well I'm not, not anymore and I'll prove it. Somehow I'm going to get him, make him squirm and crawl and cry, somehow I'm going to hurt him, I'm going to watch him beg for life and I'll smile, and he'll die… somehow I'll think of a way.'

CHAPTER 39

Matt lay in a heap next to the gate in the Tapir corral rubbing his shin. On the other side of the gate Susie was laughing.

'Gracefully done – are you okay?'

Matt got up, brushing off some of the straw that clung to his wet jeans.

'Yeah fine – just wasn't expecting it to be so slippery. So come on then, let's see if you can do any better.'

'In this skirt – are you kidding?'

Matt pondered the problem for a moment then scrambled half way up the gate and leaned over. 'Okay then, give me your hand, I'll pull you up.'

Hesitantly, Susie reached up to Matt who grasped her wrist and, with a grunt, hoisted her foot into the air. Susie's legs flayed wildly for some purchase before she lost her grip and slid, giggling, back to the ground.

'I can't do it if you don't hold on,' grumbled Matt as he jumped back down.

'I can't help it,' said Susie. 'You're too slippery, and I can't get my foot high enough with this skirt. Are you sure you haven't got the keys?'

'Of course not!'

Then there's only one thing for it,' Susie put her hands behind her back, unclipped the fastener and let her skirt fall to the ground. 'Now watch this!'

Stepping back Matt took a sharp intake of breath as Susie scrambled nimbly over the gate. With a triumphant

Tah rah she dropped down on the other side, giving Matt a little curtsy. 'Bet you didn't know that you'd got involved with a Mountain goat.'

'Mounting goats?' Matt gave her a childish nudge. 'That's illegal isn't it?

Susie groaned. 'And I didn't realise I'd got involved with a comedian, and a bad one at that.'

As they approached the Tapir's den, Matt put a finger to his lips. 'Shhh – we don't want to be interrupted by a curious, probing snout do we?'

He peered into the den, listening for the snorts and rustles of the animals. Satisfied that they were inside, he cautiously un-hooked the stable doors, closed them and drew the bolt across.

'Good idea, now come on,' said Susie. Taking his hand, they splashed through the puddles on the corrals concrete and out onto the paddock. Thirty feet below them the river now churned and gargled, feeding greedily on the gushing little streams that flowed down from the paddock. Matt and Susie squelched and slid recklessly along the slope, eager to reach the tree.

The oak provided no shelter; if anything, the deluge was even more intense as the wind shook the branches that sent a surge of water cascading down, plump wet bullets that exploded on impact of their bodies.

They stood facing each other, Matt combed aside the hair that clung wet and straggly to Susie's face. Then he held her tightly, protectively – peering searchingly into the blackness. Again, the feeling that they were being watched, stalked, flooded his senses.

Then he became aware of something else – the incessant chirp of a million crickets that suddenly burst out all around them. He looked down at Susie, puzzled by the sound. But as their eyes met the world around them melted away, consumed by a raw, primitive, lust that overpowered them, quashing all inhibitions – all self-control.

The Tapirs' eyes flickered open, their muscles twitched involuntarily, primal emotions violated their brains, overloaded their senses – flight or fight was their only response. A muffled thud echoed around the den as they hurled their heads repeatedly at the bolted door.

Matt and Susie kissed with reckless longing. The mixture of rainwater and saliva flowed freely into their mouths until they felt as though they were drowning.

He ran his hand up her blouse and began gently massaging her breast.

She held his wrist, encouraging the motion until impatience and a need for more fulfilment drove her to tug imploringly at his arm, entreating his hand to move down and between her slightly parted legs.

A gasp followed by a deep intake of breath was all the encouragement he needed; he began to rub his hand against her, slowly at first and then he allowed his movements to be guided by the circular thrusts of her hips

Her kisses became more intense, her tongue thrashed against his. She could feel herself losing control, giving in to the exquisite tingling that was pulsating through her pelvis. She heard a voice, her voice 'Harder, oh God, harder...'

Andy flinched as the rat's claws dug into his skin. He reached under his T-shirt and grasped her around the middle, dragging her out squirming and writhing, then winced again as her teeth sunk into his thumb. It's alright, Lucky, I know you can't help it, it's starting again, isn't it.'

Dexterously he adjusted his position, scruffing her around the back of her neck he lifted her up, level to his face, and looked at her with patience and adoration.

For a moment she was still, just licking the blood that dripped down her muzzle, then she lashed out again, catching Andy on the nose with her hind feet.

'Shh… shh, it's okay,' he cooed, as he carried her to her cage. 'I'm just going to put you in here, just to keep you safe until it's over.'

He fastened the cage door and returned to his window seat. He stared blandly down at Jez and the girl splashing amongst the raindrops that re-bounded on the pool's surface.

A brilliant white flash of lightening tore a gash in the sky. Andy leaned forward, his nose pressed against the window, his interest pricked as the lightening briefly illuminated two dark shapes that slipped silently into the pool with the lovers.

The sea lions began circling just below the surface, closing in on the couple with each pass as if herding prey, before sinking out of sight.

Andy stood, scanning the pool for the silhouettes whilst trying to differentiate between rain drops bouncing off the water and the popping globules of air floating up from the bottom. A minute passed…then two.

Then they struck.

The girl was first. A sudden jerk and she was gone. Vanishing amongst the ripples of the agitated water. She reappeared, breaking the surface, her hands clutched and tore at the air and her mouth thirstily gulping in oxygen before being dragged under again.

Jez was floundered in the middle of the pool, his head whirling wildly from side to side when she burst from the water again, propelled into the air like a torpedo. Jez spun around and began scrabbling to swim clear, clawing at the water as her flaying body slammed down into him.

The couple's forms were consumed by a convulsing spasm of spray and foam as Jez lashed out at the girl who frantically tried clinging to him. Freeing himself from her grasping hands Jez made a desperate lunge for the edge of the pool. His fingertips struck the side, he kicked again, gripping the concrete ledge firmly and hoisting himself up and onto the side. With a final effort he pulled his legs clear of the water.

Splayed out on the concrete, spluttering and coughing he looked back to the pool.

An immense black shape loomed over him.

His back arched as a sea lion clamped her jaws into Jez's calf and began slowly pulling him back into the water. Jez stabbed at the concrete with his fingers. He flipped on to his back, his tanned stomach scuffed and grazed white, his arms thrashing out wildly as his legs, waist, torso, shoulders were gradually dragged back into the pool. Finally, his head, lurching frenziedly from side to side, slid beneath the surface.

Andy continued to watch until the wash lapping against the pools edge subsided, then he glanced over to his rat. She was feverishly scrabbling at the bars of her cage.

He turned back to the scene below – looking down at the dark film that began to spread over the pools surface – at Jez and the girl's limp bodies, bobbing amongst the raw, puffy lumps of torn off flesh – his face relaxed into a thin, vindictive smile…He wanted to kill King. Now he knew how.

At the other side of the park Al involuntarily ducked as the thunder and lightning tore across the sky.

'Fucking hell!' Like being in the fucking trenches.' He reached into his pocket for the keys. Snagging them on the material he gave them a yank then groaned as they flew from his hand and disappeared into the darkness with a splash. '…Bollocks and fuck – less fucking haste, more fucking speed.'

He knelt down, blindly sieving his hands through the puddles and gravel like he was panning for gold. 'Now that I want a bit of fucking lightening…'

Beth stood still, sniffing the air. Her green eyes glared intensely at the door, penetrating the blackness that engulfed her.

She resumed her pacing, splashing through the urine and saliva that saturated the floor.

'Fuck this,' sighed Al, then, shouting above the rain, 'I'm sorry, Beth. I can't get in, I'll bring you a bunny tomorrow, I promise.'

Beth halted as she heard the footsteps disappear into the rain. Then her ears pricked up and her hackles burst up along her back as the crunch of footfall on gravel grew loader – returning.

'It's okay, Beth, your Dada's a fucking airhead is all, forgot about the spare,' cried Al excitedly. Groping on the floor by the door he found the slab of loose paving, prised it up and grabbed the spare key that he kept hidden beneath it. With a grin of satisfaction Al slipped the key into the padlock and twisted it; with a click it sprung open. He removed the padlock, hung it on the handle and, wrenching open the door, he stepped inside.

'Fuck me!' he cried, the thick smell of ammonia almost knocking him backwards, 'Have you been pissing yourself 'cause of the storm?' He reached out and flicked the switch, then flicked it again. 'Lightening must have knocked out the lights,' he muttered. 'Poor Beth, have you been scared? Dada is here now, everything's going to be fine.'

Beth watched as the intruder edged along the weld mesh. She crouched into the corner, pushing herself back until she felt the cold concrete pressing hard against her, frustrating her impulse to escape; flight was no longer an option. She kept still, not even blinking, trying to blend in with the stone walls that entrapped her. Drool hung from her open mouth; her lips pealed back along her incisors in a silent snarl.

Click. Another padlock snapped open, a squeal as the heavy bolt slid from its rusty home, a creak of an opening door and then the threat was with her, brazenly sharing her space, invading her territory, violating her need for safety.

Susie's legs buckled from beneath her as a shimmering wave of ecstasy swept through her body and she collapsed, half moaning and half laughing to the ground, taking Matt with her.

He tried to stand, but she pulled him back down and rolled him onto his back, his body tensing on contact with the cold mud.

Crawling predatorily up the length of his body she straddled his waist and brought her head down to meet his. Her lank hair fell around him like a tent, veiling his face from the elements and giving him the warm insular sensation that they were the only people left in their world.

'I'm not finished with you yet,' she whispered between nibbles of his ear.

'Don't be scared, darlin', it's Al...your Dada...what's up Beth?'

One step, then another, it was too close – the threat had crossed the final invisible line, its hostility unavoidable, attack inevitable. Cautiously she waited for the right moment, unaware that she had the advantage of sight.

'Beth... where the fuck are y–?

She sprung.

The force of her impact sent Al sprawling back and crashing onto the mesh door that buckled as it absorbed their weight. He hollered in pain and surprise as the leopard's jaws sunk into his shoulder. The warm blood began seeping from his wound and into her mouth giving her a rush that she had never experienced before.

Al reacted instinctively – grasping her upper jaw tightly until he could feel the incisors cutting into his fingers and howling as he wrenched back Beth's head, his flesh burning with the sensation of teeth dragging through his skin. Grabbing a loose fold of fur from under her foreleg with his free hand he lifted her clear off the ground and hurled her across the den.

The small size of the enclosure gave her no opportunity to right herself before she made brutal contact with the opposite wall. Her head struck the concrete first and she slid to the floor, flipping quickly onto her feet in anticipation of the counter attack. A trickle of blood flowed from her ear as she stood watching, with her mouth gaping like a stone gargoyle.

'Shite, Beth, what's wrong with you? It's me…It's Dada!'

Beth watched as the invader inched its way along the wall, its arm outstretched and its eyes darting around, searchingly. She crouched low until the white fur on her belly stained yellow, soaking up the puddles of urine.

Slowly she lifted a leg and crept forward, one tentative paw at a time, crawling spider-like towards her quarry.

Al reached the door. 'I'm going, okay? It's alright… I'm going!'

Not daring to turn his back, he groped behind him until his palm rubbed against the familiar smooth handle of the bolt. He tried tugging it across but the frame, bent out of shape, had jammed the door. He raised his leg, bringing his foot down hard on the mesh in an attempt to free it.

Beth paused, momentarily discouraged by the noise and the cry of anguish that accompanied it, then with added stealth, she continued her stalk, patiently getting in position, waiting for the right moment.

'Where are you? Beth…where the fuck are you?'

Al knew that he had no option; the door had to be opened, he couldn't stay in there – in the darkness.

'Shout, spin around, open, jump and close,' he murmured under his breath. 'Shout, spin, open, jump, close.'

Suddenly a thought crossed his mind — what if there was no more danger? He had heard nothing since the grunt she made when he threw her off. What if her collision with the wall had hurt her, badly hurt her, even killed her. If he had killed her... Memories flashed through his mind: Beth as a cub tripping over herself in her keenness to reach him, clambering over him with claws retracted, her mouth playfully clamping over his arm, firmly but never with enough force to penetrate. A stark contrast to the teeth that had savagely pierced and crushed his shoulder.

A yearning more powerful than logic swamped him; he needed to run his hands through her thick fur, to bury his face deeply into her neck, breathe in the uniqueness of her scent... offer her reassurance.

He stepped forward, inciting a low growl from the darkness, almost inaudible but unmistakable. His heart leapt with the relief that she was alive and with that confirmation came purpose. Comfort wasn't enough, she was hurt, needed help. He barely noticed the throb of his shoulder – only one thought consumed him – he needed help. He needed Susie.

He abandoned all sense of caution. Spinning around he wrenched aside the bolt and barged the door open.

She timed her pounce perfectly, landing on his back with a force that sent them both sprawling from the enclosure and into the corridor. Recovering first, Beth re-launched her attack, lunging at Al who caught her by the throat, stopping her jaws just short of his neck. With groaning effort, he pushed her back, holding her at arm's length whilst she twisted and writhed, attempting to free herself of his powerful grip. She felt panic swell up, and increased her onslaught as she lashed out with her claws, vicious daggers slashing at the trunk and legs of her foe. Al screamed out with each fresh laceration, attempting to lift his other arm in defence but it was by now swollen, limp and unresponsive.

A sudden pain, a slice deep into his inner thigh, leapt above the other cuts with searing intensity. Roaring with agony Al threw himself backwards, rolling Beth into him as they landed heavily on the floor so that her back was held firmly against his chest. Before she could appreciate her vulnerability he hooked his legs around hers and re- adjusted his arm lock so that all her limbs were pinned securely against her body, all her weapons immobilised.

At first he assumed the warm liquid that gushed down his leg was Beth urinating in her relentless struggle to free herself, but as the seconds passed and her fight diminished into an exhausted panting, he began to realise that a bladder could not be that persistent.

He was unable to lift his left arm but he could, by moving his hand in a caterpillar-like action, drag it along the ground. This he did, and with trepidation he worked his hand down the length of his body, squeezing it beneath Beth's leg until his fingers made contact with the hot sticky liquid. A morose realisation grew within him as he tentatively worked his way to the source.

The gash in his inner thigh pumped out a fresh stream of blood with every beat of his heart. He tried applying pressure but his attempt was futile, his blood simply oozed through the gaps between his fingers.

Beth also seemed to understand the implication and sporadically tested his hold through a fit of violent jerks, checking for signs of weakening.

With every heartbeat a little more of his consciousness seeped out of him – it was simply a matter of time.

'Fuck.' he said. His voice was weak – resigned.

Quietly he began to sing to her, hugging her tightly, rocking her gently as he had done so many times before. 'Pussy cat, pussy cat, I've got flowers and lots of hours to spend with you, so go and powder your cute little pussycat n....

Beth felt his muscles relax; she rolled onto her side taking with her the limp body of Al, his limbs still entwined around hers. The madness had ended. It had left her as immediately as it had arrived and she had no memory of what had occurred in-between. She felt momentarily disorientated, confused by where she was, but she also felt Al's arms around her and that reassured her. She was aware that somehow her circumstances had changed, that she was not where she ought to be, not where she had been before. Allowing her maternal feelings for Al to quash the urge to get up and explore her surroundings, she remained where she was. Safe and content, she didn't move, reluctant to disturb his sleep.

Sweeping her hair back Susie looked down at Matt, gradually reducing the gyrations of her hips from gallop into canter, trot to a gentle rocking walking motion. Matt lay sprawled out beneath her with his fingers buried deep into the earth and his eyes tightly shut.

She made no effort to conceal the elation in her eyes or the glee in her wide, satisfied grin. She wanted him to see it, couldn't wait for him to open his eyes and understand with one glance at her expression the way that she felt about him. 'Matt…'

'Hmm…? He kept his eyes closed, still relishing the last dwindling sensation of the movement within her.

'Matt, look at me.' She wiggled her hips to secure his attention.

He opened his eyes. 'Yeah?'

'Matt – I don't know what just happened. It's not like me to… It's like we… I…had no control. It was amazing. Matt, I think…'

Matt's eyes, at one moment lazy and sanguine, had suddenly flashed open.

'Matt – what's wrong?'

Susie felt her hair tighten on her scalp, then brutally yanked back, her hands involuntarily grappling at the thick, powerful fingers that dragged her to her feet.

'Whore!'

King released her hair and drew his arm back. Before she could respond, he brought it back down and hit her.

'King…Stop!' Matt staggered to his feet, attempting to hoist up his twisted jeans.

'And you…' said King, turning on Matt. 'Shit, boy… What did I tell you about respect?'

'King…Wait…'

With the goad grasped firmly in his hand King lashed out. The metal hook struck Matt's shoulder and sent him tumbling down the slope.

King strode after him. 'Get up.'

Matt slipped and scrambled, trying to stand. He felt something vice-like grab his arm and hoist him upright, then a winding blow to his gut and a kick to his side and he was spiralling downwards.

He lay sprawled on the bank, coughing up a mixture of mud and bile, and looked up. King was now looming over him, screaming something at him, his voice lost to the seething swell of the rapids that roared past. Reaching up Matt grabbed a clump of reed, and heaved himself onto his knees.

King bent down and pressed his mouth against Matt's ear.

'Too late for prayers boy.'

PART THREE

'The Indian elephant is said sometimes to weep.'
Charles Darwin

CHAPTER 40

Wash basin, mirror, sofa, even a radio. Everything. Christ – no wonder Julian spent so much time in his office!

The mirror – Clean off all this mud, crud and blood. Christ, look at me…just two days and look at me…My eye! Just wash it – it's not as bad as it looks – give it a clean and–

What's that noise – was that the door – someone outside?

It's nothing – your imagination – you're safe. He can't get me here – can't get me if he can't find me.

The phone. Please work – please be a tone…Fuck. Fuck. Fuck!

It's okay – you knew that. Andy said. You knew the phones wouldn't work. Just need to relax – I'm safe now.

Stick to the plan, write it down – write it down and expose the bastard. Get it all down quick before he finds you…You've got time. Just need to relax, clean yourself up…see to your wounds…then stick to the plan – write it down. Find a pen … paper.

Where the fuck does Julian keep his pens?

I don't remember much. Just snatches of pain, darkness, movement. I don't even know how long it lasted. When I did wake up I was surrounded by a stink of rotting meat and urine that burned my eyes and my throat.

Andy was looking down at me, asking me how I was. In answer to his question I threw up.

He told me off, typical Andy, told me if I was going to vomit again, that I might consider doing it outside, said we could be stuck in here for a while – that conditions were bad enough as it was. Then he started to explain, how he'd found me, dragged me here – to the wolves den.

While he talked I looked around. The den was basically an underground dug-out, perhaps twelve feet deep and eight feet wide. On the sodden clay floor lay clumps of straw bedding and a scattering of bones. The only indication that this was a man-made structure was the access, a two-foot-high sliding metal door dappled brown with rust which sat in two metal runners. Sunlight streamed through a one-inch gap where the slide met the earth, dimly illuminating my surroundings. Andy was kneeling at my side, his head bowed against a ceiling criss-crossed with the roots of plants above ground.

'It's brilliant' he said 'no one will ever find us here, and I've got us loads of provisions.' He gestured towards the corner of the den, 'I raided the shop. See.'

I glanced at the small pile of Lucozade bottles, crisps and Marathon chocolate bars, then at his face, grinning with pride over his stash. 'Where's Susie? I asked.

Andy's grin slid from his face. 'A lot happened last night, I guess I should–'

'For Christ's sake, tell me!' I shouted.

'Okay, okay, don't shoot the messenger... she's dead Matt, they're all dead...Lucky's okay though, I left her in her cage when she started having one of her moments.'

That's how I found out. I felt dizzy, bile rose in my throat. In the background Andy's voice droned on about Lucky – his fucking rat – being safe.

I screamed at him that I didn't care about the rat. That it was all his fault she was dead. That if he hadn't pissed off King, if Susie hadn't seen what he was really like. Then she would still be alive. It wasn't fair, but I told him anyway. Andy protested, saying that it was my fault for getting off with her and that I would also be dead if he hadn't pulled me from the river.

Then I began coughing and vomiting again.

'We mustn't argue,' he said, it just makes you worse. It's neither of our faults, it's King, he's the bastard not us, but don't worry about him, I've got a plan, a way to get him.'

All the time Andy talked he fussed over me, lifting my head and offering me some Lucozade, picking out pieces of straw from my hair. Once he was satisfied I was okay he lowered my head back down and began telling me what had happened.

I'll try and write what I remember, what Andy told me. You need to know his state of mind – what had happened to him – about the last few hours of his life. I owe it to him; he saved mine.

He told me that he'd been sitting in his flat, the night of the party, trying to think of how to kill King when it started happening again – the animals going crazy.

'I can always tell when it's about to start because of Lucky' he said, 'she's always the first, I guess because she's so intuitive, and then I noticed the sea lions, they started attacking Jez and his date, drowned them in less than three minutes, and that's when I had the idea.

It was like a message from God – I knew exactly what to do.'

He said it so casually – Jez's death – with such bland indifference, I had to ask him to repeat it. He did, adding that it was no great loss.

I was stunned by his indifference. He'd worked with Jez for years; he was his friend! I told him so.

'Hardly a friend, an arrogant, lazy sod,' he said, 'always parading his girlfriend's past me, bloody show off.'

I didn't understand; I didn't realise then what was happening with Andy. Furious, I began shouting that he was a callous, selfish, bastard, until my rant was cut short by another coughing fit. I slumped back onto the damp, piss-stained straw, allowing Andy to fuss over me until the attack subsided.

Then he carried on. 'I didn't say I wished him dead, it's just that I won't miss him. And anyway, he didn't die in vain, like I was saying, it was seeing that happen that gave me my idea on how to get King, and you must want that as much as I do.'

He paused to swig some Lucozade, probably hoping I would agree with him – I said nothing.

'Anyway,' he continued, 'I was just coming back along the paddock walk when I saw King walking away from her body. Once he was gone I went down to her, but it was too late, she was already dead.'

I rolled on to my side and turned my back to him, wishing he'd go away, leave me alone, stop talking. I didn't want to hear anymore. I was suddenly exhausted. Andy didn't seem to notice, he just carried on talking.

'I was just wondering what had happened to you when I heard footsteps on the gravel path above me and just had time to dive behind the tree before King reappeared from around the corner; he must have had second thoughts about leaving her body there. I risked a peek around the trunk and, I don't know, it could have been the rain, but I'd swear he was crying. Anyway, he threw her over his shoulder and was about to leave when he hesitated. Man, that really freaked me out. I thought the bastard had sensed me or something, you know, what with all his Vietnam training, but instead he peered down the slope and into the river, like he was searching for something, and that's when I realised, it wasn't something, it was someone…you. So as soon as I knew it was safe and that he had definitely gone I came looking. Good thing I did, I don't think you would have lasted another five minutes in the water.'

I rolled over to face him. I had hoped against hope that Susie was still alive, that Andy had got it wrong, that King had held back, but no…Andy had seen her. She was gone.

'This plan,' I said, 'your idea to get King, tell me about it.'

In the murky half-light of the den his eyes briefly grew wide and bright, before a thin, wolfish grin forced them back into their familiar weasel-like slits.

'All we've got to do is sit back and wait,' he said.

And then I realised what he'd done. 'Christ,' I said, 'you're fucking crazy.'

Andy chuckled. 'Relax, will you. I've not let them all out, just a few choice ones: wolves, lynx, and some primates.'

'But what about Gajadhar,' I said, 'and Al? They're out there too, you're going to get them killed as well!'

Andy stopped smiling and stared at me as though I was a child failing to grasp some basic concept. 'They're dead. I told you already, they're all dead.'

I felt the dizziness return; my mouth was suddenly parched. I reached out for the Lucozade and Andy passed me the bottle. I took a sip, the glass rim clattered against my teeth. I steadied my hand then drank some more, draining the bottle. 'Was...was it King?' I asked, 'who killed them?'

'He didn't kill Al, no, just Gajadhar.' replied Andy, 'I only found out this morning. You were still unconscious so I decided to risk the trip to raid the shop. I was just coming out of the wood and I was being really cautious 'cause of the wolves, you know, really keeping my eyes peeled, and bloody lucky I was. I heard a crackle just ten-foot away, and just managed to get under a bush before Colin appeared. He was talking on the walkie-talkie, asking if King had found anything. King said that he hadn't and that the bastard – I think he meant you – has either crawled under a bush or done like any injured critter and made for home. Then there was a long silence before King spoke again, said that you definitely weren't in the river and that they should try your flat, he said that it was still early and that even if you weren't there the mahout would still be in bed, said that he was going to give him a wake-up call, going to fix him once and for all.'

'So, you didn't actually see Gajadhar dead then,' I said.

'Come on, Matt, you know what he meant by that. He can't leave anyone alive now, he's gone too far, gotta get rid of all the evidence and make it look like the animals did it. I wouldn't want to be in Colin and Gary's shoes once they've outlived their usefulness.'

Briefly I considered his point. He was probably right. 'What about Al... How do you know about him?'

'I found him when I was returning from the shop' said Andy. 'I didn't really need to come back past Beth's enclosure but it only took me slightly out of the way and I guess I was half-thinking of releasing her as well – just thinking about it; I wasn't sure what Al would do if I did. Anyway, turns out I didn't have to worry, Al was lying dead in the corridor – that's how come you're wearing his jacket. I thought it would be more use to you than to him. Anyway, Beth was nowhere to be seen. I guess he must have gone to see her last night, when the animals turned. Poor bastard, makes you realise how powerful Dan's influence is.'

At that phrase, 'Dan's influence', I was briefly transported back to the party – to me, Susie and Gajadhar discussing the animals' behaviour. I could still hear their voices, still see Susie's mischievous smile. I could still smell her.

'Are you listening to me?' asked Andy.

I ran my palm across my cheek, pushing away the tears, 'Yeah, you just reminded me of something.' I gazed briefly at the wet sheen that coated my hand. 'Susie and Gajadhar, they'd been talking about that...at the party, saying about Uddanda, about him being somehow involved.'

Andy pounced on my words. 'Really? Wow – what did they say – what did they reckon? I think telepathy, what did they say, did they think the same? What about you, you must have an idea, what do you know about telepathy?'

'It's all crap,' I said. 'There's absolutely no scientific basis in it and animals are incapable of feeling revenge.'

He looked briefly wounded by my comments. 'But if you had seen what I saw last week you wouldn't be saying that. There's definitely something going on, look.' He pulled out a little notepad from his back pocket. 'I've been keeping a tally on when it all started, you know, after Devi was killed, remember, when we all had that shared dream about being chased by the elephants. Every time the animals went weird I wrote down the time; I even did a chart,' He proudly flashed a childishly drawn graph at me. 'I guess I'm more in tune with all the activity 'cause of Lucky, it's kind of hard to ignore her when she's under Dan's spell. Anyway, you can see how much more frequent they've become. At first it was once or twice a day, but it's gradually increased. Yesterday it happened six times. But what I can't work out is a pattern. I'm sure it's not random and if I could discover what precedes it, you know, what kicks it all off, then I got my proof. Might even write a paper on it. That would be a kick in the teeth for King, wouldn't it? 'A Study in Elephant Telepathy' by world famous animal expert Andy Marshall. I just need to find the pattern. Maybe you can help, you know, fresh pair of eyes, what do you think?'

He thrust his pad under my nose and I pushed it away, irritated by his enthusiasm. 'I think its bullshit, a group of animals feeding off each other's hysteria, that's all.'

'I don't believe that,' he insisted, 'they've never done it before, so why now?'

'How the hell should I know?'

Andy looked hurt. 'Well, that's a pretty poor attitude coming from an education officer.'

'Christ, Andy, who cares,' I shouted. 'No one's left alive to fucking care.'

'Alright, calm down will you, you're not the only one emotional about everything. I'm upset too you know, I just deal with it differently to you is all, some of us don't like to wear our hearts on our sleeves.'

I ignored him but he carried on regardless.

'Anyway, you said that Susie thought it was likely… And elephants have got really massive brains for an herbivore, that doesn't make sense unless they use them for something other than just munching on grass and leaves.'

'Look,' I said, 'they probably use most of their brains for orientation, okay, and yes, possibly communication but not bloody telepathy, Susie dismissed that idea as well. I think she only said it to tease me, she had some thoughts that Uddanda – that all elephants – were capable of some kind of infrasonic communication, I think she thought that was a feasible explanation but–'

'But she wasn't sure – and my theory could still be right.'

I ignored his interruption and carried on. '…If Uddanda was out for revenge and had power over the minds of others then why doesn't he just tell King to go hang himself and that would be an end to it.'

For a minute Andy was quiet. 'You're right,' he said finally.

'Thank god for that.' I closed my eyes, feeling drained.

'No, I mean you're right that it should be Dan that kills King, of course it should. I've been so caught up in just wanting him dead that I forgot about justice. It's Dan who's been wronged and it's his right to get his revenge. And there's a symmetry to it as well – Jez was killed by his sea lions, Al by Beth, even Roger, it was his deer that gored him. It makes sense that an elephant should get King, or should I say fix him.'

He started laughing, a hiccupy kind of laugh. 'Just imagine it, King's face when Dan gets him, squeezes him until his eyes pop from their sockets. It's brilliant, perfect, I can't believe I didn't think of it before. What was I doing letting all the other animals out when it has to be Dan. It just has to be Dan.'

I sat up, alarmed by the malice in his voice and looked at him. It was then that I realised…something inside him had snapped. 'Christ Andy, you can't release Dan, you'll never make it.'

'Why not, it's the last thing King would be expecting, as long as I'm careful.'

'But what about the animals you've already released, what if you bump into one of them?'

'I told you; I'll be careful.'

I couldn't believe it; he was serious. I watched him start stuffing his pockets with chocolate bars, muttering that he'd just take a few provisions. 'Andy, what the hell has got into you, this isn't like you, you're neurotic, self-absorbed, cowardly, you don't go on half-arsed missions–'

'Fuck you!' he snapped.

He was on his hands and knees, scrambling towards

the sliding door of the Den. I grabbed his ankle, dragging him back to my side.

'What about Lucky,' I pleaded, 'what happens to her if you get caught?'

He paused and I let go of his ankle, relieved as he shuffled back to my side.

'Look,' I said, 'just give it some time – someone will be along soon. They'll wonder why no one's answering the phone, why the gate is still locked. Help will come; we just need to give it time, that's all.

He smiled and rested his hand on my shoulder. 'Matt, no one's coming.'

'You're wrong – you don't know that. The phones – people will wonder…'

'Matt, I tried the phone, in the shop I tried it but it was dead, knocked out by the storm probably. The last time that happened it was over a week before they got around to sorting it. And the gate? King would have thought of that, stuck some sign up saying 'closed for reasons beyond our control' or some such bollocks. He would have thought of that; he wants us alone, and that's just what we are, trust me Matt, it's the only way.'

'Then I'll come with you.' I said.

'No, you're not well enough, and if he got us both then there would be no one left to tell the truth about him, he would blame all the deaths on the animals, he would win.'

As he began to crawl back towards the sliding door I tried one last effort to stop him, asking again about what would happen to Lucky if he didn't come back. He looked at me. I hadn't noticed until then. I should have. His gaunt face, his skin saggy against his jaw line, his eyes haunted and sunken, deeply ringed.

'You'll look after her, won't you Matt,' he said. 'If anything did happen, you'd see she's okay, she likes you, we both do.'

He dragged open the door, squeezed through, slid it shut behind him, and was gone.

CHAPTER 41

Maybe I should put on Julian's radio. Help keep me awake. I don't want to sleep – don't want to risk another dream. Christ that dream – Dan – enormous, towering over the trees, sucking up everything into his trunk like a giant hoover. Buildings, people – Tommy, Roger, Mickey – their screams, like the screams of the animals outside.

Maybe I should risk it. Maybe if I put it on quietly. Christ, to hear some music. And human voices – normal voices instead of just listening to King's fucking ramblings on the walkie-talkie and the animal's going insane outside.

Shit! What if I screamed in my sleep – during that dream? Could King have heard me – if I'd screamed loud enough? Screamed...like Andy had screamed...

It was dark, night-time dark, I could tell by the small shaft of moonlight that cut though the gap in the sliding door. All night I'd been kept awake by scratching and sniffing noises from outside. Now they'd stopped, but there was something else out there. I was convinced.

I whispered Andy's name; he should have been back.

The noise outside got closer; I was sure it must be Andy and was about to call his name again when I was cut short by another voice, muffled by the shrubs and greenery.

'College boy...hey, college boy... come out, come out, wherever you are.'

I actually felt relieved. I thought that was why Andy hadn't come back, he couldn't. King was out there – searching. I thought he was safe. Then the bastard spoke again.

'Hey, college boy, come look what we found skulking around the eles, seems like the little weasel's grown some balls since our chat in the reptile house. Like I always say, what don't kill you will make you stronger.'

I crawled to the metal slide and looked through the gap. I could just see them with their backs to me. Colin and Gary were holding Andy whilst King paced around them.

He started talking again. 'What about you college boy, what's it gonna take to grow you some balls, huh?'

Andy said something I couldn't hear, then King punched him.

'See what I mean? Hell, almost seems like a new man. Weren't too long ago he'd be shaking like a fifty-cent ladder. I think he's even got to liking these beatings, some folks do, heard about a man once, could only get it off by putting his balls in a vice, don't know what Andy here feels about that'

Andy howled in pain.

'Nope, he don't seem to like that none too much.'

He reached down and pulled his knife from his boot. 'Heard of someone else who liked the sensation of cold steel up their ass,' he said. 'Man, there's some sick folk around. I mean, what the hell's wrong with some people, but then s'pose it takes all kinds, gotta respect that I guess. What you reckon, Matt, think that's more to Andy's taste?'

Andy whimpered.

'What's that, Andy? Speak up. Matt can't hear you when you snivel … you want me to stop? Of course you do, you think any of us are enjoying this, but it's not up to me.' He raised his voice, 'what about you, college boy, you enjoying this? You want me to stop? You got the balls to come out from wherever you're skulking and come and stop me? You got the balls for that? Just you and me, the boys won't interfere, hell, I'll even give you the first punch, tie one hand behind my back if you like… man, what's it gonna take to rile you into action?' He paused. 'It's gonna happen sooner or later so why not make it sooner, save the rat boy here some discomfort. What do you say, let's us get it over with.'

Colin or Gary said something. Something about me not being here. King told him to shut up. Said I was. That he could feel it.

Then King continued. 'Well, you sure got me fooled, thought you had more fight, guess I was wrong, guess you're just all talk. Fooled Susie as well with your smooth, high and fucking mighty college talk, taking advantage of her when she was at her most vulnerable, getting her hurt like that, making me fix her. Seems to me you're a dangerous person to get close to. Since you arrived, what is it eight or nine days? Since then everyone who befriended you, they all got hurt…'

I buried my teeth into my forearm, fighting the urge to scream out yeah…and it was you who fucking hurt them!

Still he went on. Christ I hated him.

'Now I start to think of it, all kinds of bad shit has happened since you arrived, you know. Big Al's dead, and Jez and his girl. Shit Matt, you got some kinda jinx thing going – you piss off a Ju Ju man or something?

Perhaps you screwed his girlfriend too, got her drunk first, like you did Susie. And now Andy. You're just gonna sit back and watch him suffer. Hell, boy, how you gonna live with that, when you could have prevented it...'

He was right. Nothing was stopping me other than my fear. But that was now gone, he had replaced it with something else. I grasped the handle of the slide, ready to wrench it back, wanting to get it over with... then I hesitated as a dark shape brushed passed.

At first I didn't know what was happening. I thought maybe Colin or Gary had circled around and discovered my hiding place. I pressed my eye up against the gap – Colin and Gary were still there, holding Andy. Then an eye appeared, just inches away, staring back at me from the other side. I fell backwards, and then scrambled back, peering through the gap at the glimpses of phantom-like movement that passed by, at the pack of wolves circling the trespassers.

'King...King! Colin's voice was shrill and fearful.

'Yeah...I see them, just keep still.'

'What we gonna do King? How many of 'em are there?'

'How the fuck should I know...enough okay, now let me think.'

The wolves started snapping at them. King stood motionless; his knife grasped in his hand.

'King, let's just leg it,' pleaded Gary, 'Matt can't be here, or if he was they've got him, come on, let's get out of here.'

'Maybe he is, maybe not... but don't you fucking move, you'll get us all killed,' snarled King, then addressing me. 'What do you reckon college boy, how would you get yourself out of a fix like this?'

Then I knew… not how I would escape… but what King intended to do. I watched in mute horror as King told Colin and Gary to hold Andy still.

Then I heard Andy, his voice rose clear above the deep snarls of the wolf pack.

'King no – for God sake, no.'

He started to struggle, writhing against Colin and Gary's grip.

'Hold him steady boys.'

'Shit, King…what… what you gonna do?' Colin's voice was hesitant, 'you can't…there must be another way?'

'It's him or us,' bellowed King.' Hold him still.'

Andy's back was to me, I didn't have to see the look in his eyes, only hear his high-pitched scream as King stuck his blade into Andy's gut and slid it up. The scream ended, there was a slopping sound, then Andy slumped to the ground.

I puked violently.

When I finally looked back through the gap, Andys' body was buried beneath the pack of wolves tussling over his remains. Colin and Gary were cautiously edging away. King was a few steps behind them, staring in my direction, smiling.

I lay awake shivering for the rest of the night amongst the stench of vomit, urine and discarded animal remains, trying to shut out the noises from outside. I didn't attempt sleeping for fear of the dreams that I would have. Al's jacket was my only protection against the cold damp straw.

I didn't know what to do next.

I couldn't stay there. He'd guessed where I was. Probably heard me throw-up – it was just a matter of time before he returned.

Then I had the idea of Julian's office. The door was never locked, 'one doesn't lock one's door to one's family' he once said. I remember because Al had answered, 'yes one fucking does.'

It wouldn't occur to King to search there. It wouldn't fit in with his model of the hunted. Prey doesn't sit in an office. Prey panics, prey bolts, prey sacrifices its cunning in favour of escape. It runs on instinct, that's what King would expect, I was sure of it.

I left at dawn.

I crawled on my stomach. Even with no wolves in sight, the main thing was to remain low and get to the footbridge as fast as I safely could. Once there I could disappear into the river and make my way the hundred yards or so downstream. If I got that far I reckoned I'd be ok.

It took ages, crawling like that, and it took all my willpower not to get up and run.

I'd got about fifty yards, reaching the point where the path split – left for deer paddock, straight on to camels, the footbridge, the walled garden and safety – when I thought I heard something just ahead of me – voices? I rolled off the path and into a bank of nettles and lay still, my face buried in the earth. Then silence. I pictured King standing triumphantly over me, his elephant hook raised high in the air, and I waited for its strike, the finishing blow, but nothing happened. Slowly, I lifted my head, not knowing what to expect. There was no one there, just the clump of nettles swaying in the breeze. I was beginning to believe that I had imagined it, that even my senses had turned on me, when I heard King's voice.

'Look again, goddamn it... he's gotta be here somewhere, King out'

I looked over to where the voice was coming from and saw a black, stubby aerial poking out from a small pile of leaves lying across the path.

One of them must have dropped the walkie-talkie last night. I clambered out from the nettles and rushed over, reaching into the pile of leaf litter for my prize.

Then the pain...

CHAPTER 42

These four walls – Julian's four walls. Brown, fading wallpaper, swirling felt patterns, fuzzy and peeling. The paintings: the grazing antelope silhouetted against a blazing red savannah sun. The snow leopard draped listlessly over a rock. That lion's gaze following my every move.

And that grandmother clock, tick, tock, tick, tock, bequeathed to Julian, no doubt, by some spinster aunt. I can imagine him visiting her on her death bed, tick, tock, greedily surveying his inheritance, tick, tock, the clock counting down the old woman's life in reverberating tick fucking tock seconds.

This feeling of being trapped – no hope, no point. It's not a sanctuary, it's a prison. A drab, lifeless, hope-sapping cell. Christ, is that what Gajadhar meant by unperceivable madness? Is that why all the animals in the park are going insane? Is that why the wolves behaved that way?

What made them so savage?

Was it the taste of freedom? Is captivity such a delicate state? Wildness always bubbling just under the surface. Does that mean every bloody thing here is insane? Maybe even me! I'm captive. I'm a caged animal. No, I'm not – I can think. Abstract thought – that's the difference between man and beast. I can change my situation; I have a choice...did have a choice – but not anymore. So now there's no difference – between me and the animals.

But…something's different. The answer's there – to what's happening – just need to concentrate. Just concentrate. Keep writing down what happened. Maybe it'll make sense if I write it down…Thank Christ it was my left arm. If it had been my right…if I couldn't write…Thank Christ is was my left…

I writhed on the ground hardly daring to look at what had happened, at what remained of my left arm. Reaching up with my good hand I grabbed at the object that held me, at the blunt, rough metal.

With the pain came confusion, panic, a primal desperation to get myself free. I clawed at the mechanism, trying to prise open the jaws, but it was futile. Then I tried the chain. It was still half-buried by the leaves, one end welded onto the trap and the other wrapped and padlocked around the base of a holly bush five feet away, the same gauge as the chain King used to tether the elephants. I looked around for a rock, a brick, anything to smash against the welded end.

After many blows I gave up and collapsed back down. I must have lain there for at least ten minutes, until the tears of pain, frustration, and anger subsided and the rational side of my brain was able to take over.

The mantrap was designed only to grip, not to sever limbs. It was made to catch and to hold its victim prisoner, to bait and trap, to hold them until the hunter returned to finish them off. Using the walkie-talkie as bait was perfect, I could never have thought of it, which I guess is the idea, to think as your quarry would and then do what they wouldn't consider.

I thought of how a fox would attempt to gnaw off its own leg to free itself from a snare. And wasn't there a mountaineer who had to amputate his own foot with a Swiss army knife when it became frostbitten? What links them – man and beast? It can't be fear of death that causes them to take such measures; the fox doesn't understand death does it? It must be the will to survive that links us, the need to live that drives us to defy the inevitable.

I looked down at my rock, shaped like a stone-age axe. Four, maybe five blows, pain that could not, should not be imaginable, but I would live...But live for what? A long, fruitful life, to meet and fall in love with a girl, a girl like Susie...or for revenge, revenge on King? Was that worth the pain? I imagined him standing over his trap, unlocking it and pulling out the remains of my arm, scanning the immediate area with a look of admiration on his face, 'at last a worthy opponent.'

It was that final image more than any other that made up my mind. I raised my arm, gripped the rock firmly in my hand, and clenched my teeth.

Whether I would have gone through with it I don't know. I hesitated – long enough to hear the approaching footsteps, the whoops and jeers of delight. I turned and saw Colin and Gary bounding towards me and grinning with triumph.

'Got you, you bastard!' they cried in unison.

I hurled the rock at them, missed, and then slumped to the floor.

'Just get me out of this thing,' I said.

Colin stepped forward, pulling what looked like a key from his pocket, but Gary stopped him, 'King'll kill us if we let him go.'

'Fuck King!' I screamed.

They looked at me horrified, like I'd blasphemed, denied the existence of their one true god.

'Look at me,' I said quickly, 'do I look like I'm in any condition to escape? My arm's busted, I've got so much river water in me you could wring my lungs out, I'm half dead with exhaustion. I'm not going anywhere, but this thing is hurting like hell.'

They looked at me blankly, unsure of what to do. I realised that I had confused them, that suddenly I was no longer the prey that they had been manipulated into treating me as. I watched as their faces struggled with the strain of making a decision of their own. They were just kids, barely seventeen or eighteen, kids who had stood by, even helped commit cold-blooded murder, but still kids, and I was their senior, the only authoritative figure in the absence of their master... and I could use that. Treat them like King would.

'Don't just stand there like a couple of fuckwits. Hey you... Gary.'

'I'm Colin,' said the one with the key, apologetically.'

'Colin, Gary, who gives a fuck, just unlock this fucking thing now.'

It worked. They looked confused, then nervous. Colin slipped the key into the lock and the jaws sprung open. I felt a tingle in my hand as the blood began to pump back through my veins, and gently I tried wriggling my fingers. Reluctantly, they responded. I was almost tempted to pounce, fight my way out. But if I did that – if they overpowered me – they would call King for sure.

Already Gary was raising his walkie-talkie to his mouth and was about to press the talk button.

'Wait!' I shouted.

'What for?' said Gary. His arm slowly fell back to his side as he waited expectantly for my reason.

'You know that once you make that call you've as good as killed me as well.'

Furtively, he shrugged. 'We didn't kill no-one.'

'For Christ sake, haven't you heard of accountability for your actions, aiding and abetting? You're accomplices to murder.'

'No-one's gonna get done for nothing; King'll look after it, said he would.'

'King's full of crap, he's only going to look after himself. When I'm gone you're the only ones who'll know what really happened here – he's not going to risk that.'

'That's bullshit!' said Colin angrily, 'you're the one full of crap, King respects us.'

It was hopeless. In their eyes King's word was unquestionable.

'Okay,' I said, 'but I saw your faces when King gutted Andy, you even threw up. I did the same myself,' I added quickly, realising that I was in danger of offending them again. 'Christ, anyone would, but that's what's going to happen to me if you call King, is that what you want?'

They looked at one another, then Gary spoke, still defensively.

'King had to do that to Andy, otherwise them wolves would've got us, he saved our lives, he had no choice.'

'Perhaps, but he didn't have to enjoy it so much. You saw the look on his face when he stuck the knife in – do you think that's normal?'

'In war it is,' said Colin.

'What are you talking about war, who's at fucking war? It's a wildlife park, not the Somme.'

'Well King don't see it like that,' said Gary. 'He says it's a personal war, says when you're given an opportunity to right some wrongs then it's your duty to act, and then, when the animals started killing...Well, King reckoned it was his chance to fix things, a gift from God he said, get things back to normal.'

'What do you mean, 'righting wrongs...back to normal?'

'With all the business of the mahout, King says the boss was questioning his authority, then you turn up and start hitting on Susie, shit, even Andy had a go at him over the radio, calling him queer and stuff. Don't you see? No respect, and King says respect is everything – it's what makes a man, he says. When people are trying to take your respect you got two choices, lay down and die with the rest of the sheep or look 'em straight between the eyes and take it right back, ain't no in-between.'

'And you think that's alright?'

'King says...'

'King says!' I shouted, 'I'm not asking what King says, what do you think?'

They looked at each other then back to me.

Colin shrugged his shoulders. 'King says it's not about what you think, it's about what you do.'

Christ, they were brainwashed. I tried again. 'Look, just because someone is right most of the time doesn't mean that he's right all of the time. Isn't it possible that King is wrong on this occasion, that he has… lost it?'

'Bet you wouldn't say that to King's face?' said Gary, smirking.

I ignored him and carried on. 'Sometimes life isn't black and white, but some people don't like that, they prefer to keep it simple, but it's not, it can't be, things are complex, people are complicated. King's attitude to life and death, it's not normal, you must see that?'

But their expression told me that they didn't, or wouldn't. It was like talking to a brick wall. 'You can't think that it's normal,' I continued, 'you must be able to see that what's going on here is fucking insane?'

To acknowledge a flaw in King, to even think it was heresy. They reacted in the only way they could.

Gary slammed his fist into my cheek and knocked me to the floor. Instinctively, I scrambled into a ball, shielding my bad arm with my knees and cocooning my head with my good arm as they lashed out with their boots. I felt a stinging pain to my eye, and then the beating stopped.

I could hear one of them speaking into the radio, 'Yeah, it worked, caught him in the trap, sure, where are you? The eles, okay we'll wait for you here, about ten minutes, Okay, Gary out.'

He had done it, made the call, sealed my fate.

I opened my eyes, (or one eye, the other didn't respond, the lids held together by something thick and sticky) and focused it beyond the legs of my attackers and tried to make sense of the hazy brown and grey figures that were padding stealthily towards us. I smiled.

'What are you fucking grinning about?'

I nodded in the wolves' direction and Colin and Gary turned around, then staggered back in fear.

'Shit, what we gonna do! Gary, what should we do?'

They were kids again, their voices weak and lost amongst the snarls of the approaching wolves.

They looked to the only authority they had.

Matt, what do we do?'

I didn't hesitate. 'Run,' I said quietly.

'What…But King says…'

'Run!' I said again, firmly.

I didn't have to speak again, the boys turned and pounded up the path, triggering the wolves' keen response to chase. I felt a rush of agitated air as the pack brushed past me, then watched as the hunt began.

Gary was the first to be brought down, his legs knocked from under him by the swipe of a massive paw.

'Colin, help m–'

His screams became muffled, buried beneath three wolves.

Colin looked back, an instinctive response to his friend's cry. He stopped running, and turned slowly; Gary had disappeared, replaced by a seething mass of red dripping fur.

Looking around Colin grabbed a stick and hurled it into the pack. 'Get off him, you bastards!'

Three wolves pacing the periphery of the mauling turned towards Colin. Slowly they began their stalk. The boy grabbed another stick from the floor and began waving it ineffectually at them.

'Fuck off – just fuck off.'

Drawl hung from their muzzles as they closed in. Colin began to stagger back as two more wolves left the feeding frenzy in favour of a fresh hunt.

He launched his stick at them, turned and ran.

I didn't wait to watch the result, his screams told me all that I needed to know. Slowly, I picked up the radio and backed around the corner of the path. Only when I was completely concealed by a large laurel bush did I begin to run.

There was no longer need for caution, no slipping into rivers or wondering how to cross the play area, I was as good as free. King would be coming down via the top paddock path, (the most direct way from the elephants), and, as long as I crossed the bridge before he reached the deer paddock, I could run unseen along the path that led to the walled garden. By the time King discovered what had happened, I would be past the gate and half way up the lanes to the Hunters Moon pub.

I must have sounded like a steam train – gasping for oxygen to feed my unsteady legs, tacking drunkenly along the path – yet it felt like I was floating.

I entered the walled garden like a marathon runner approaching the finishing line. The Lemurs howled their delight, monkeys chattered and cheered, and a peacock fanned and shimmered his tail like national flags flapping in a breeze.

Only then did I allow myself to relax, gulp down the air that my lungs were screaming for. I slowed down to a steady trot.

King would have just about arrived at the wolves, but, even assuming that they didn't get him as well, I had at least a fifteen-minute head start and in my head I was already bursting in through the pub doors. Annie, a picture of concern, was escorting my exhausted body into a chair and bustling the landlord outside to call the police whilst locking the doors behind her.

'Hey, college boy.'

Even King's rasping voice, breaking into my fantasy from the crackling walkie-talkie didn't dampen my euphoria. If anything, it added to it; he sounded as distant as a bad dream. The bravado was there but it lacked the usual menace, his voice almost lethargic in defeat.

'Hey college boy, you there? You hear me, course you do…don't know how you wrangled that little disappearing act, guess Colin and Gary must've fucked up somehow. Be the last time they do going by what's left of them. Come on, college boy…talk to me.'

I shouldn't have answered; I should have left his question hanging in doubt and uncertainty, but I was confident that I had won, that the tables were turned, and that I finally had the upper hand – just a taste of misplaced arrogance made the urge to reply irresistible.

'Yeah, I'm here, but not for long. Tell me, King, how's it going to feel spending the rest of your life behind bars, locked up like …' I paused, briefly drowned out by the shrill call of the Lemurs and then continued, 'like an animal.'

King was silent for a minute before replying, a hint of his old menace returning in his tone. 'You're up at the walled garden then, going for the gates, huh?' There was another silence.

'Well, guess I may as well amble up there myself. 'Hey, college boy, you be sure to give my regards to Andy when you see him, okay….'

He barked out a short dismissive laugh and was gone. I felt a chilling shudder run up my back and had to remind myself that there was nothing he could do to me now.

The animals' intensity seemed to grow as I wound my way through the walled garden. Screeches, rattling bars and beady, manic, little black eyes keenly followed my every move. I realised why, they hadn't been fed since Saturday and it was now...I had to think... Monday. I felt guilty, even apologised to a group of marmosets that squeezed themselves against the mesh, their little arms reaching out imploringly to me. Worst were the otters. Hysterical at the best of times, they screamed with shrill outrage at the sound of the gravel crunching under my feet.

After passing Julian's office and the aviaries, I slowed into a walk and massaged the fingers on my left arm in anticipation of climbing the gate. It was, as I remembered, a large, wrought iron construction with fancy spiralling ironmongery in-between the bars, essentially a large climbing frame. I felt sure my arm was up to it... It had to be.

A chattering noise above my head drew my attention and I looked up at three Capuchin monkeys sat in the branches overhead, part of Andy's released vigilante. They glanced from me to something up ahead, then back to me. Something disturbed them, I doubted it was me as they were used to people, but something made them tense, and they began flashing concerned glances up ahead of me. I kept looking at them, as their grunts of warning increased. Cautiously, I turned the corner and stopped dead in my tracks. ...Solid, impenetrable, standing between me and the gate. Her lips curled over her canines...then she snarled.

CHAPTER 43

God that feels good, cool, soothing. My eye's looking better – can see out of it now. Think it's going to be alright – Fuck! What does that even mean? Susie's dead – nothing's going to be alright again. What's the point to all this now she's gone? Stop. Don't think about her. Don't cry. Think about something else...stop crying. Christ the tears sting.

What's that? The animals...It's happening again – the madness outside. That's three times. Three outbursts in the last two hours. Andy was right about the madness – it's getting more frequent.

What if King's been caught? He hasn't spoken on the walkie-talkie...not for ages. Maybe the animals have got him... ripped him apart. He's alone now. No one to help him – not even his dog.

Shadow's eyes were fixed on me.

I couldn't outrun her. I couldn't climb, no weapons to protect myself, and with every second that passed King was getting nearer. I had no more options.

King had trained her well, of course he had. She launched herself at me, slamming into my body with a force that sent us both sprawling to the ground. She recovered first and lunged, and her jaws snapped tightly around my calf. I could feel the sting of her teeth puncturing my skin, then an intense, burning pain as she shook her head, like the wolves had to Gary ten minutes earlier, tearing and lacerating my flesh. I lashed out with my other foot and caught her muzzle. She yelped, I wrenched my leg free, staggered back and fell onto my hands and knees.

Quickly, she regained her composure, her hackles raised, her ears flattened as she crept towards me. I crawled crab-fashion backwards along the ground, dragging my injured leg. Beyond her was the gate, the gateway to freedom, but to get there I had to pass Cerberus.

She took her time, relishing the stalk as her master might, getting nearer with each slow, purposeful step. Even the baying screams of the Capuchins didn't distract her. But then something did.

I didn't dare look away but I could tell by her reaction that it wasn't the welcome sight of her master. She stopped mid prowl and her malignity shifted to the intruder. Over my left shoulder I became aware of a deep rumbling growl, and then I felt the firm but affectionate nudge of Beth's head against the sleeve of Al's jacket as she passed and planted herself between Shadow and myself.

With the mocking contempt of a feline she swiped tauntingly at the air with her claws fully extended. Shadow, her muzzle stained red with my blood, stood motionless. They remained in that hypnotic state, each sizing up the other's weapons and scrutinising any weaknesses.

Which animal pounced first I couldn't tell. It seemed like an instantaneous clash, a blur of fur and claws and teeth that kicked up a cloud of dust in front of me. Briefly, they separated, Shadow knocked back by a blow from Beth's paw, and then they were locked together again, both rearing up on their hind legs. Shadow's teeth sunk into Beth's shoulder as the leopard bit into the dog's back. The leopard let out a roar, releasing Shadow from her jaws, and rolled onto her back, taking the dog with her. I heard the howl of pain as Beth hooked her claws into Shadow's back and drew her close enough to fasten her mouth around her throat. The dog's eyes bulged and she tried to wriggle and kick her way free but Beth's technique was an innate part of her being, she was a leopard and she knew how to kill, how to suffocate her prey with quick and ruthless efficiency.

Shadow collapsed limply on top of her, but still Beth maintained her hold, squeezing the last breath from the dog. Then, satisfied there was no life left, she rolled over and stood panting over her victim, looking warily around for any sign of interlopers who may try and poach her kill. She glanced at me blandly, obviously regarding me as no threat. Then she tensed – her panting ceased, alert to the sound of approaching footsteps.

Between where the wall next to the gate met the aviary was a space, about nine inches wide, almost completely concealed by a thick curtain of clematis and ivy. I tried to stand, forgetting about the damage done to my calf, and fell sprawling back to the ground. I forced myself back up and dragging the useless leg behind I hobbled passed Beth to the gap, squeezed into the crevice and peered back out from the dense greenery, just as King appeared around the corner.

'What the...you fucking bitch!'

I don't know whether he meant Beth or if he was berating Shadow for her failure, it could easily have been either. It surprised me, I don't know why, but I expected more emotion over the death of his dog.

'Fucking bitch.' he repeated. 'Hey boy, you here?'

I froze, numbly aware of the trace of relief in his voice.

'Thought you'd left the party for a minute back then.' He was staring hard into the leaves where I was hiding. He took a step closer then stopped as Beth, guarding her kill, growled.

'Not a bad idea, bringing a leopard to a dog fight... Man, if I had my rifle with me she'd sure make a pretty trophy – have her stuffed and mounted before you could blink.'

He took another step. Beth hissed.

'Always been a passion of mine, hunting and tracking, got pretty good at it too, and going by this track I'd say Shadow did some good after all. Gonna be hard for you to get out of here with your leg all mashed up like that. I'm guessing your arm must be broke too, can't climb, can't fight, shit boy, you're running out of options.'

Beth's growls intensified; King backed away.

'Yup, always been a passion. Even as a kid I loved tracking, a broken twig, a blade of grass laying different to the rest, it's a real art, that's why you gotta start young. I've been doing it all my life, so you see it's just a matter of time before I find you...'

I held my breath, terrified that just a movement of a leaf would give me away.

'Playing dumb, huh? Not feel like talking? I don't see why you don't just come on out right now, you must be hurtin' some, might as well get it over sooner than later, save yourself a lot of pain...'

I could hear his voice growing fainter in the distance.

'Ain't no skin off my nose, you understand, shit I'm having a ball... and I ain't in no great hurry, got some other business to take care of anyways, you ain't the only fun to be had in this place...'

His voice faded away and he was gone. I didn't know what he meant and I didn't care, all that mattered to me was that he'd left. I looked up at the Capuchins who were watching King's movements and could see by the angle of their heads that he wasn't doubling back.

The space I had crawled into seemed to run the entire length of the back of the aviaries, a narrow tunnel overgrown with ivy, buddleia and clematis. I was confident that King wouldn't fit down the gap, and that would make it harder to track where I went. I could still hear his words, 'a broken twig, a blade of grass laying different to the rest'. I edged my way along, wondering where I could go. King was right about my lack of options. But I still had one. Julian's office.

After what felt like an hour, I re-emerged to where some stepping stones separated the path from the flower beds and led almost to the office door. No twigs or blades of grass to give me away, just the practicalities of balancing on one leg and hopping from stone to stone. A couple of times I slipped, then painstakingly squatted down and smoothed over the footprint in the soil until I was satisfied that it was undetectable.

At the door I suddenly had a surge of paranoia, convinced that the office was an obvious hideout, that King had anticipated my move and that behind the door would be another of his traps. Perhaps it was hunger or exhaustion, but I couldn't shake the idea from my mind.

A sudden outburst of the crickets snapped me back into action. Startled by the noise I grabbed the handle and yanked it to the right, then to the left and then sharply back again. It was locked. Julian, with his 'the door to my office is always fucking open' had betrayed me, shattered my last glimmer of hope. I had nowhere to go, nowhere to hide, I may as well do as King said, hand myself over, end this misery…and at that moment, as though mimicking my despair, the park exploded with a wail.

Like some deranged animal asylum. All around me caged animals were committing acts of wanton violence, clawing, tearing, biting, launching themselves at their bars and all of it, every hateful, malicious scream of frenzied torment and rage seemed to be directed at me. Hundreds of possessed eyes pleaded that I should come to them, allow them the opportunity to sink their claws and teeth into my flesh.

Something heavy fell onto my back, a blur of black and beige that bit and scratched at my head. I grasped hold of a clump of fur and launched a Capuchin across the path where it was joined by two others. I flattened myself against the door, searching for some kind of weapon and grabbed the only thing to hand, a plant pot that sat on the ground. Something underneath it, a flash of silver caught my eye, a key. I slid it into the lock, turned the handle and collapsed through the door, kicking it shut behind me.

I lay on the floor until the ruckus subsided. Five, maybe ten minutes, then everything went quiet. Painfully I got up, shuffled over to the door and locked myself in. I was safe…for now.

CHAPTER 44

Christ, it's so stifling in here. How does Julian stand it – even if there was a window I couldn't dare open it.

Is it the weather? Could it be that simple – affecting the crickets? No, it's cooler since the storm – it can't be that. But it always starts with the crickets...then the other animals. How? If I knew how it might help – help make sense.

Crickets...insects – what is it about them? What makes them special? They can tell when there's going to be an earthquake. I've heard that.

People on fault lines use them as an alarm. They're sensitive to tremors – but there's no earthquake. What then?

Vibration? What causes vibration – sound – infrasound? That could explain the crickets...but why the other animals? Christ, what if it's not just the animals! What if it's affecting us? The party, the primal lust, the sex between Susie and me, Andy's madness, King's relentless hate. Could it all be linked, enhancing our primitive anxieties – without us even realising...if that's true can I trust myself to do what's right, to do what is rational?

I've been trapped in Julian's office for about 30 hours – it feels like forever. I keep telling myself the longer I'm here the better – at least I'm alive – give my injuries a chance to heal – maybe help will come. But the truth is,

*I'm just counting down the minutes till the inevitable –
till he finds me.*

I finished this journal early this morning – but I couldn't
sleep, King wouldn't let me – either through my own
paranoia that at any moment he's going to burst in, or
from one of his calls to me on the walkie-talkie.

'King to Matt…King to Matt…'

Yes, I'm still here, you bastard. Still alive. But you
can't find me, can you. With your Vietnam expert
tracker training, I've outsmarted you…

I never answer any of his calls. I doubt if he either
wants or expects me to, they're just part of the process
of psyching me out – taunts of how he's going to 'fix'
me, or the demands for me to come out and face him
like a man. Those no longer have any effect on me, I'm
used to them, desensitised. It's his monologues, the
'world according to King'. The glimpses into his
obscene, twisted mind. It's those that drive me crazy. He
always starts off the same – just a long, monotone
ramble about righting wrongs, about respect and justice
– wild justice as he calls it. Then his voice – it changes.
It's like he's not talking to me – not talking to anyone –
just hate filled reminisces of his time in Vietnam – of
how good he was at his job…how efficient. Of how he
got court-marshalled for being too efficient.

He rages on like this for ages, like he forgets I'm even
listening. I try not to… I try to block him out, look for
distractions, search the office for hidden treats, ideally
cigarettes, but all I found were sweets in increasingly
weird places -loose toffees in between files in his filing
cabinet, liquorice allsorts buried under stationary.

I even found a sherbet fountain crushed between the pages of an animal encyclopaedia.

At first it amused me – then it made me nervous. The more I sit in his office, go through his stuff, the more I realise how pathetic, how ineffectual Julian is. What if his fear of King and desire for a quiet life overrules his sense of right and wrong? Can I trust him to do the right thing? I'm relying on him to give this journal to the police – to expose King if I don't make it.

It's finished; this is my last entry. I don't know what's going to happen to me, what I'm going to do next. All I know is King won't get away with what he's done. Not when this is found. I've beaten him. Now I need to think – concentrate – got to decide where to hide this journal.

CHAPTER 45

Genius. I'm a bloody genius. No one will look there. King wouldn't check an envelope, not addressed to Julian's accountant. Why the hell would he? I've got him. It'll take a while but it will be delivered. And King will be exposed...eventually. I've got him.

I should celebrate... put on the radio. I've earned it. I want to hear music...voices...normality. If it's on quiet King will never hear it, not from outside. And it will help me think. Focus ... work out what I'm going to do.

Christ! It's kicking off again... seems to be getting louder...each time more intense... more hysterical. The screams and howls. I know how they feel...I want to scream and howl too. Maybe living like this – being captive. Maybe I'm becoming more in-tune with the animals? Shit. Maybe I'm turning into an animal?

Lack of choice...was that what Gajadhar was talking about? His 'sounds of the forest' theory. No – not choice – loss...losing touch with that part of you which made you who you are. That's what he meant. Christ, I get that!

Is that how animals feel? I'm part of a gregarious species; I can understand loneliness, security in numbers, loss. But a solitary species, a leopard, like Beth – a leopard doesn't have emotional needs, does it? Why would you have emotions if you live your life on your own? But look at Al and Beth – the joy that companionship brought to her. Does captivity force a change in emotional needs; with the loss of a natural state does the company of others act as a kind of surrogate for the 'sounds of the forest', drawing comfort from something that, in the wild, she wouldn't tolerate?

And why would a leopard, why did Beth, act like she did, put herself at risk. Was it just mistaken identity – Al's jacket? What emotion compelled her to protect me? Is it just because she's hand-reared – giving her an unnatural bias towards humans, or has she picked up on some of our emotions like some kind of zoonotic disease?

Christ! This isn't helping – it doesn't make any sense. So what if animals have complex emotions, it doesn't help – not if it's Uddanda. If he's the source...then it's not about emotions – it's about control. And how the hell does an elephant control others?

He'd need to be self-aware. No, more than that – he'd have to know that other things feel, tap into their fears. Is that even possible?

They mourn – I've seen it on TV – a mother standing over her dead calf for days. Is that bereavement – understanding death...mortality? Christ – she might just be waiting for it to get up for all we know?

And what about elephant graveyards? Is that just bollocks – elephants sensing their own deaths. What if it's true?

La, da, da, da – this song on the radio, I know it – heard it recently. Ignore it – don't lose your train of thought. You're onto something...

Apes are self-aware, and they can understand the feelings of others. So why not elephants – why can't they have a greater emotional awareness? No one knows when emotions evolved – elephants may even have begun the evolutionary process earlier. Maybe they have a better understanding...understanding of what? Revenge? Bitterness?

Uddanda... Uddanda, nemesis of evil and vices.

Why not? Christ – am I going mad – can I trust myself – why not?

Susie's idea – infrasound – it fits. Their evolution – their nomadic lifestyle – loose family groups that need to stay in contact. Their physiology – if whales can adapt a vocal means for long distance communication then why not a terrestrial species – producing and receiving frequencies over a vast distance. Why not?

Tremors. Vibrations – that would explain the crickets – their alarm.

I know where I heard this song – it's from the party – Al played it. 'I'd rather be a free man in my grave...than living like a puppet or a slave'.

That's all I am, a puppet to entertain King. Just by staying here I'm giving him pleasure – the satisfaction of the manhunt. I don't have to stay – not anymore. I've written down the facts, King won't get away with it now.

I can turn this around – I can win – I have an advantage. I know about the crickets – the vital few seconds of warning they give before the madness begins... And I know about Uddanda. If I could release him, succeed where Andy failed. Give Uddanda a chance to right the wrongs done – to dispense justice, his own kind of wild justice. That's what I'll do. Andy was right.

I must release Uddanda . . .

PART FOUR

The torn boughs trailing o'er the tusks aslant,
The saplings reeling in the path he trod,
Declare his might—our lord the Elephant,
Chief of the ways of God.

Rudyard Kipling, The Elephant

CHAPTER 46

Tuesday 7th

Matt was jolted abruptly from his thoughts as the walkie-talkie crackled into life.

'Hey college boy... you receiving, you ready for a little chat with King yet, or are you still sulking?'

A feverish sweat coated Matt's forehead. He held the walkie-talkie to his mouth and depressed the button on the side. 'Fuck you!'

He slammed the radio back down on the desk, flicking the switch to the off-setting and cutting short King's derisive laughter.

It was just before dusk when he grabbed the walkie-talkie and crept tentatively from Julian's office and back into the park. Crouching, limping, it was in stark contrast to the man who had strode out of that same door on the day of his interview, proud and confident that he would be offered the job of his dreams.

He crept cautiously, tucked up tightly against the low walls of the enclosures, hunched within the fall of the long shadows. Even the animals were silent; they weren't sleeping and yet they weren't awake, suspended in some place in between the two states. Everything was still, compounding the noise of the gravel as it ground beneath his wary steps.

Crunch

Past the otters

Crunch
Past the tamarins
Crunch
Past the lynx

Blank eyes staring at him, apparitions with expressions of listless detachment.

He came to the 'staff only' door and hesitantly turned the handle. The door swung open with a squeal from the hinges that seemed to last an eternity. He braced himself, half expecting to be greeted by the sadistic grin of King waiting for him on the other side. He raised his arm and clenched his fist, determined to strike first, to punch, kick, scratch and tear at his foe with all the hate-fuelled strength he had left, then his arm fell back to his side – no one was there. He continued nervously through the gloom, down the short corridor and out onto the path that ran past the zoo kitchens, his head reeling with the memories that the place evoked: his first walk with Susie to meet the elephants: Andy preparing food with Lucky perched on his shoulder, the rat greedily anticipating the next piece of melon that her master plucked from his chopping board: Al looming over the table next to him, a huge joint between his lips and booming along to T Rex on radio one: Roger, Jez and Tommy playing French cricket with a cucumber and some grapes, heedless of Julian's sudden appearance to 'jolly everyone along'. The memories evoked the smells of the zoo kitchen and his stomach groaned with desire. He forced the thoughts out, quickening his pace past the kitchen and towards the elephant house…almost there.

The doors were open. A sign, Matt concluded, that either King never even considered such a brazen assault on his territory, or that it was another trap. As he approached the outer door, the neglect of the routine cleaning was immediately apparent. The air that had previously been thick with the scent of molasses and fresh hay was now swamped by the odour of urine. He waited a moment, allowing his senses to acclimatise. He peered into the dimness and listened for any indication that he wasn't alone.

The first time that he had visited the elephants and stood in this porch he had found the clanking of chains and low rumbles that emitted from within thrilling, this time however it was a completely different kind of exhilaration. His pulse quickened, he was trembling, Uddanda knew he was there, Matt was certain of it, he knew who it was and he knew his purpose for coming. He felt transparent and exposed, envisaging the elephant's eyes fixed upon him from the other side of the wall, searching deep into his soul. Apprehensively, he peered around the huge metal door, and into the barn. There was barely any light, it felt as though he was staring into a vast chasm, teetering on the edge of an abyss. A wave of dizziness surged through him and he steadied himself against the door frame. The vertigo subsided as his eyes adjusted to the darkness. Gradually he began to make out vague shapes, the nearest corner with the stacked mound of hay, to his left a stash of pitchforks and shovels. As his eyes grew more accustomed to the low light, one particular shape attracted his attention. A silhouette of a man, a broad, powerful back leaning over something indiscernible that lay on the floor at his feet.

A pile of straw... A sack... An animal?

Matt's instinct was to back away – he still hadn't been seen, he could still return to the relative safety of the office, check the phone; it had been a mistake to come. Had he checked the phone before leaving? He couldn't remember, he had been in such a state it was possible that he hadn't. What if it were fixed... but it wasn't too late, he could still go back. But his hate was driving him on, demanding he grasp the fork that lent against the wall and drive it deeply between the shoulder blades of his foe, but neither emotion would give way, he stood rooted to the spot by the contradiction.

Suddenly, the silhouette moved to the left, and at that same moment he heard a moan from the shape lying on the floor, barely audible, but enough to snap Matt out of his frozen state. The moan was instantly recognisable and Matt's eyes began to make out the curls of hair and the curve of the waist... the figure lying on the floor was unmistakable. Susie... It was Susie!

Matt felt a surge of purpose and hope. The figure that loomed over Susie, his back to Matt, just one man, a man who has taunted, tortured, killed...but just a man.

Silently Matt picked up the fork and began his approach. He neither blinked nor breathed, he didn't dare; he just focused on the moment, on his one chance. At each step nearer he raised the fork a little higher above his head, oblivious to the aching throb in his left arm, he must not fail. Ten steps, then eight, then six, he was almost within striking distance, five, four...

'Ahh Matt,' said a warmly familiar voice, 'I am so very relieved that you are finally here, although I must admit to have been expecting you sooner.'

Gajadhar turned around, looking from Matt then to the fork as it clattered to the ground.

'And what,' added the mahout rather sternly, 'were you planning to do with that?'

Matt was momentarily too dumbstruck to answer. 'But…they went to the flat…they caught you…I thought you were dead!' he said.

'They may have gone to the flat but I wasn't there to be caught, and so it would seem, to quote the delightful Mark Twain, that rumours of my death are greatly exaggerated.' His jovial expression quickly changed to one of concern as he looked Matt up and down. 'But please, you must forgive my flippancy, I had no idea that your injuries were so severe.'

'It's nothing.' Matt knelt next to Susie, discarding the walkie-talkie that dug into his hip. 'Is she's alright? Christ…why's she unconscious!.' He noticed a chain, padlocked around her ankle and secured to the steel girder next to her, and he began to feel incensed, turning irrationally on Gajadhar. 'Why didn't you escape, go and get help?'

The mahout looked taken aback by the accusation in Matt's eyes. 'I felt it better to remain, for Susie and for you…And you are forgetting that I am not familiar with these surroundings, my only experience beyond the walls of the park was on my arrival and, although I did not pay much attention then, I had the overall impression that I could easily get myself lost and as likely as not find myself walking deeper into the moorlands.'

'I'm sorry,' said Matt, 'you're right.'

'Do not give it another thought,' said Gajadhar. 'Your frustration is quite natural, but Susie will be fine.

I have kept her in this unconscious state myself to aid her recovery, the swelling has greatly reduced and her fever has now passed. It is a simple matter of understanding pressure points,' he added, 'I was actually in the process of bringing her around when you arrived.'

Gajadhar knelt down and began gently caressing her scalp. In the dim light his fingers took on the appearance of tentacles hovering over Susie's head and for the first time Matt acknowledged the mystical aura that the mahout commanded.

'It is extraordinary the rejuvenation powers of the young,' said Gajadhar, concluding his manipulation and scooping some fresh straw under her head, 'but of course she has also had the benefit of having Uddanda watching over her.'

Matt looked over into the dim recess; it was too dark to see anything clearly but even the darkness couldn't conceal the force of the presence that stood staring back out at them. He felt a shiver run down his spine. 'It's him, isn't it. It's Uddanda who has been…influencing all the other animals. Have you seen it? Is it like Susie said? Is he communicating using infrasound?'

'It would appear so. I admit to feeling slightly ashamed that I have never made the connection myself but…I suppose that it is the nature of spirituality that it can, occasionally, lead us into complacency, leaving too much in the lap of the gods and therefore into accepting without questioning. But of course, one should also never underestimate the usefulness of a fresh young pair of eyes,' he looked down at Susie, 'and it was a truly remarkable observation.' Tenderly he picked out a stray piece of straw from her hair before continuing. 'Yes, I have witnessed what you aptly call his influence; I have seen the subtle vibration of the trunk, felt its power and yet heard nothing, and then…a minute later… the park is alive with the screams and cries from the other animals.'

'But is it conscious behaviour, I mean is he aware of what he is doing, the effect he is having, is it…' Matt hesitated, almost embarrassed by the word, 'is it revenge?'

'You credit me with more wisdom than a humble mahout has a right to be credited with,' said Gajadhar, the familiar twinkle back in his eyes. 'I cannot tell you what is fact but, if you are interested in my opinion, then I shall be happy to share with you my feelings, but only on the condition that you allow me to take a look at your own injuries.'

Matt looked nervously at the door and then to Susie. 'But shouldn't we be… what if…?'

'Do not worry about Susie,' said Gajadhar. In response to a loud splashing sound the mahout stood up, muttering thanks to Joti, who had just commenced urinating. He removed his shirt and held it under the cascade, talking casually to Matt as he did so. 'And if Mr King returns we shall have plenty of warning, the elephants will make sure of that, they have a way of expressing the approach of evil. That is how I knew that it was you and not Mr King who was coming…you see they become extremely agitated when they sense his presence.' He returned to Matt with his urine-soaked cloth. 'Now, 'he added, 'shall we first look at the cause of your limp?'

Matt automatically snatched his leg away from the mahout. 'What are you doing, that's elephant piss!'

'I am aware of that,' replied Gajadhar testily, 'it is also antibacterial and antiviral and has many other cleansing and healing properties, now if you would allow me?

Reluctantly Matt rolled up the leg of his jeans and lent back onto his elbows whilst the mahout, tutting at the wound, began dabbing the cloth onto Matt's tattered leg whilst resuming with the discussion.

'You ask me if Uddanda acts out of revenge. I cannot blame you for thinking that, and at first it was also what I believed, it is after all as his name suggests, and certainly he has every right.'

Matt winced and jerked his leg.

'I am sorry, I will try to be gentler...So, dear Uddanda, only a calf, wrenched from his home, witnessing the slaughter of his family, brought up in environments full of unfamiliarity and fear, raised in a world with no understanding, no kindness. All his life torture has been his only constant, torture in his dreams, torture in his reality,' He glanced over at Uddanda. 'Truly, no creature has suffered or should ever suffer the pain that this poor creature has been subjected to, and no creature has a greater right to claim his revenge for that pain, and yet...I have been fortunate to have shared my entire life with elephants, I have known many and, as with people, some have been good and some bad, and the bad ones...' Gajadhar paused as if reliving some memory. 'Let me assure you that there is nothing in nature to compare with the magnificent, life affirming terror of an elephant baring down on one with his eyes ablaze with wicked intent. But with Uddanda, despite his right, despite his name, when I look into his eyes I

294

see only nobility, nobility and a deep, deep sorrow. I believe he is profoundly troubled, but to intentionally and randomly kill, for me it is inconceivable that he would do that without extreme provocation.'

'But aren't you forgetting,' said Matt, 'he has killed, that other keeper, and almost Tommy.'

'But that was different. Have you never heard of the plea of temporary insanity? That is what musth is, temporary insanity; there was no intention there, no malice. And look at how he reacted when he understood what he had done, he shut himself down, cocooned himself in remorse. He knew that to kill a man was wrong, but he was powerless to change what had happened. What was there left for him to do? It was, as I perceive it, a coping mechanism, when emotions become too powerful then there are only ever two options, allow them to devour you or, if you are strong enough, find a way to bury them.'

Matt shuddered, the concept was only too real to him and he wondered which way he would have gone, which option would have won the battle within him, had his imprisonment continued.

'And then,' continued the mahout, 'Devi died... a terrible, terrible death. I think that it was the horrors of that event that provided the jolt required to bring Uddanda back to the present after a year of self inflicted exile. Perhaps to provide comfort to Kali and Joti, or perhaps not comfort but protection, the urge to look after his family that is so strong in elephant culture. As for the reasons for his emitting these calls, I could not say whether it is a cry for help or an attempt to contact and reassure the spirit of Devi, but I believe that the deaths caused by the animals in the park is a by-product of the infrasound and not I think, and as you have suggested, as an act of revenge.

Matt flinched as Gajadhar dug deeply into his cut with a corner of his shirt.

'I am sorry, it is a piece of grit that is stubbornly embedded, there...got it!'

'Thanks,' said Matt, rolling the trouser leg back down. He was silent for a moment. 'But you say that, under provocation, he may kill?' he asked tentatively.

'Under extreme provocation, who knows how one may react? I have always regarded myself as a peaceful man but even I was so repulsed by the atrocities that they committed on poor Andy's person that I was forced into feelings that are repugnant to my philosophies.

'You were here when they caught him?'

'I have been here all the time.' Gajadhar cast his eyes to the floor. 'I am afraid that the events that have occurred here do not reflect well on me. I am ashamed to say I lied to you, telling you that I was returning to our flat after the party when in fact my intention was always to come here, to the elephants.'

'It's lucky for you and Susie that you did, otherwise...' Matt shuddered.

'Perhaps, but my presence here couldn't help poor Andy... I shall never forgive myself for not intervening when I had the chance.' Gajadhar looked at Matt. 'Perhaps I should explain what happened.

CHAPTER 47

'I had been concealing myself amongst the hay, tending to Susie when they left to search for you. Then they returned with Andy... They had caught him just outside the zoo kitchens so I never had an opportunity to warn him. It will haunt me forever, the sound of his screams, but I had to keep reminding myself that my priority was Susie's welfare, and later, when I heard them discussing what had happened...I never dreamt that they would actually kill him.'

'I know what you mean. I was only a few yards away when it happened. But if we had tried to help then we would be just as dead as Andy, and King would have got away with it.'

'You are right in what you say, but it doesn't make it any less a burden.' Gajadhar looked into Matt's eyes. 'He was very brave you know, physically there was nothing that they could do to make him talk, in the end it was what they threatened to do to his rat that made him confess, but even then I think that he held back. It is the only source of comfort to me that such a tragedy reaffirms the true depth of the human and, for that matter, the animal spirit. That it can tolerate all manner of horrors for itself but if others are threatened then it is compelled to protect them, forsaking any thoughts for self-preservation. There is great beauty in such an unselfish and altruistic death,' Gajadhar paused before adding, 'and is she safe, Andy's rat?'

The question sounded ridiculous, and from anyone else's lips and under different circumstances it would have hinted of sarcasm or flippancy, but Matt knew Gajadhar well enough to recognise the genuine concern in his voice.

'As far as I know, Andy said he'd left her in her cage in his flat... Christ, if we ever get out of this I'll build her a rat palace, I owe him that.' Even now he found it difficult to associate Andy with words such as beauty and unselfish, suspecting Andy's stoicism was more likely borne out of an insane hate for his captors.

Susie groaned and Matt turned back to her, hoping to see her eyes flicker open but she just shifted her position slightly and then was still again. He thought that he noticed a slight change in her expression; her forehead had become furrowed by long wrinkles that hinted of troubled thoughts, but he couldn't be sure because it was now very dark, the only source of light coming from the moonlight bouncing off the metallic surfaces as it filtered in through the large opening of the door. Even the colossal forms of the elephants were swallowed up as they stood within the blackness, a slight clink of their chains growing in its intensity.

'You've got to go,' said Matt as a sense of urgency suddenly gripped him. 'I'll look after Susie while you get help.'

Gajadhar's reply was long in coming. 'I would much rather stay with you.'

'Yeah, well I don't exactly relish staying here alone, but it would take me forever on this leg, so what choice do we have? And it's pretty much dark now, chances are that King won't see you.'

'No, but I won't see *him* either, the disadvantage is too great. Really…I think it would be much better that we stay together.'

'Look, I see what you're saying, but either you try and find help or we stay and fight.'

'But what about the darkness? It will make it even harder for me to traverse. And the lanes, they are likely still to be flooded after the rain' insisted the mahout.

'Maybe, but you'll find a way, I know you will.'

Gajadhar sighed. 'You have forced me to make a rather shameful confession. I believe from what I have overheard that the leopard reared by Al is roaming free, having killed her unfortunate master.'

'I'm afraid so, yes.'

'Excuse me, that was meant as a rhetorical question. I am aware that it is true, I am merely trying to explain something rather…difficult. Do you remember, on our drive here, I told you of a leopard that Amish and I hand reared? Well, that was not the end of the tale. After it was discovered by my mother we were instructed to dispose of it; the wisdom of our elders knew the dangers that would exist in such an animal that had lost all its natural fear of humans. However, we were young and had not the heart to carry out our instructions to the letter and instead we released it at a distance that, in our innocence, we regarded as safe.'

'I think I know where this is going,' said Matt with resignation, 'sort of Androcles and the lion, but in reverse.'

'Unfortunately, you are right. It was about two years later and I was on my own, returning from my schooling at Amish's house when the leopard… *our* leopard appeared. I knew that it was ours, he had a slight deformity in his tale, a kink six inches from the end, and my heart leapt with the joy of seeing him again. Maybe I startled him, I would like to believe that perhaps he didn't recognise me, but as I rushed to greet him in childish enthusiasm he responded as any wild animal whose innate fear of humans had been removed…It was Lalite who saved me – you recall her? I showed you an old photograph that I have of her during our journey from the airport. I believe it amused you that I considered an elephant as my surrogate mother, but perhaps now you can understand why I should feel that way. She came charging through the undergrowth, she must have sensed the danger long before it occurred, and the leopard took off, leaving me badly mauled. Lalite scooped me up and took me to my parents. It was my first experience of wild altruism and it affected me deeply. It humbled me that such a magnificent creature should care enough about, not only one so insignificant as myself, but also a different species, as to come to its aid.'

'And after that…' urged Matt, sensing Gajadhar was about to digress onto the subject of altruistic behaviour.

'Ahh, well, as for the leopard, I discovered later that the night I spent recuperating, my and Amish's father's, along with a few others, hunted down the beast and killed it. They didn't tell me at the time, I think to spare me any more distress. They knew how strongly I felt about animals, and in time I recovered and my scars healed, all but one.'

'You're terrified of leopards,' offered Matt.

'One could say that I have a slight phobia, yes,' admitted Gajadhar sheepishly.

'Okay, then that decides it. We go to plan 'B'. We fight.'

The Mahout shuffled uneasily.

'What?' sighed Matt.

'It is not that I am scared,' said Gajadhar defensively, 'at least not for myself, it is simply that I do not believe I could be of any use to you – if anything, quite the opposite.'

'What are you talking about, you've got shoulders like a Sumo wrestler.'

'You misunderstand, it is not a question of strength but of will – to take on a man like Mr King one must be willing to do real harm to him, any weakness of intent, any hesitation on my part would be fatal, it may even get *you* killed.'

'But surely…after what he's done?'

'Even with that knowledge I know that deep down that I could never be responsible for killing another being, whatever his crime.'

Gajadhar was resolute and Matt, sighing with frustration, knew it.

'Okay, okay, so we can't get help and we can't fight… any suggestions?'

The mahout's eyes brightened. 'I can pray. I find great solace in prayer, and it can often lead to finding answers.'

'Great, you get yourself all solaced-up and I'll try and think of a plan C.'

Suddenly Gajadhar leapt to his feet, almost bowling Matt over as he rushed off into the blackness.

'What the…what is it?' Matt squinted into the darkness after his friend. He became aware of the cool, agitated air, air stirred up by the swaying of a trunk, the flap of ears, the sway of an immense head. Then the trunk lifted high, the sound of a deep intake of breath, releasing a bellow like a siren.

'Quickly, we must hide,' hissed the mahout.

Matt felt a powerful grip on his arm as Gajadhar tugged him across the floor towards the large pile of hay. Before he could ask what was happening he was thrust forcefully into the soft heap, followed immediately by the mahout.

'Quick, dig!'

Like startled mice burrowing into the safety of their nest they twisted and wriggled their way down, reaching its core just as the figure of King appeared, a flickering of light, followed by a decisive buzz and the barn was bathed in an orangey neon glow.

'Hi honey, I'm home!'

Matt shuddered at the notion that King was genuinely enjoying himself.

He felt completely vulnerable. In the lair of the hunter...unable to see and guessing King's whereabouts by the sound of his footsteps, getting louder...louder. The dust and the kernels caught in his throat; he needed to cough...*had* to cough. The slightest noise would be his death sentence. The footsteps...still getting closer. He had to cough...he felt it coming, an involuntary action...if he smothered his mouth with his hands, muffled the noise...

Then the footsteps stopped, somewhere in the middle of the barn and near where Susie lay, where the acoustics released a more prominent echo. A sound, something like a shoe scraping along the floor, then muttered words that Matt, straining, failed to pick out. This was followed by a long moment of silence and then the footsteps again, receding back to the entrance.

A squeal resonated around the barn, the sound of metal wheels stubbornly grinding into action as King closed the huge door, trapping them inside as it closed with a decisive bang.

The remnants of the metallic echo faded away and King's voice took over, calm and thoughtful, dotting Matt's skin with goose bumps.

'Hey college boy, you know you gotta be more careful where you leave your walkie-talkie laying around. Anyone could find it.'

CHAPTER 48

Heavy, lazy steps, accompanied by the scraping of metal against concrete, continued getting nearer. Matt couldn't see but he could picture the hulking figure, the wolfish grin, the pale greedy eyes, and in his hand, dragging behind him...what? With horror Matt remembered the pitchforks leaning against the wall.

The steps halted.

'Ain't but one place to hide in this barn. You gonna come out or am I gonna make you?

Groping in the hay, Matt found the mahout's arm, giving it a squeeze that he hoped conveyed to his friend to stay where he was. Then warily he crawled out from the haystack and stood up, spitting and coughing out husks whilst brushing off loose strands of hay that fell to his feet.

King didn't speak, not immediately; Matt felt his cold, piercing gaze bore into him, trying to read him.

Eventually King's thin lips stretched into a wide grin. 'I gotta say, this is the last place I expected to find you. Did you finally get yourself some backbone?'

Matt didn't answer. Caught between fear and rage he stared unblinking back at King.

'No, that don't ring true,' continued King, 'you look about as nervous as a chicken with a stock cube. So, what *are* you doing skulking around here? Ain't 'cos of Susie. Andy said you both thought she was dead, tell the truth I was about to radio you to let you know she was still alive, thought that might lure you from wherever it was you dug yourself into.' He scratched his head with exaggerated puzzlement. 'Where in hell were you, anyway? You may not be one for fighting, but man, you could give a chameleon a run for its money when it comes to concealing yourself.'

Matt continued staring blankly, determined not to give anything away. If King didn't know of his hiding place then he would never find the journal.

'Not talking huh, lost your voice? No matter…let's see if I can't work it out for myself?' He folded his arms with the relaxed manner of a man who knew that he'd won. 'Let's see now, what made the quarry come to the lion's den? If you were here to confront me then why hide. An ambush? Nope, you know well enough you couldn't ambush an old pro like me. There must be something here, some kind of weapon, something you couldn't find anywhere else…' King's eyes darted around the barn, then his gaze fell on the massive form of Uddanda and a smile crept over his face. 'Hey, you got the same fanciful idea as Andy, figured you'd let Dan do your killing. Guess it could've worked,' he added with a grin of satisfaction, 'worked once for me.'

'What…what do you mean?' Matt stared at King, trying to gauge the implication. 'What worked for you?'

King grunted out a derisive laugh. 'Hey, you found your tongue, good, now we can have a proper conversation, man to man.'

'What did you mean by that,' repeated Matt, 'how did it work for you?'

'Shit, Matt, thought you were supposed to be bright, even Andy figured *that* out.'

'You mean Jack? What happened to Jack and Tommy? I don't understand…it was an accident…'

'Course it was an accident.' King smiled blandly and his eyes glazed over with nostalgia. 'Poor old Dan, man he got it bad. Do you know they reckon that a bull's testosterone can rise to sixty percent above the normal during musth? With him I reckon it was more like eighty percent, maybe more, never seen a bull like it. Natives say it's a time when they remember, where their past comes back to haunt them. Shit, Dan must have had one hell of a life to put him in that kinda rage. I figured anyone who came within striking distance wouldn't stand much of a chance once the mood took him. All I had to do to improve those odds was take off his chains, pull out the light fuse and send Jack and Tommy in with some half-baked instructions. Let Dan do the rest. Yup, one hell of an accident.'

'Christ, you're insane,' he cried, 'why would you do that, why would you want to kill them? To satisfy your sick blood lust? Your twisted sick hobby?'

'Careful, college boy, you don't know what the hell you're talking about.'

His voice had become quiet, venomous. Matt held his tongue.

'You didn't know Jack,' he continued, 'he was a sanctimonious fucker like you, didn't approve of my techniques, thought he knew better. He never joined in with the training, reckoned it was barbaric. And then I started to notice Tommy holding back, not showing willing, questioning my orders, and I knew that Jack had turned him against me. I used to catch them in cosy little huddles, whispering, plotting, undermining my authority. I recognised the signs, seen it happen before, in Vietnam... my platoon... my own men.' Briefly he was silent, his forehead furrowed by the memory before snapping back to the present. 'I'd be damned if I was going to let it happen again.... You know why man is the top predator? It's because we're opportunists, we see a moment of good fortune and we grab it. See what I mean?'

'All I see is a psychopath on a killing spree.'

'Boy, you got it all mixed up. A psychopath, he kills for kicks. I don't get no pleasure from it, but I won't be wronged, I won't be wronged. And Jack, he wronged me, about to go and spill his guts to the boss. Tommy, now that was a shame, a nice boy, but weak, easily swayed. He's what we call collateral damage.'

'You're kidding yourself. I saw the look in your eyes when you murdered Andy.'

King laughed. 'You got me there boy. I guess every now and then killing can be a pleasure. That little weasel had it coming – been sniffing around for months. The others may have suspected something, but they knew their place, respected me enough to keep quiet. Andy, he just couldn't keep his goddamn mouth shut.'

'And that gives you the right to kill him?' Matt was surprised to see King thinking through his question, scratching his chin like a college professor considering a student's point of view.

Finally, King answered. 'What you and your kind never understand is that killing is easy. It's natural, a law of nature, you know, survival of the fittest. The problem's not the killing, it's the getting away with it. Try walking in my boots, see things from my perspective.

You coming onto my girl, the mahout brought in to undermine me, even Andy conspiring against me. I could feel you all snapping at my heels, trying to topple me from my position, stripping me of my respect. Then, and how about this for luck, the animals start going crazy, start killing. The perfect cover for re-asserting my position, thinning out the deadwood.'

'What, so you're blaming fate for your murders?'

'Like I said, I'm an opportunist. I don't believe in fate.'

'Gajadhar would disagree with you...' Matt regretted saying it the moment the words leaked from his mouth.

'The mahout?' A streak of concern flashed across King's eyes, 'What do you know about that son of a bitch, have you seen him?'

'Not since he left the party.' Matt concentrated on giving his voice the right amount of baffled concern, trying not to falter under King's suspicious gaze.

'No. Guess you can't have' King answered hesitantly. 'Anyway, If he was still alive I'd have found some sign by now – reckon the animals must've got him, dragged him into the undergrowth or up a tree, fancied an Indian take-away.' He let rip one of his rasping laughs.

'So, what about me? Matt said. 'How are you going to explain my death?'

King's mouth formed a wide grin that lay easily across his face, no hint of his usual snarl. It was the expression of genuine joy and before Matt could even question its motives, King gripped Matt by the throat.

Matt tried to fight back but King's fingers sunk deeper into his trachea, lights churned around his vision, a loud whooshing filled his ears, and his limbs went limp.

King released him and Matt slumped to the floor, coughing out the bile that flooded into his mouth.

'Don't worry, college boy, much as I'd like to wring your neck, your death has to be in keeping… it has to look like the animals did it.'

He grasped Matt by the arm and dragged him over to where Susie lay, still unconscious; deftly he adjusted the chains until Matt could feel each individual link draw tightly around his ankle and wrist.

'If it's any consolation, Susie ain't gonna feel a thing. You, on the other hand…' King laughed and walked over to the table. Seizing his mattock handle, he strode towards Kali.

Matt struggled against the chain, his tethered limbs burning with the effort. He knew what was in store, and judging by the sudden bedlam of that exploded outside, it seemed the entire population of the zoo realised as well. He looked at Uddanda, hoping to witness some form of insurgence, hoping that the source of the madness would rip his shackles from the wall and come to his rescue, but the bull was motionless. Matt looked over to the other elephants.

Kali's head was rolling wildly from side to side, mirroring Joti who stood swaying on the opposite side of the barn. As King drew closer the steady pendulum swings of Kali's trunk grew more erratic, taking heavy, futile swipes that fell well short of her tormentor. She tugged at the chain, trying to lessen the distance, then reared back in response to the stinging blow that landed on the tip of her trunk.

Kali took another swipe at King who nimbly avoided it and retaliated with another well-judged swing, followed by yet another, each proceeded by a command, 'nahii', no.'

Kali's hate retreated, subdued by the incessant blows and the contagious effect of Joti's fear. King had regained control.

He moved behind her, loosening the nut and bolt that dictated the length of her chain and peered over, judging the distance between her and his two captives, then dragged out a further ten feet.

The mattock handle slapped sharply against her flank as King boomed out an instruction, 'chalo, walk,' and in dull response Kali lumbered forward, each step vibrating through the floor and into Matt's body as she advanced slowly towards them.

He looked with desperation towards the hay pile, imagining Gajadhar laying within, repetitiously chanting his prayer, oblivious to the desperate situation. Matt was on his own; it was up to him to save both himself and Susie.

He began manically writhing from side to side, trying to draw Kali's attention, but her ponderous form kept growing, throwing a shadow over where they lay. Then an idea struck him, the journal. Matt thought of the techniques King would employ to extract the information of its location, but he swept the images aside, he had to end the immediate threat. He called out to King, his lips forming the words, but nothing intelligible came out, just a strangulated, rasping whisper, all that his bruised and swollen larynx could produce.

Kali was now towering over them, her foot lifted to take the next step, then she paused, allowing her trunk to roll exploratively over their bodies. Tenderly, it moved on to Susie's face, then slid slowly along her body, probing her with gentle caressing movements whilst inhaling her fragrance. She set her foot back down again carefully and manoeuvred around them, wincing with pain as King unleashed a second beating.

'Kali nahii, no.' He moved to her side and hooked his goad under her knee and began hollering new instructions. 'Kali, Utho, lift.'

She didn't respond.

'Do as I fucking say,' cried King returning to her flank. He launched the weapon at her, screaming for her subservience until his face glowed red. He went back to her foreleg and tried again, tucking the sharp metal point behind the leg and yanking it up. 'Utho Kali… lift!'

Hesitantly, she obeyed, slowly raising her foot and dangling it over Matt's torso.

King yanked the goad from her leg and began to stab her knee. 'Kali, Baith, down, Baith.'

Matt twisted beneath, attempting to move clear of the crushing foot, but each new position only left another part of him exposed to the pulverising weight that hung over him. The waiting became excruciating, unbearable, and still the foot hung suspended over them.

'Kali baith, baith.'

A long shrill cry came from Joti. It was a call that contained so much dismay that it instantly seemed to trigger something matriarchal that lay dormant within in Kali.

She roared back, a roar of confidence and defiance as she stepped away, mindfully lowering her foot onto the concrete floor as she reversed back into her corner.

'Wanna play the bitch, huh? Sure, I'll fucking play with you.' King rammed the goad back into its holster then shortened Kali's chain so that her movement was restricted to barely nine inches. 'Just gotta make you more fucking comfortable.' He tightened the nut, then stormed over to the table and seized the cattle prod. 'Look,' he announced, grinning through the sweat that ran down his face, 'I even got your favorite toy!' He pulled the trigger and a blue spark crackled from prong to prong.

Kali leaned away, as far back as the tether would allow, then launched herself forward allowing the momentum to carry her trunk towards King. He threw himself to one side and the trunk brushed harmlessly past him.

'My turn.' Stepping neatly to her rear he rammed the prod between her legs and pulled the trigger, holding it down with sadistic force until his knuckles turned white.

Kali bellowed and thrashed, hurling herself back against the wall in an attempt to crush King who rode relentlessly with her movement, pouncing clear and then ramming the prod back into her.

The stench of singed, burning meat drifted across the barn, the smoke swirling around Joti's head on its journey up into the rafters. She sucked in the smell as though she were inhaling a part of Kali, then wailed her anguish at what the taste evoked, a long melancholic shriek of desolation that ripped through the building like an aftershock.

'Enough... that is enough!'

Matt and King stared into the corner of the barn and towards the haystack which shook and surged into life. Hay scattered and tumbled as a figure slowly emerged, stepping towards them through a cloud of dust and straw husks.

King turned fully to face him, the redness of his pallor fading into white, as if he were seeing a ghost rising from a mossy grave.

'What kind of monster are you?' cried the mahout, stooping to pick up the pitchfork. He brandished it, bayonet style, pointing it at King. 'Is this the only language you understand?'

Matt looked over at King and noticed the familiar snarl back on his face. Then he turned back to Gajadhar. 'Be careful' His voice was rasping, too weak to be heard. He swallowed painfully and tried calling again. 'He's insane. Be careful.' Neither man heard him.

The mahout walked cautiously towards King. 'You know, Mr King, there is an old Hindu proverb that says, when an elephant is in trouble even a frog will kick him. I believe that you are just such a frog.'

King stood his ground. His composure had returned and his expression was now one of savage amusement.

'A frog huh? I kinda like that, an American bullfrog, takes me back to my childhood. You know the thing about the bullfrog is they'll eat pretty well anything that'll fit in their mouth. Yup, I'm a bit of an expert on those critters, used to go hunting for bullfrogs after prayers every Sunday...'

Matt watched the scene in front of him with a growing trepidation. He had heard enough of King's monologues to be wary of where they led. Gajadhar hadn't had his experience, wasn't aware of the subtlety of King's manner, of the tricks he played with one's psyche. He wished the mahout would stop him, just thrust the fork into King's chest and end this hell, but he knew he wouldn't, he knew that he was condemned to listen and to watch the scene play out to its inevitable conclusion.

'...can you picture it, me in my cut-off denim dungarees bursting out of that church door like the good lord himself were after me, grabbing my line and charging down to the river like a regular Huckleberry Finn...'

Matt looked over to Gajadhar. The mahout's expression was transparent, he was imagining King as that child, vulnerable and full of aspirations and potential. King was humanising himself, playing on the mahout's sentimentality and it was working. *Stab him... stab him now.*

'...Man, I loved those days, running feral like nature intended, and them bullfrogs, man they sure taste good. Hell, I guess when you're a kid everything tasted good, even the air has a kind of sweetness to it. Know what I mean? Sure you do, that's the thing about childhood, in those early years we all have the same feelings...the same dreams. I bet you always wanted to work with elephants, I know I did. From the moment I saw my first Tarzan movie with Johnny Weissmuller, he was the best.

Lex Barker was okay as well, damn sight better than that one on TV, what's his name, Ron Ely, man, what a faggot. No, Johnny was the best Tarzan for my money, you ever get them movies where you grew up?'

Gajadhar didn't answer at first, the surge of rage so unfamiliar to his nature had passed as quickly as it had risen. Lines appeared in his smooth forehead, looking from King, smiling broadly, almost warmly, and then to the exhausted form of Kali. 'Please,' he said, 'I would be grateful if you would stop talking.'

'I guess not huh,' continued King, 'not many drive-ins in the jungle. You know I envy you that, growing up there. I had to wait years before I saw my first elephant. The sheer size, the power, damn near bowled me over. That's the thing with us, the thing that sets us apart, ain't many who could command an animal like that. Man, I still get a kick having that much power under my control. Guess you do too, huh? Funny ain't it, the two of us, raised continents apart and yet alike in so many ways.'

'I am nothing like you,'

'You think not? Reckon we're about the same age, give or take, both of us live by natural law, both elephant keepers. It's only the experiences we've had, the journey from boys to men that separate us.'

'You are mistaken. I am not and could never be a violent man,' said Gajadhar quietly.

'No? All evidence to the contrary.' King flashed a glance at the pitchfork and barked out a laugh. 'You say you're not a violent man when you've got me pinned down with that, hell, you say that 'cause you ain't got the balls to take me on man to man.'

'I am not a violent man and I will not fight you,' insisted the mahout.

'You won't huh, well as I see it you ain't got much option. You either run me through with that fork and escape or you take a chance and fight me... hand to hand. That's quite a choice for a pacifist.' He spat the word out like he'd swallowed a bug. 'But let me tell you this, if you stab me, you better finish me off... you won't get no second chance.'

For a moment Gajadhar was silent. He looked down at the weapon in his hands, then over to Kali. Finally, he looked back at King, his eyes half closed as if in meditation. After a long pause, and to Matt's dismay, the pitchfork slipped from the mahout's hand and clattered to the floor.

King laughed mockingly. 'Hand to hand, that's perfect ain't it? More... natural.'

The mahout's eyes opened wide and sparkled with life. 'I'm not going to fight you,' he repeated, and he took a step towards King.

Matt felt he must be hallucinating, but it seemed that Gajadhar's mass was changing before his eyes. That his bulk increased with every step he took towards his foe.

The distance between them was now only six yards, then five. King was like a Pitbull, salivating with eager anticipation. When only two yards stood between them, he could restrain himself no more and launched himself at the mahout.

There was a blur of arms. King's muscular fists powerfully lashing out, each attack obstructed by the defensive motions of Gajadhar's shorter but no less powerful limbs. The struggle lasted no more than a few seconds, the frenzy suddenly halted and the two men stood motionless. Matt quickly assessed the situation, his heart sinking as he realised that the clash had merely been a struggle for positioning. And King, with his hands wrapped firmly around the others throat, had won.

And yet Gajadhar's eyes appeared to betray no fear, no concern, if anything they shone more brightly. King must have also noticed the change and his face reddened as he squeezed even tighter. Matt watched intently as the mahout placed his hands firmly on King's waist and leaned into him, his muscles bulging as he began to heave forward, pushing against King and forcing him backwards.

King readjusted his fingers, probing for some way of penetrating the thick swollen muscles and rhino-like hide that layered the mahout's neck. The veins in King's forearms stood proud; a sheen of sweat coated his forehead, his face now crimson. Still the mahout pushed, driving King's back up against the rough, hard blocks of the barn wall.

Matt tugged fruitlessly at his chains. Gajadhar couldn't resist that grip for much longer, the muscles in his neck must be screaming to be relaxed. Neither man was giving in, yet someone would have to... eventually one of them would have to.

Gajadhar's hands moved slowly, following the line of King's spine. Creeping up past his neck, they reached the base of his cranium and spread, each stubby digit working independently, seeking out the pressure points.

Matt watched, aghast, as the mahout's eyes slowly closed. Gajadhar was losing consciousness, mumbling something as his strength faded.

King pulled Gajadhar closer to him. What's that? What you saying?' He bent down and put his ear close to his lips.

The mahout's voice was quiet, raspy, but had lost none of its clarity. 'I told you I would not fight you, but to restrain, that is different.'

Then it happened. Matt stared wide-eyed as Gajadhar unfurled King's fingers and removed his hands from his throat, ducked under his arm and, grasping his wrists, gently lowered King's stiff, unreceptive body to the ground.

'You see, Mr King, for a peaceful man there is always a choice.'

CHAPTER 49

The mahout rushed past Matt in his hast to reach Kali, offering her gentle words of reassurance that Matt didn't understand, although the tone of concern was apparent.

'*Daro mat, ab tum salamat ho, bhut chala gaya.*'

Running his hands down the length of her trunk, he cupped the tip and softly blew into it, murmuring more words of solace until, finally, the elephant began to respond. The swaying eased and the rumbles sounded more content. Gajadhar moved along her flank, maintaining contact the whole time with his hands. Caressing her in sweeping circular motions he worked his way to the chain on her rear leg. Locating the nut and bolt he began working on its release.

Matt watched with growing frustration as the mahout struggled with the chain. His back throbbed and ached, his wrists and ankles were rubbed raw and stung. He turned his head towards King's incapacitated body, laying just as Gajadhar had placed him, on his back staring up into the rafters, his arms held up in front of him and his hands still gripping some invisible throat. He looked fossilised, trapped in time. Matt shuddered at the image and glanced down at King's trousers and at the pocket that contained the keys to the padlocks. He rolled his head back to the mahout and slapped the souls of his feet on the concrete floor, but Gajadhar, focused on his task, paid no attention. Giving up on him, Matt turned back to King, and froze. King's head was now facing him, staring at him. Then, very slowly, he blinked.

For a moment they both stared at each other, then King's finger twitched, then another. Bit by bit, his body began to respond, his movements becoming more fluid with each passing second as he shook off the debilitating influence of Gajadhar's spell. Urgently Matt tried shouting but his voice still wouldn't cooperate. He slammed his feet down repeatedly, desperate to attract Gajadhar's attention. The mahout didn't even look up.

King was struggling to his knees, rubbing the joints in his wrists, his eyes fixed malignly on the mahout's back.

Matt kicked and writhed, moaning with as much force as his bruised larynx would allow.

King was now on his feet. He bent down, staggered, regained his balance and bent down again, snatching up the pitchfork as he began his stalk.

In Matt's mind he screamed – a clear, loud sound, projecting his fear, his warning. But the reality was a small, gargled cry of helpless despair that barely reached the mahout's ears.

'Please Matt, a little patience would be helpful. I will deal with your chains once I have sorted Kali's.'

King limped past Matt, every step becoming more sure-footed. He was now only yards away.

Gajadhar look up, 'please, please look up?'

Even Kali's sudden relapse into agitation couldn't deter the mahout from his task. 'Shanti Kali, be calm, I am doing the best that I ca–'

Gajadhar's body stiffened, his shoulders arched as his hands briefly fumbled behind his back, trying to make sense of the pain. He turned his head and Matt met his eyes. There was no terror in them, no fear, but the sparkle was gone, replaced by a look of regret that Matt instinctively understood. He could almost hear the mahout's voice, *I have let you down, forgive me my friend*, and then he tumbled onto his side.

King wasted no time; dismissively, he kicked Gajadhar onto his stomach then grabbing the fork handle, he yanked it free, leaving the mahout groaning and coughing on the floor.

'Looks to me like we both severely underestimated each other,' he said, examining the blooded prongs with curiosity and pride. He gave Matt a sideways glance, it was only fleeting and yet unmistakable in its meaning... *I have won.*

'I know what you're thinking, boy,' he said. 'You think it's going to be tough explaining a dead mahout with fork prongs in his back.' He put his hand up to his nose and sniffed with contempt the blood on his fingers. He looked briefly at Kali then, burying his head in his hand he began to holler. 'Kali went mad, like all them other animals. She killed Matt and Susie, then turned on me. I grabbed the first thing I could, the pitchfork, and I tried to protect myself.' He wiped away imaginary tears. 'Then the mahout came out of nowhere, went crazy, leapt between me and the elephant and before I could stop...it was a horrible accident.' His voice relaxed back into its familiar drawl. 'Just need to set the scene...make it a little more convincing.'

He turned to Kali, adjusted his grip on the handle, planted his feet firmly on the ground and lunged with the pitchfork.

Kali's momentous cry tore through the barn, slamming into the walls and shattering against the steel girders, flooding the building until it dripped with the echo of her pain. As the cry slowly ebbed, another sound appeared. Low and powerful, it seemed to roll beneath the wave of Kali's wail like an undertow.

Matt felt as much as heard it, and so, is seemed, did every other creature, as the world outside the barn exploded with howls and roars, screeching and squawks. He glanced over to Susie, her eyelids began to flicker, then his attention was drawn back to King, standing at Kali's side, his eyes closed in rapturous delight as he whirled the pitchfork over his head as though conducting the cacophony.

As the noise gradually subsided, he lowered his arms and prepared to thrust again with the fork. Then he hesitated, becoming aware of the deep, thunderous growl that was resonating from the ground up; rising like flood water, slowly consuming the barn with its intensity until it became an omnipresent roar. King's head was jerking up, down, side to side, searching for the source, then he paused. Slowly he turned, peering into the darkest recess of the barn; towards the bull.

Uddanda lunged. The chain snapped taut between his ankle and the breezeblock wall. He took a step back and again threw himself forward, hurling his six tons against the strength of the mortar. The wall shook and a web of stress-lines appeared. The third attempt was his last – a cascade of crumbling rubble, and the elephant was free.

King took a step back, then another. He raised the pitchfork above his shoulder, javelin style, preparing for the charge. But the elephant just stared, his ears flattened against the side of his head, his trunk curled underneath.

'What's the matter you son of a bitch... scared?' He hurled the fork, then, snatching his ivory handled goad from his side, he pounced.

Uddanda brought his head down, sweeping it to one side and catching King across his midriff with his tusk. The impact sent King sprawling across the floor, his head colliding with a girder. He tried to get to his feet but his legs buckled and he slid back to the ground. Slowly he looked up. Uddanda was looming over him.

The bull's thick, heavy trunk reached down, probing King's body for purchase. It flipped him over, slid under his chest, and enveloped him in a swift, rolling movement, lifting him high into the air.

A popping sound, then another as the trunk tightened around King's chest. King screamed and threw his arms down, both hands gripped around the ivory handle as he drove the point of the hook through the elephant's hide. Uddanda applied more force, more popping sounds. King bellowed, wrenched the hook free and brought it down again and again and again.

Matt watched with a growing sense of desperation, the impossible becoming a reality. What if King was to win? Matt looked back at Susie, calling out her name, his voice weak, raw, but growing in strength. Her eyes flickered, a series of rapid blinks bringing her a little closer to consciousness. Then they opened fully. A quiet moan leaked from her lips. 'Matt?' He gazed at her large, green, questioning eyes, at the thin, wan smile. He couldn't lose her again.

King was hacking down at the Bull's head, blood flowing freely from the elephants brow and coating the pearl grey handle of the goad red. How long could Uddanda take such an onslaught?

The mahout was thinking the same. Lying as King had left him, on his stomach, his head tilted towards the horrific scene, tears were streaming down his cheeks.

'Gajadhar, can you move...can you get to me? Susie, she's awake.'

The mahout didn't seem to hear. He appeared transfixed by the tragedy in front of him. Then, finally, a tentative arm reached out; fingers clawed at the ground as, inch by inch, he began to drag himself toward Matt and Susie.

A sudden shriek from King drew Matt's attention back to the ongoing horrors. King's expression was barely human. His features had contorted into a creature from our primeval past. An apelike apparition from some prehistoric time lost to us. He shrieked again. A lingering cry of pure hate. Wielding his goad high above his head he reached back, further, and further and further... Then silence. Then one last crack, quiet, subdued, like the snap of a dead twig. Then nothing... just silence.

King's torso was flopped over Uddanda's trunk like a split sack of corn, his head almost touching his limp, dangling legs.

The bull tossed King aside, his body, a lifeless, twisted heap, landing just three feet from where Matt, Susie and Gajadhar lay, his goad, sticky with blood, still clutched in his hand.

Gazing up at Uddanda, Matt met his eyes, expecting to see some sign of satisfaction, even jubilation. Maybe it was his imagination, but he sensed only pity as the bull slowly turned and lumbered over to where Kali stood waiting, her trunk reaching out to him.

CHAPTER 50

Matt and Susie limped slowly out into the night. It felt cool and refreshing and a bright moon lit their way.

Once Susie had reassured herself that both Gajadhar and Kali's wounds were not life threatening they had made Gajadhar a makeshift bed, a pile of fluffed up hay, which they placed next to Joti at the mahout's insistence. 'Uddanda is so busy with Kali that Joti will need my support, and I hers,' persisted Gajadhar. 'Had I mentioned the strong resemblance that exists between her and my beautiful Ananda back home?' he added, his eyes sparkling with fondness.

Leaving Gajadhar chatting reassuringly to the elephant, they wound their way along the path towards the curators office.

'Andy, Jez, Al... and Colin and Gary.' Susie's voice was quiet, contemplative. Matt hadn't wanted to tell her until she had fully recovered but she had insisted. 'I just can't quite believe it.'

'I'm just grateful that we aren't on that list,' croaked Matt, massaging his throat. He was quiet for a minute. Thinking. *Uddanda nemesis of evil.* 'Have you noticed, the animals... they're all quiet...they seem, calm.'

'Naturally,' said Susie, grateful for a distraction from her thoughts. 'Now that Dan's content. That the wrongs have been righted.'

Matt smiled, 'I think you've spent too much time with Gajadhar.'

'I was unconscious the whole time!' protested Susie.

'Well, too much subliminal time then.'

'Subliminal? Oh, so *now* you accept the concept of the subconscious human mind being violated, as well as the animal mind?'

'If anything,' said Matt, as much to himself as to Susie, 'I'm starting to wonder just how much difference there is between the two.'

She slipped her hand into his and they continued in silence along the path.

***

Buried deep within the foliage of some conifers, two large green eyes stared out as the couple passed within three feet of her. She caught the scent of Al's jacket, drawing in the recognition and the fond memories it evoked, her longing to greet the source barely contained by another impulse. She looked towards the wall and then back to the couple. As they disappeared behind the door Beth emerged, savouring the last lingering molecules of familiarity that hung in the air before turning up the path. In a single bound she leapt on to the perimeter wall and stood perched on the top. After surveying the moorland that rolled into the distance she gave a final glance back into the zoo.

Emitting a long, deep purr, she jumped down from the wall, her sleek form immediately swallowed by the darkness as she dissolved into the moors.

Extract from the Bridgeworthy Echo
Tuesday 12th October 1976

Issue 3512

LOCAL RESIDENTS PACK THEIR TRUNKS

Lankin Moors Wildlife Park has said a sad farewell to three of its largest occupants.

The elephants, two females named Joti and Kali and the male called Uddanda, left in the early hours of Saturday morning to begin their epic voyage to India under the expert guidance of their Mahout.

Also accompanying the elephants on their journey will be the zoo's education officer Matthew Flynn and local vet Susie Turner.

'We hope to establish a reserve and have been fortunate in receiving a very generous offer to fund the project,' said Miss Turner, conducting the press interview with a rat perched on her shoulder.

Neither could be pressed on the identity of the mysterious benefactor who has requested to remain anonymous, however it has been rumoured that he is an extremely wealthy Indian industrialist and a close personal friend of the Mahout.

The departure is not believed to be linked to the bizarre and tragic events of six weeks ago.

'We still have not found a satisfactory explanation for the animals' uncharacteristically aggressive behaviour, but whatever the cause, it appears to have ended and there have been no more incidents,' commented Acting Curator Roger Harman, himself a victim of a deer attack. 'Also, you will be relieved to hear we have successfully rounded up all of the animals that escaped with the exception of one leopard.'

When asked what to do if the public came across the leopard Mr Harman said, 'I would urge anyone who sees her not to approach. Although born and reared in a zoo, she is still a wild animal.'

Footnote

In 1984 Bioacoustics researcher Katy Payne discovered the elephants' ability to communicate through infrasound, publishing her findings, 'infrasonic calls of the Asian Elephant (Elephas maximus), in 1985. Studies have since revealed seismic communication through infrasound, leading to speculation as to the effects of noise pollution on captive elephants.

In 2009 the Central Zoo Authority, the Government agency responsible for India's zoos, recognised that zoos cannot provide a suitable environment for elephants and ordered the relocation of all elephants in zoos in India to sanctuaries, national parks and reserves. The CZA also confirmed that there is little or no benefit to the *in situ* conservation of wild elephants derived from keeping elephants in zoos. In the UK, America and Europe, despite scientific studies comparing wild, captive and working elephants that has found that living in zoos can significantly shorten elephant lives, no such directive has been revealed.

Further reading.... Elephants in Zoos: A Legacy of Shame. 12/05/2022 https://www.bornfree.org.uk/resource/elephants-in-zoos-a-legacy-of-shame/

Acknowledgements

I'd like to thank those who, either directly or indirectly and out of obligation or coercion, have supported me throughout this process.

In particular... My clan, Susannah, Lara and Elissa.

The editorial skills of Rosie.

Jackie, Judy, Heidi and Oscar for their feedback and encouragement.

And special thanks to Zawahir (for her translations), and Martin Moir, whose help made this book possible.